I0564350

RUINED

THE ETERNAL BALANCE SERIES

JUS ACCARDO

Entangled Publishing, LLC
2614 South Timberline Road
Suite 109
Fort Collins, CO 80525
Visit our website at www.entangledpublishing.com.

Edited by Liz Pelletier and Heather Howland
Cover design by Jessica Cantor

Manufactured in the United States of America

First Edition December 2013

For my parents…

Chapter One

Jax

Why? Why the hell had I picked up the phone?

Because I was a damn masochist, that's why. Finally, the years of violence and torment had fried my fucking brain.

I'd already been on a bus speeding down Route 11, no more than six miles from Uncle Rick's house, when the cell went off. I ignored it at first. Picked it up, saw the number on the caller ID, and tossed the phone back into my pocket without giving it a second thought.

Then it rang again. And again. And again.

I caved. It was either that or hurl the thing out the window. Since money wasn't something I could magically pull out of my ass, replacing the phone wasn't an option. But listening to it scream wasn't either. The bastard calling wouldn't have given up anyway.

Now, instead of sticking to my vow to stay the hell away

from my hometown, I was standing in the shadow of the alley next to McCarthy's, the local diner. This was my uncle Rick's fault. The only reason I'd agreed to come back to this pit was because he swore my twin, Chase, would be out of town.

He'd lied.

Or maybe he hadn't. Maybe Chase had played him. The guy was sneaky. I wouldn't put it past my brother to weasel the info out of the old man. It wouldn't be the first time he'd done it.

Rick had a blind spot when it came to Chase. The whole damn town did. He was the golden boy. The shining example of perfect manners and intelligence wrapped in a snappily dressed charmer.

I on the other hand was rotten fruit. The deformed apple that fell to the ground too early and had gotten picked at by animals. I was all the bad habits and diseased bits from the drain of the Flynn family genetic tub.

But none of that mattered now. Chase had called and said it was an emergency. There was something he needed to talk to me about before I went to see Rick.

So here I stood. On the sidewalk. Trying to drum up enough strength to walk inside.

There were so many reasons I shouldn't be here. At the diner. In town. *On this godforsaken earth…*

The main one, though, was a nasty little affliction passed down from a family curse that forced me to share my body with a demon. A violent, cruel monster that survived on the pain and misery of others.

Descendants of Cain, the world's first murderer, some of the male children in my line came into this world with a demon attached to their soul. *Infested,* my father said once. Cain killed his brother, Abel. I figured that was why the thing inside hated Chase so much. We were destined to keep repeating the same mistakes.

Fratricide at its fucking finest.

Unhappiness was like chocolate to the damn thing. And rage? Like pure crack.

Demons, in general, were like that. They fed on negative human emotions, sucking them down like high-end whiskey. There were differences between them; for example, I was unique. A human saddled with a demonic stowaway, while the others were purebreds. They did share common traits, though.

I stepped out from the alley and took several steps toward the diner. Wanda Falkner walked past with an armload of groceries. She stooped down as she went, lifting a hand to wave, then froze when she saw me.

I knew that look. Horror and disgust mixed with fear. It was the expression everyone in this damn town wore when staring me down. Just another reason to get this shit over and done with and leave this place in the dust forever. I was like a plague to these people. The Antichrist and Hitler rolled into one horrible package.

Wanda straightened and scurried away as fast as she could.

I was proud of myself. I hadn't even flipped her off. That was progress.

Three years ago I'd walked away. Turned my back on everyone and everything I loved. It was fine. I did what needed to be done. It wasn't a huge loss. No one here missed me. Uncle Rick was able to move on with his life without having to worry about finding a corpse in Chase's bed each morning, and Chase, well, he'd moved on just fine, too. He spent his days as a successful photographer, and his nights screwing a path across Jensen County.

The only thing that made leaving hard was *her*. Samantha Merrick. The girl who, to this day, still pulled me from the mire and made it possible to go on, even if she didn't know it. She was my anchor and kryptonite all at the same time. Salvation and damnation in one beautiful, unattainable package.

Thank fucking God she wasn't living in Harlow anymore. She'd gone off to college several months ago. I could probably suffer being in the same room with Chase for a few minutes, but being forced to pull a face-to-face with Sam? That would have gutted me.

The smell of demon wafted through the air, faint but noticeable. A quarter mile, tops. They were everywhere. Schools, shopping malls, local food stores. No place was safe. Like a permanent rodent infestation, they were always around. Always lurking in wait for scraps.

I could see my brother through the diner window, at the back booth. Of all the horrible things I'd done, none were worse than what the demon wanted me to do to Chase. The monster hated my brother.

It flashed an image of Chase, pinned against the wall and struggling for air. I could feel his skin beneath my fingers in the all-too-real vision, and as I leaned in closer to savor the fear and confusion, Chase let out a scream that made the hairs on my arm dance. It wasn't real, but it sure felt that way. One quick movement. That's all it would take to snap his neck. Dead, brown eyes would stare into the distance as the demon rumbled with satisfaction. The contented warmth it felt would flow through my body, and for just a moment, I wanted to do it. To walk into the building and end my brother's life, if only to gain a moment of peace.

The flash ended and left me breathless. I slammed a fist into the tree behind me. "Fuck!"

I waited until everything evened out before turning back to the building. One step toward the alley. Then another. This wasn't going to happen. It couldn't. Chase was leaning forward again, as the person sitting across from him did the same, giving me a perfect view of her profile.

A wave of fury rolled over me. "Motherfu—"

Samantha Merrick, who was supposed to be away at Huntington College, was about to kiss my brother.

Chapter Two

Sam

Chase Flynn flashed a lopsided grin as I slid into the booth across from him.

"You never get anything different. Always pie." I tugged the menu from my best friend's hands and skimmed the dessert section.

McCarthy's was his guilty pleasure. They made the best key lime pie on the East Coast—according to Chase. The tartness of lime always turned my stomach.

I preferred excessively sweet things like chocolate mousse or strawberries slathered in homemade cream. One of the few vivid memories I had of my mother was Saturday morning strawberries and cream…

"Amen to pie, baby," he said with an easy laugh, eyes fixed on mine. Today he was dressed in a tight-fitting forest-green T-shirt and well-worn jeans with a small hole in the left knee. On another guy, the outfit would have been week-end casual. On Chase, with his classic features and Greek god cut, it was runway chic. Although he could have donned clown shoes and a series of strategically taped paper bags and still caught the attention of every girl in the room.

Chase had lived in the house next door with his uncle and brother from the time I was six. He'd stolen my Aunt Kelly's heart from the instant he'd arrived on the doorstep with a plate of warm brownies and that infectious charm that seemed to ooze from every pore. From that moment on, my aunt was determined to hook us up despite the fact that Chase—ironically named—was with a different girl every other day. Pass. I wasn't interested in being anyone's flavor of the week.

"So the movie was fun." He flashed a sultry smile, and my pulse hastened despite the fact that I wasn't interested in him that way. It was just the effect he had on people.

The two women at the next table were not-so-subtly eye-humping him in addition to the occasional, pointed giggle. They were older—midthirties if I had to guess—and apparently saw no shame in cougaring it up.

Chase ignored them and focused on me. "I liked the shower scene. I didn't think it was possible for human beings to bend that way. We should test it out some time."

He'd delivered countless lines to girls over the years, but none had ever been aimed my way. Not seriously, anyway. I laughed and leaned forward, elbows on the table. We'd played this game a thousand times before. With a wink, I joked, "And after we're done there, we can do it doggy-style in the rain."

Of course the waitress chose that moment to stroll over

and set down two plates of hot apple pie. With a disgusted shake of her head, she turned to the table across from us to take their order. I was more tired than hungry, but Chase grabbed his fork and went to town.

"Just name the time and place, baby." His lips tilted into a mischievous grin. Guys like this were dangerous. They knew the sway their smoldering stare held over girls, and exploited it at every turn to get what they wanted. I'd seen many a girl fall to that overpowering, swoon-worthy stare and heart-stopping grin.

I yawned and poked at the pie with my fork. Apple wasn't my favorite, but it was better than cherry. "Yep. And after we do that, we'll shave a llama and take it to dinner."

He pushed his pie aside and took my hand, grin morphing into a solemn expression. "What if I said I was serious?"

His words were like a punch to the gut, stealing my breath and sending goose bumps across my skin. I didn't know whether to laugh or jump up and run like the hounds of hell were on my ass and looking for a new chew toy. I wasn't his type. Not even close. There were runway models and sorority house fashionistas with enough artfully applied makeup to warrant a flammable sign—and then there was me. Jeans, T-shirts, and a small tattoo of my favorite Disney character, Stitch, masterfully hidden away on my left hip. "This is a joke, right?"

Chase was smiling again, but his eyes darted over my shoulder for a moment. "Is it a bad thing if I say no?"

"It'd be a confusing thing." I pulled my hand away and said, "For starters, you're not known for having actual relationships, and I'm not into the one-night-stand scene." I'd done it while away at college and wasn't interested in repeating the experience.

He leaned back, subtly glancing around the room as though he was looking for someone. Feigning insult, he said, "You think I'm itching to make *you* another notch in my post?"

Distraction was one of the biggest tools in his arsenal. I'd seen it at work a thousand times. Whenever he wanted to avoid a question, he'd answer with one of his own. But there was no way I was playing into that crap. "Secondly, I'm not your type. You're not my type, either."

"You're not dating anyone at the moment, correct?"

"Have I mentioned anyone lately?" The truth was, the last time I had a date, it ended with a clammy handshake and a forced smile. The time before that, the guy kissed me, and it was less like a kiss and more like an ice cube with a slimy tongue and sweaty palms.

I was too picky, according to Aunt Kelly. But that wasn't it. I knew exactly what I wanted. Screaming need and desperate kisses so hot, they'd melt the sun. Something that had slipped through my fingers... A fire I'd been chasing without success ever since. "But so not the point."

"I know I have a certain...*reputation*. But it's not like I'm proposing marriage." He winked. "Even though that would make Kelly happy..."

I couldn't believe we were having this conversation. Out loud. He was right, though. My aunt would shit bricks of happy, since she'd been shoving us together for years, but ick. He was like a brother. "Don't you think it'd be a little weird? Us? Together?"

"Is this because of my brother?"

Silence. I didn't answer. Couldn't. The subject of the

other Flynn was off-limits. An unspoken rule, and I intended to keep it that way.

Chase shook his head and stuffed another forkful of pie into his mouth. His eyes all but rolled back as he swallowed. "He made his choice and he has to live with it. I don't."

I opened my mouth, then closed it. He had to be screwing with me.

"What do you say? Interested in giving it a try? No expectations. No pressure. Maybe just one little kiss…"

It was a thought I'd entertained deep in the *never-in-a-million-freaking-years* part of my brain more than a few times but had never considered actually acting on. Chase was one of my best friends, and yes, he was hot as hell, but not in an *I-want-to-hook-up-with-him* kind of way. The attraction was less about how he looked and more about who he looked like. His twin brother, Jax…

"I—"

Standing, he leaned across the table, and his cologne drifted pleasantly through the air. I'd been with him when he bought it for the first time. Some expensive thing imported from Italy in a tiny bottle that cost more than my monthly rent. Eyes darting to the door again, his lips bloomed into a wicked smile. "Kiss me, Samantha."

I have no idea what possessed me to actually do it, but I kissed him. When our lips met, the sensation caught me off guard. His tongue slipped across my bottom lip, teasing for just a moment before capturing it between his, and my pulse quickened. He seemed eager to show me what I'd be missing if I turned him down, and when he deepened the kiss, my insides ignited.

But not because I was kissing Chase.

I couldn't stop myself from imagining it was Jax's insistent lips doing the nipping, his name a desperate plea falling from my lips. Any minute now, he'd take mercy on me, sweep me into his arms, and…

That's when reality crashed back like a semi through a china shop. Holy shit! I'd just used Chase as a fluffer in my own low-budget porno.

Slowly I opened my eyes, guilty heat rushing over my warm cheeks at the thought of Chase misinterpreting my enthusiasm, but it was a different gaze that gave me pause.

A towering figure stood in the doorway, his large frame blotting out the sun. With a mop of dark, unruly hair and eyes the exact shade of gray that graced the skies right before a violent storm decimated the city, he wore a long leather trench coat and an expression that was both fire and ice at the same time.

His eyes met mine, and the top right-hand corner of his lip hitched. Just a hair. I wouldn't have noticed if I wasn't staring. Which I was. How could I not? The newcomer's presence was one that demanded attention. Painfully beautiful, yet deadly. Like the poison apple from the Garden of Eden. Sinful and seductive, yet eternally damning.

I pulled away and blinked twice, sure his appearance was nothing more than imagination. Maybe even an apparition of guilt. But he was still there. Still staring. He looked rough, like he'd been to hell and back. There was a gleam of something close to madness in his eyes, and for an insane moment, I almost slipped from the booth and went to him. "Jax…"

Identical twins, yet as different as oil and vinegar. Chase kept his face cleanly shaven and his hair trimmed short, while

Jax had let his grow out. It was long enough that the tips of his bangs curled slightly, giving them a sexy, *wild* look. But it was their expressions that defined the difference between them. Chase was always smiling. There was something warm and welcoming about his expression that just drew people to him. Jax's expression on the other hand, screamed *keep the fuck away*.

Kind of like the way he looked like right now.

Chase pushed forward again, lips tickling the tip of my chin. "Why are we talking about him?"

I pushed him back to his seat and nodded to the right where the tall, dark figure loomed, cloaked in a leather trench coat and black skullcap. "Because he's *here*."

Chase swiveled and met his carbon copy with a shit-eating grin. With a nod and an all-too-cocky smile, he said, "Big brother. When did you get back to town?"

Jax lunged forward and knocked him out cold.

Chapter Three

Jax

After Chase hit the floor, I made for another go, but Sam jumped between us. She checked on my brother, then reluctantly agreed to deliver me to Rick's where I couldn't do any more damage.

"Still dealing with that impulse control issue, huh?" she said, starting the engine with a flick of her wrist and a yawn — the third one since we'd gotten into her car. There were dark circles under her eyes, and I couldn't help wondering how she'd been spending her nights.

Or with who.

Her lips twisted disapprovingly, and I found myself having to recite the alphabet backward to keep from paying too much attention to the little details. The way she tilted her head, sending soft strands of chestnut hair across her shoulder. The soothing tone of her voice. The way she moved. I'd dreamed about these minute details a million times over the last three years.

This girl was the one thing I couldn't outrun. The only piece of my life I couldn't seem to shake—and a part of me hated her for it.

"Someone sounds bitter," I said, keeping both eyes on the dash. Mud. Think of mud. Zombies. Anything to keep from focusing on her. "You were hoping to deck him yourself?"

The engine sputtered and revved and the car jerked from the parking spot, indicating that little had changed when it came to her driving habits. She was hell on wheels. Not a bad driver, but she certainly liked her speed. I didn't know what asshole thought it'd be a good idea to give her a license, but if I ever found the guy, there'd be a serious fucking beat-down in order.

She stomped the gas, and the car lurched forward. "You're the one with anger management issues, not me."

I snorted and bit down hard on my tongue. She was right, in a way. I had anger issues—only they weren't necessarily all mine. The demon had a nasty temper and just about zero impulse control. To keep the thing in check, I'd forced myself to feed it, committing one truly violent act every two days since I was seventeen. That, coupled with little nibbles of the darker side of human emotion here and there, had been enough.

She tightened her hands around the wheel. "Besides, I think we're dating…"

Fury churned in my gut like a tornado, and the scene from the diner played on repeat inside my head. My brother's greedy hands trespassing in places they didn't belong.

It'd been nearly impossible to stop from ripping my twin in half. I'd lost control for a moment, but was determined not to let it slip free again. Not while I was in town. And not around Sam. Logically, I knew I had no right to be pissed about the kiss between her and Chase. I was the one who'd walked away.

Unfortunately, logic wasn't on my side.

"Dating?" I gave a short laugh. She was full of shit, but it still pissed me off. Chase knew the rules. Sam was off-limits.

The whole thing had been a show. My brother knew I was standing there. The bastard probably saw me walk up outside. He'd kissed her to get a reaction, I was sure of it. Which was ten kinds of dangerous, considering how short my fuse could be. But that was Chase. Always living life on the edge.

Sucking in a breath, I forced a smirk to cover up the anger and said, "Are you serious? Chase is dating *you*? I find that impossible to believe. For starters, you have no ass." She had a great ass. "Also, your arms are too long. Kind of apish." They'd be perfect for wrapping around my waist. "That's good though. You're short. I bet it helps with the top shelf."

She opened her mouth—then closed it, slamming down hard on the car's brakes. The tires screamed against the pavement as I shot forward, face smashing the dash with a loud crack. I didn't feel much—one of the only perks of living with the demon—but rubbed the spot for her benefit. The slight, satisfied tilt of her lip made the whole show worthwhile. Shit. I'd bleed myself dry if it would get her to smile like that again.

No. That was against the rules. Rules I'd put in place for a reason.

She was still the same—and that made her dangerous. Every moment I spent with her was a precarious balance of control and self-discipline that couldn't be trusted. My only defense was to act like a dick and hope she kept her distance. It was the only thing that would keep her safe—and me sane. "Guess that'd be a resounding yes…"

"I guess so," she snapped, and yawned again.

"So if you guys are together, was that disaster I stumbled into a *date*?"

"Don't sound so shocked," she mumbled. Another lie. If she and Chase were really dating, then I was the damn pope. "Not every guy feels the need to run to the other end of the earth to get away from me."

Her words were like a donkey punch to the nuts. She had every right to be angry after what I'd done, and if that's all it was, I could have taken my licks like a man. Sucked it up and moved the hell on. But it was more than that. I could hear the thinly veiled pain behind the snipe, and it killed me. I'd wrecked a lot of lives, a tornado of destruction and pain wherever I went, but none came with as much regret as Sam.

"Still haven't gotten over that, eh? They make therapists for shit like that, you know." God, I was a fucking bastard. "And you shouldn't have left your *boyfriend* alone. He's probably picking up your replacement as we speak. Did you get a load of the rack on the waitress at the counter? I bet he's already down on that."

Sam held her breath for a second before exhaling through pursed lips. "You're an asshole."

There. That had done it. I'd hit a nerve.

Like the purebreds, my demon enabled me to see and sense negative human feelings, making it easy to find the most potent ones to feed on. Each emotion was represented by a different color and had an exclusive flavor. Its favorites—fear and anger—were sweet with an almost fruity aftertaste.

The car flooded with crimson—anger—and the cloying scent rose from her shoulders and began swirling around her head. The faint taste tickled my throat as my muscles started to ache. Physical pain was an indicator that the demon wanted to feed, and the longer it went without getting what it wanted, the more I suffered. I pushed back hard and focused on a dark spot on the dashboard. After a moment, the feeling began to pass.

My life was twisted. The more misery I caused people, the happier the demon was. The happier the demon was, the more I wanted to kick my own ass. I could walk into a room of people, push their buttons and suck down the resulting darkness to calm the thing inside, but for an ounce of true peace, I needed something dark. Something violent. Day in and day out. Same damn thing. It was a vicious cycle—one I'd never wanted Sam to be a part of. I'd left town once to save her from what I was, and was counting down the minutes until I could do it again.

Sam's posture was stiff as the swirl of red faded. No matter what, I had to maintain as much space between us as possible. It would be easier to deal with her if she stayed annoyed. The minute she flashed those big browns my way, I was fucking toast.

"Yanno… Putting yourself alone with the sexier brother is just plain cruel. It's like dangling a juicy carrot in front of a starving horse," I baited.

"Did—did you just refer to yourself as a carrot?"

"I think the better question would be, did I just refer to

you as a starving horse…"

Biting her bottom lip, she held her breath as the red waves of anger intensified. I made a fist, digging my nails deep until I felt the skin of my palm break. The subtle stinging gave me something else to focus on besides the increasingly sweet taste in my mouth. I could take a bite, taste the anger without doing her any real harm, but I was afraid I wouldn't be able to stop. The only rule I had was no feeding off people I knew. Any kind of emotional connection always fucked things up. There was too much of a possibility of losing control. Letting the demon rise too close to the surface was risky.

Sam kept her eyes on the road, and it was obvious she was trying not to engage in confrontation. Unfortunately, the harder she tried, the sexier she looked. It made her lingering anger more intoxicating, and the demon struggled for control. I held my breath, depriving the thing of the scent of her fury.

She cut the wheel to the left, turning onto Beekman Avenue. "So why did you come back?"

"Could ask you the same thing." I turned away as more of the crimson dissipated. I'd gone to see her—in secret, and from a distance, of course—just last month. She'd had a few problems, but I hadn't known she left college. "Aren't you supposed to be at school?"

When she didn't respond, I forced myself to look at her again. The anger was gone, the waves of red replaced now by a smoky swirl of gray. Fear. "Sammy?"

It was like the arctic had settled across her face. "School didn't work out. I've moved on. End of story." And that was all she said. After a moment, some of the tension left her body, along with the rush of gray, and she sighed. "And you're back because…?"

I wanted to know what happened with school, but it was a bad idea. Getting involved in her life—even the smallest bit—would only give her the wrong idea. Plus, it would make leaving again that much harder. You didn't hand an ex-junkie a needle without expecting a relapse. That's what this girl was to me. An addiction I'd been trying for years to kick. No. Better to stick with the plan. Keep it casual and cool. Act like a dick. I'd do what I needed to do in town, and then get the hell out. "Would you believe nostalgia?"

Sam's brows rose. "Nostalgia? For what, kicking the crap out of your brother?"

"Someone's funnier than I remember," I said. "Are you going to tell me to stay away from your man?"

"How about I just ask you to crawl back to whatever hole you've been hiding in for the last three years?"

The words stung even though I could see the conflicting swirls of color dancing around her head. Anger, hurt, and something else. Something that said underneath it all, she was glad to see me. Hopeful, even. And as much as it ripped away another small piece of my soul, I couldn't have that. Samantha Merrick needed to hate me. "I won't be here long. There's nothing worth staying for."

The words tasted bitter, but they did the trick. Her colors turned deep crimson again, and she squared her shoulders and shrugged. "Then I guess it really is my lucky day, eh?"

"Seems like it." I focused on the dark spot on the dash again. Coffee. I could smell it. Another perk of the demon. My nose was better than a border collie's. All my senses were enhanced. I could hear a whistle from three blocks away. Feel the minute fibers in a single piece of paper. Even see the delicate veins in the wings of a fly.

I turned away and watched the town pass in a blur of green and brown from the passenger-side window. Things hadn't changed. Most small towns didn't. I'd always hated that about Harlow. The landscape. The people. All so narrow and static.

Sam took the corner of Mercer Avenue and hung a hard right onto River. The street sloped at a sharp slant and ended in a thin guardrail that ran alongside the river. I'd always hated this road, and being in Sam's passenger seat only amplified that because of her aversion to the brake pedal. "You might wanna slow down, Sammy."

"No one likes a side seat driver." She jabbed a finger at me.

Her nails were gnawed to the quick and unpolished. Another thing that hadn't changed.

"And no one calls me *Sammy* anymore. You'd know that if you hadn't fallen off the edge of the planet."

"Oh, for fuck's sake," I snapped, leaning back in the seat. I should have known we wouldn't get through the ten-minute drive without her bringing that up. It was 100 percent justified, but I couldn't let her know that. I'd practically kissed her clothes clean off, then disappeared without a word the next day. "I knew this was a bad idea."

"I wasn't exactly thrilled about it, either." She thought I meant the car ride. The truth was, I should have never come back to town. The urge to return had been building slowly, but when I found out that my Uncle Rick, the man who'd raised me, was terminally ill, I couldn't put it off any longer. I needed to say good-bye.

Sam wasn't supposed to be here. Neither was Chase,

who was scheduled to visit a friend in Jersey. Wrong on both counts. Two strikes. One more and it was game over for someone. I planned to see my uncle, then make a run for the city limits like someone had lit my ass on fire.

"I *was* serious though," I said, inclining my head toward the road. The car barreled toward the river and showed no signs of stopping. "Feel free to slow down."

Her foot pushed the brake as each of her fingers turned white, wrapping tight around the wheel. The car didn't slow.

"Any time now…" I prodded, gripping the "oh shit" handle above the door. The demon shifted, sensing distress. There was never any privacy. It was like I lived in a house with glass walls. Every thought—every emotion—was on display for perverse entertainment of the monster inside.

The car picked up speed as it slipped past the final hill and closed in on the last few feet before the railing. Thick gray mist filled the car. "I'd *love* to…" she spat, violently stomping the pedal now. *Thunk thunk, thunk.* The sound echoed through the small space.

"It's not working?"

"Of course it's working. I think I'd rather just drive over the edge!" She smacked the wheel and smashed her foot down once more, throwing all her weight behind it. It didn't do any good.

Time was up, and we were out of road. "We're not going to stop. Open your window!" I slammed a hand against the dash to brace myself, then started pushing furiously on the window button with the other. Like the brakes, nothing happened. "Fuck. Why isn't it working, Sammy?"

"They're broken," she yelled in a panic, yanking up on the buckle of her seat belt. "College dropout. Piece of crap car!"

A growl rose in my throat. "Why the hell would you not get that fixed?"

Sam ignored me, fingers fumbling with the belt release button, jabbing randomly until it clicked free. She cursed and reached for the door, but it was too late. The car crashed through the guardrail in an explosion of twisted metal and clamorous sound as it careened off the road.

For a minute we were weightless. Suspended in midair like spiders from a string. Sam had unbuckled her safety belt, and her body lifted from the seat like a rag doll. I threw my arm across, pinning her down to keep her from smashing forward into the windshield.

"Hold on," I grunted, bracing us both. We jerked forward on impact, the car slamming into the water with a deafening crash.

Sam pulled up on the handle, but the door wouldn't budge. The pressure of the water had us trapped already. "We're stuck!"

"Stay calm," I said, withdrawing my arm.

I closed my eyes and fought hard to keep control. The excessive waves of panic rolling off Sam made tucking the monster away that much harder. "The *worst* thing you can do right now is panic."

"Don't panic?" She pounded the dash. I almost pointed out beating up the car wouldn't do a damn thing either, but now wasn't the time to play the asshole card. Not with her on the verge of losing it and the demon licking its nonexistent lips at her fear. The taste of it had the thing churning, restless, and hungry. "Are you kidding me? We're going to die!"

"We're not going to die." My voice deepened. Shit. I was

losing it. "I can get us out of here."

The car slipped beneath the surface and the water rushed in through the floor and vents. It was cold and rising fast. "Really? Did you develop *gills* while you were away?"

"Sammy, calm the fuck—" The ache in my muscles ignited, turning into an all-consuming fire. It stole the air from my lungs. Her fear was too much.

I closed my eyes and counted to ten, fighting like hell against the darkness. If I lost control, Sam would drown. The demon wouldn't care about anything except self-preservation. It pushed. I pushed. But it was a losing battle. The black thing convulsed, driven by the heightened emotions, and with a flash of sharp pain and a flare of bright light, I became a spectator hovering on the edge of consciousness in my own body.

The demon wasted no time. Though faster and physically more powerful when in control, it was still subject to most human vulnerabilities while living inside my body. It made me tougher and stronger, but if my body died, the demon died with it.

It made a move to grab the door, but Sam intervened. She grabbed its face—*my* face—and pressed her lips to mine as the water inside the car closed over our heads.

Danger.

Sammy.

Death.

Sam.

Violence.

Samantha.

Pain. Sammy…

The instant our lips met, the watery inside of the car

was gone, replaced by a wooded area surrounded by large rocks. Two teenagers—one angry boy and a damaged, but determined, girl stood in the center.

It was a memory—one I remembered all too well, but it was different somehow. This was from someone else's perspective. It took a second, but I realized it was the demon's memory. The thing was remembering Sam and the kiss we shared the night I left. A rush of emotion hit hard. The soft, warm feel of Sam's small body crushed to mine. The way her hair smelled like raspberries. Lips. Longing. Need. A moment of absolute peace and perfection in a life full of violence and pain.

The memory faded, and Sam pulled away and opened her eyes—then her mouth. The mist bled into the water around us, swirling like colored ink. The dark blue of sadness tainted with regret and mingled with smoky gray fear. The demon was in control, but I felt it all. The sensation was overwhelming. It was pleasure and pain and necessity.

A single bubble escaped Sam's mouth and her eyes closed. I let out a rage-filled roar—or maybe it'd come from the demon. In that moment, we were so tangled up and twisted, I couldn't tell where I ended and it began.

Just when I was sure it would abandon her, it gathered Sam in my arms, shielding her, and crashed through the glass, kicking hard for the surface.

Chapter Four

Sam

Before I dared open my eyes, I moved a finger. One by one, each in turn, they did as commanded. Next came the toes. All ten piggies wiggled exactly as they had before. An arm here, a leg there, my limbs appeared to be attached and functioning properly.

"Samantha?" asked a voice thick with concern. "Samantha, baby, are you awake?"

Oh, God, no… Someone put me back in the river.

The voice belonged to my aunt, and I made the decision to keep both eyes closed tight. No doubt the moment they opened, Kelly Merrick would be flinging disapproval like monkey shit at the zoo. The unsafe car—which she just happened to be right about; the decision to drop out of school; my less than snow-white past—she would have whored me off to Chase at fourteen if she could have legally gotten away with it. Everything in my life was subject to the older woman's constant nagging.

It was the main reason I'd applied to an out-of-town college. There'd never been any real interest in school for me. I was nineteen and had no idea what to do with my life. I had sketchy people skills, and no marketable hobbies. The only real talent I had came from my earlier years of troublemaking. I could pick a lock and hot-wire a car in record time, but the chances of turning that into a lucrative career that didn't end in the pokey was pretty nil.

As far as I was concerned, there was plenty of time to decide. Life right now should be about hitting up frat parties and pulling all-nighters ending by 7:00 a.m. at the local diner with a missing shoe and no memory of the evening. Living off mac and cheese and wearing flip-flops all winter. Proving to Aunt Kelly that I could stand alone. Huntington was supposed to be the path to finding myself and where I belonged in the world.

Or, it had until I'd walked away from it all. Nowhere in my wildest fantasies had there been anything remotely resembling scenes from a B-movie horror flick.

Lately disaster seemed to follow me around. There'd been a string of increasingly bad accidents since I'd turned tail and run from school, and my mind had been nudging the possibility that maybe there was something bigger going on. But this was an accident. The car was a piece of shit. Brakes failed—especially when you didn't have the money to maintain them.

"Are you happy? This is your fault," Aunt Kelly spat. "You've always been a horrible driver. Disaster just follows you along wherever you go, doesn't it?"

"Kelly," Chase said from somewhere to the right. He sounded tired and in need of caffeine. "Jax wasn't—"

"I'm responsible for global warming, too. Haven't you heard?" Jax snapped. "I bet you could place me at the assassination of Lincoln if you tried hard enough. Oh. And I killed that stupid deer, too. What's its name? Bambi?"

Kelly gasped and I felt an internal eye roll coming on. The surprise over Jax's response was nothing more than an act played by an old pro very much deserving of an Emmy. Where she viewed Chase as a saint—an exemplary specimen of a man that could do no wrong—Jax was the devil incarnate.

"Do the authorities know you've come back to town?"

Jax ignored her. "What's the rabbit's name? Humper?"

Chase sighed. A sound like paper crumpling was followed by, "Thumper. The bunny's name was Thumper, Jax."

"That's right," Jax snickered. "Thumper. Made excellent stew."

Kelly gasped again. Really, it was a wonder the woman didn't pass out more often. "You are a menace. How many people will you harm while you're in town?"

I waited, sure he'd declare his innocence, but Jax remained silent.

"The best thing you ever did was leave," she continued, no doubt interpreting his silence as an admission of guilt. "Everyone's life was better without you here!"

Jax hadn't done anything wrong—this time—other than being his not-so-charming self. There was no reason for Kelly to rip him to shreds for my mistake. They were standing over me bickering like five-year-olds. I'd almost just died, for Christ's sake.

I'd almost just died…

Everything came crashing back and my heart began to pound. The car had gone over the edge and into the river. *Under the river.* A shiver ran through me and I could almost feel the icy water kissing my exposed skin again. No wonder Kelly was flipping out. She thought Jax was driving and had almost killed me.

I pushed the terrifying thought aside and forced my eyes open. "I was driving." If he wouldn't come clean about his innocence, then I would. They'd been telling me to take the car in for service for months now. As with everything else, I kept putting it off.

When my vision cleared, Kelly stood at the foot of the bed, arms folded with a typical scowl firmly in place.

To the right of the bed, in the chair by the door, Chase sat with a coffee cup. He'd changed at some point. The jeans were gone, replaced by worn sweats and a white T-shirt. It was the most disheveled I'd seen him look since the morning he was caught sneaking off Kiki Muller's porch after prom night.

"You're nineteen, Sammy. I don't think you owe her an explanation," Jax said. He slouched in the corner, as far away from Chase as the room would allow, and when my eyes met his, those last moments in the car came flooding back with a vengeance. There was a flush of embarrassment and a rush of heat.

I'd kissed him. Granted, I'd been sure we were about to die, sentenced to a watery grave, but still… How was I going to live this down?

Wait…

How was I *able* to live it down? Everything was so fuzzy.

"The car was under water," I said, eyeing Jax. "The doors were stuck. How did we get out?"

He returned my glare, eyes narrowing so that only the slightest hint of gray was visible. I knew that look. A challenge. "Does it matter? Maybe I should put you back in? It'd give you an excuse to grope me again."

Aunt Kelly choked and Chase was instantly alert. "She groped you?"

"Hell, yeah, she did." Jax tapped his lips, then puckered up, blowing a kiss in my direction. "Laid one right on me."

I swallowed. "That's not—"

Chase balked. "How was it?"

Seriously?

Jax shrugged. "Eh. Definitely inexperienced."

This is not happening.

"Is this true?" Aunt Kelly snapped. Her face was pale and she looked ready to drop.

I glared at Jax. "Chase didn't seem to have a problem with my kissing expertise."

My aunt went from livid to over the moon. "You kissed Chase?"

"Annnnd getting back on track." Chase grinned. He was watching Jax, who was positively seething on the other side of the room. Served him right.

Jax seemed to pull it together and flashed a tight-lipped smile. "Consider the source, Sammy. Do you have any idea where those lips have been? They should come with a hazmat sticker"

"Her name," Aunt Kelly spat with a dramatic flip of her hair, "is *Samantha*. Sammy is something you'd name a puppy. Or—or a tool."

Jax nodded to his lap. "Of course it is. That's what I named *my* tool."

"If you two keep going at it, I'm ringing the nurse to load me up with the biggest sedative they've got," I said, pushing myself up into a sitting position.

"So what happened?" Chase asked, pulling his chair next to the bed. He was every bit the troublemaker Jax was, but knew enough to filter his behavior, where his brother didn't care what anyone thought. Because of that, he'd been dubbed the golden boy and Jax the bad seed.

Aunt Kelly came behind him and clutched his shoulder as a justified smile creased her lips. I was so tempted to say something that ensured her hand's removal—something shocking and unladylike—but settled for the simple truth. Verbal sparring with my aunt, while awesome, took more energy than I had at the moment.

"I think my brakes must have failed." The memory of fruitlessly pumping the pedal as the car sped toward the river at breakneck speed sent an icy tremor up my spine. I was never driving that road again, even if it meant going an hour out of the way. Hell. I might never drive again. Period.

But Aunt Kelly couldn't know I was rattled. She'd insist on them keeping me here. Squaring my shoulders, I plastered on my game face and said, "Assuming they're not going to keep me here for swallowing half the river, can we get the fuck out of Dodge? I'm beat."

"Samantha!" My aunt paled and clutched her chest. Cursing was something ladies didn't do—especially in front of gentlemen. In that moment, I wanted to find an excuse to say "cock knocker" in front of the *flawless* Chase Flynn. That would really get her going.

"Relax," I said, throwing the covers aside. The room spun a little, but otherwise everything seemed fine. The sooner I got out of this sterile, bleach-scented environment and back to my nice cluttered apartment where coffee lived, the better. Hospitals gave me the creeps. Sliding from the bed, I planted both feet on the ground and felt a subtle updraft.

"Cover yourself up!" Spreading her arms wide to shield me, Aunt Kelly whirled on Jax, who politely averted his gaze and turned to the door. His brother, on the other hand, made no attempt to hide his stare—which of course went unnoticed.

I sighed and tugged the impractical hospital gown closed at the back.

Jax stood. "I'll find the doctor. See if we can't get things moving along."

As Chase busied himself with trying to calm Aunt Kelly down, Jax turned. Our eyes met and the bottom dropped out from my belly. *Whoosh.* I was at the top of a roller coaster, just before the car plummeted over the edge. Excitement and fear so tightly wound together that they were one and the same. It was a dizzying rush that warmed my skin and made my head swim—in a good way—while wreaking havoc on my heartbeat. The missing spark in my life, the one I'd been chasing since the night he'd left...

With the slightest nod of his head, he disappeared around the corner and my heartbeat evened. Not good...

I wasn't over Jax Flynn.

Chapter Five

Jax

My bedroom was exactly the same as I'd left it three years ago. Hard-rock posters lined the walls, and the dartboard Rick had gotten me on my fourteenth birthday still hung above the bed, the last dart I'd ever thrown, a bull's-eye, poking out from the center.

I'd been at the window watching Sam pace the length of her old bedroom next door for the last hour. Instead of going home to her apartment, she let her aunt talk her into staying at the house for the night.

She'd always hated the silence. The television was on in the background, a repeat of the press conference the police chief had given earlier about a series of murders by someone the press dubbed the Gentleman Stalker. A handful of girls had gone missing from Harlow and the surrounding towns recently and authorities were stumped. I'd heard about it, but hadn't really followed the story.

Sam ignored the news and stalked the floor of her old room. It was easy to see she didn't want to be there. Every once in a while she would slide the fingers of her hand through her long brown hair, tug at the sides, then tilt her head back and sigh. Tufts of gray fear trailed behind as her heart hammered an erratic rhythm. Twice she'd reached for the phone. I'd listened as she dialed the first five digits of Rick's number before slamming it back to the dresser and cursing softly.

Another person would be curled in a ball, rocking themselves to sleep after what just happened. Not Sam. Even though she was shaken to the core, she put up a brave front. Alone in her room and away from prying eyes, she continued the ruse like there was no other choice. Like showing even the smallest hint of weakness would send reality crumbling down around her. She was the savior and never the victim.

There was space between us—wood, plaster, and glass— but I heard every sound as clearly as if she were standing next to me. Every movement, the smell of the lake still on her skin, the subtle rub of her clothing as she moved across the room, everything was razor-edged and on the verge of driving me mad. I knew I should leave, but the only thing I wanted to do was hold her. Be there so she could let it out.

But that wasn't going to happen. If I didn't get out of here before my brother showed up—which was inevitable— I couldn't be held responsible for my actions. Or the demon's. The monster, always so predictable, had pulled a 180 by saving Sam. I was grateful, but it was more incentive to get the fuck out of Dodge. I didn't know what it might do next.

Thinking I could breeze into town, see Rick, and leave

without complications was ridiculous. Thankfully, it was
something I could rectify. Grabbing my coat from the bed, I
hurried down the stairs, taking them two at a time.

"Freeze, pal."

I stopped mid-stride, a few inches from the door. So
fucking close. I slowly turned to face my uncle. "You prom-
ised. You swore they wouldn't be here, Rick." A knot of
anger formed deep in my chest. My control had improved
with age, but that didn't mean I wanted to wave my biggest
trigger in front of the demon's face. "Are you trying to put
me on *America's Most Wanted*? Cause that's what's going to
happen. The shit I wanna do to my brother is sure to get me
on the ten o'clock news."

"I'm sorry. I should have encouraged you to stay away.
The last I heard from Kelly, Samantha was supposed to be
in school. I don't know what happened. I didn't even know
she'd dropped out until Kelly called me on the way to the
hospital. Apparently she's been living on the other side of
town for the last month." Rick frowned and a pang of guilt
needled me. Three years had aged him more than it should
have. The lines on his face were deeper, his hair now thin
and solid gray. But there were other things. Signs of decay.

Cancer. The doctors had given him a month—possibly
less.

He alternated between leaning against the doorframe
and using the old china cabinet to support his weight. The
knickknacks inside were full of dust and still in the same
spots as the night I'd left. "As far as Chase being in town,
he found out you were coming home at the last minute and
insisted on being here. I warned him to stay away, but you
know your brother…"

Of course I did. Stubborn, cocky, and invincible—or so he believed. He'd pushed me at every corner as we were growing up. Determined to prove he wasn't in danger. He was wrong, though. My twin had no idea how close he'd come to death the night I left town. "Every time I see him, I imagine myself covered in his blood." I smashed a fist into the wall next to him, and Rick flinched. The last thing I wanted to do was upset the old man, but he needed to understand that I couldn't stay any longer. I couldn't control the demon and its sick desire to end Chase's life. "This thing inside me *hates* him. All it wants is to rip him apart."

When we were five years old, I pushed Chase down the basement stairs. That was the first time I got a taste of the demon's hatred for him. The sound he made as his balance shifted. The distinct cracking of the bones in his left arm as he crashed down the concrete stairs. The surprisingly soft thud that filled the stairwell as his body fell still at the bottom. It was one of those defining moments in life. A span of six or seven seconds that I'd never, ever forget.

The night I kissed Sam in the woods behind the house pushed things over the edge. It'd been the tipping point. The line. Those few moments with her—happiness like I'd never imagined—had driven the demon into an enraged frenzy. That kiss was what I'd wanted more than anything, as well as the single most regretful moment of my life. It'd changed everything. It'd changed *me*. Changed me so drastically that I'd found myself standing over my brother's bed in the early morning hours with a kitchen knife in hand, at war with the demon inside. I'd won—barely—and did the only thing I could think of to spare the people I loved. I'd left.

"The best thing I can do for you—for everyone—is get

out of town. I wasn't supposed to see Chase. I wasn't supposed to see Sam… This has gotten too complicated already."

Rick placed a hand on either side of my shoulders. He
wobbled a little, but used me to steady himself. Seeing him
like this tore me apart. He'd always been a rock. Now, he
looked like a gentle breeze would knock him to the ground.
"I want you here. You know that. But I think you're right. I
know how hard it is for you to see Sam. And your brother,
well, that's difficult on an entirely different level. He may
think himself ten feet tall and bulletproof, but you and I
know better. I'll never forgive myself for telling you to leave,
but—"

Rick had been the one to talk me into leaving town in
the first place. I'd only been seventeen at the time, but we
both recognized the need for distance. After tearing myself
away from Chase's bedside that night, I ran straight to my
uncle, who gave me a wad of cash and a gentle shove toward
the door. The guilt had likely been eating at him ever since.

"I can't control this thing when he's around. And Sam…
She's an entirely different issue for me." I clasped a hand
over his. It was so cold. "You didn't let me down, Uncle Rick.
You helped me do what was right for everyone."

"I sent a child onto the street on his own. What kind of
a father does that?"

"The kind that can make the hard choices. I owe you."

I'd never once questioned Rick's motives. The old man
loved me. There was never any doubt in my mind. But he
loved Chase, too, and he'd done what was best to keep us
both safe and sane.

The demon flashed the encounter at the diner through
my mind again, only with a slightly different ending. In this

version I attacked Chase, ripping the still-beating heart from my brother's chest as Sam stood by and cheered. At the completion of the morbid vision, the demon settled down again, content. Of course, the things that settled the demon had an opposite effect on me. They left me feeling edgy and sick. My muscles began to ache, signaling that the demon was ready to feed again. Not the scavenger bits of anger and fear, but true violence. "I need to leave. Chase will be here soon. I don't want to take any chances…"

Rick nodded, grim. "I understand."

"I can't come back again." This was it. The last time I'd see him. I'd return for the funeral, but it would be from a distance. "The thing is always nudging me toward darkness, but when I'm here—when I'm near Chase—it's worse."

Rick hesitated, like there was something more he wanted to say. Another moment passed, and he pulled me into a hug. "I'm proud of you, kid. I think—I think you're going to be all right. Stay away from your brother and everything will be all right…"

Chapter Six

Sam

I stuffed the car keys into my back pocket and slammed the rental car door. The sun was shining and there was a chill in the air to tell us winter was on the way. I hadn't slept last night, so by the time 9:00 a.m. rolled around, I was the walking dead. To make matters worse, my aunt didn't drink coffee. The woman wasn't human… I ended up being late to work to sate my caffeine addiction, because going without *wasn't* an option.

"Sam," someone whispered. "Psst. Over here."

I whirled around, almost losing my footing in the loose gravel, and squinted into the darkness of the alley. A hunched figure hovered in the shadows by the dumpster. "Hobe?"

A small-framed man in his early thirties with a nasty nervous tic and a serious acne issue stepped from the dark. He refused to look directly at me and kept both hands stuffed in his pockets as he came closer. If I didn't know Hobe, I probably would've crossed the street to avoid him. Not dangerous in a bruiser sort of way, he had an entirely different kind of vibe. Creepy in that "it's always the quiet ones" way. Our boss usually made him work mornings to clean up because he tended to freak out the customers.

The Viking was Harlow's only nightclub. The club opened two years ago—despite an enthusiastic campaign from residents to keep it out—and had become a hot spot. Even people from four towns over visited.

"Boss man is on the war path."

"I'm running late for my shift. I know, I'm sorry." I wasn't a morning person, but I was stuck coming in early, before the club opened, to do grunt work because I'd been late four times last week. Normally Martin stuck me behind the bar. I wasn't the prettiest, but I knew how to water down a drink better than anyone. The big boss was nothing if not cheap. "What's his deal today?"

"This Gentleman Stalker thing. He's pissed. Says it's bad for business."

I'd heard about that. Some of the girls who had gone missing were from Huntington campus. It just reinforced that I'd made the right choice. I could have ended up like them. In fact, I had a feeling I almost had.

The decision to leave school was prompted mainly because I'd been attacked one night on the way home from a party. No one knew about the Gentleman Stalker at the time, but who knew? I could have ended up his first victim.

Yesterday, after the accident, I'd even had myself convinced that the near miss at school and the sudden streak of bad luck here in Harlow were somehow connected. But with the clarity of a new day, I realized that was insane. That would mean whoever attacked me on campus had followed me all the way home. There'd be no point. I'd never even seen his face.

"Boss is going to stick you on cleanup crew with me for the next month," Hobe said as I made my way around the car and to the back door. "Then you'll have to deal with the monsters."

I bit my tongue as I slipped in through the back. The running joke at the club was that Hobe's mother had dropped him on his head during a monster movie marathon.

He followed, shaking his head. "Fangs and shit. Horns, scales, tentacles…" he continued seriously. "You're nice. I'd hate to see you hurt."

"Tentacles? Really?" And I thought I'd heard it all last week when he'd told me aliens were running the Dairy Queen on Eighth and had offered him a job. "Well, thank God I have you to protect me."

It was going to be a long day…

As punishment for being late—again—Martin made me clean out the bathrooms. When I was done with that, he had me scraping the vomit from the side of the building. It was a good thing I had an ironclad stomach.

"Hey," someone said, coming up behind me. "This where the cool kids are hanging?"

No.

The universe was testing me. That was the only explanation. I nodded without turning. It was bad enough he'd come back to town, now Jax Flynn was stalking me at work? While I cleaned puke from a wall? What the hell had I done in another life to piss off karma so badly? "Sure is. Guess that means you'll have to stand someplace else."

"And deprive you of the chance to experience my godlike body?"

I threw down the rag and straightened, turning to him with a sneer. "Godlike? Try pasty and…" Yeah, I had nothing. Godlike was a good word. Drool-worthy. Focus-stealing… Holy shit. I couldn't stand there, looking at him, without wondering what his lips would taste like. Or how his skin would feel as I ran my fingers over the hard planes of his muscle.

In the same trench coat as yesterday, he was swathed in black from head to toe, looking every bit as dangerous as he did delicious. It burned that the sight of him still revved my engine. He was *cut*, too. "What are you doing here, Jax? Something tells me you didn't come down to watch me scrape puke."

A waggle of his brows and a not-so-subtle wink. "But you scrape it so well." I geared up to tell him to shove off, but he raised his hands, sobering. "Okay, okay. Kelly told me where to find you."

"Why would she do that?"

"I told her I was leaving. Wanted to say good-bye and see how you were doing."

A tangled knot formed in my chest. I hated that he was here, yet a part of me wanted so badly for him to stay. How was that for twisted? I should have the words "perpetual indecision" tattooed on my ass. "Good-bye?"

He tilted his head to the right. "Missing me already?"

Hell, yes. "Counting down the seconds to departure, actually," I said. I stepped away from the building and twirled around, ending with a little bow. "And obviously I'm right as rain. Feel free to move it along to whatever hole you plan on crawling into for the next three years. I'm working, after all."

"Oh, yeah." He folded his arms. "I can see that. It must be exhausting to clean puke. Bet they pay you the big bucks. Tell me, do you have a corner office yet?"

I turned back to the wall. The stain was all but gone, but I contemplated scrubbing it some more. I would not engage in a bickering match. Would. Not. "Like I said, I'm fine. Obligation complete." I wiggled my fingers over my shoulder in a dismissive wave. "Run along and irritate someone else now."

He made a noise low in his throat—a cross between a snort and a growl that was both hysterical and sexy at the same time. "*Obligation?* What kind of sense does that make? *You* were driving. How could I possibly feel obligated?"

Shit. He had a point.

"Speaking of…" I turned to face him again. But not stare at his chest. Or his arms. Or his lips. God. Definitely not his lips… Wow. Had someone cranked up the heat? "What was up with that, anyway? If I hadn't piped up, you weren't going to say anything."

Silence.

"About driving the car?" I prodded.

He narrowed his eyes and I had to remind myself to breathe. That look, all attitude and danger, used to be the death of me. Apparently, things hadn't changed. "Why bother?"

"Why—? Kelly thought you almost killed me. You didn't even defend yourself."

He stiffened. "I don't need you to stick up for me. Maybe I didn't care what she thought?"

"Hey, Sam," Margret Guinness called as she passed on the sidewalk. I didn't miss the look of disdain that crossed the old woman's face as her eyes passed over Jax.

He didn't miss it either. He glared at Margret, and without turning back to me, said, "Maybe I don't care what any of them think—and that includes you. "And with that, he turned on his heel and started toward the back of the parking lot.

Was he kidding? With a quick look at the door to make sure the boss wasn't watching, I took off after Jax.

"You're really something." I caught him as he reached the edge of the parking lot. Grabbing his arm, I spun him around. "And a big, fat liar."

He snorted, eyebrows rising slightly. "Someone needs to update their vocabulary. Scoundrel. Rogue. Criminally hot badass. You can do better than *big fat liar*, Sammy." He pulled away and kept walking.

Some people called it stubbornness. I called it determination. Proudly inherited from my mom right along with my crooked toes and too-wide smile. I caught up to him again, this time jumping in front to block his path. "You care what I think. Granted, you may not care what Kelly thinks—most people don't—but you care what I think."

"You're delusional," he growled, all the humor draining from his expression. I knew that look. It was the *about to go postal* expression I'd seen on him a thousand times before. "You can't possibly believe—"

From inside my back pocket, the cell phone started ringing. Without waiting for him to finish, I fished it out, hoping it pissed him off. He'd always had a thing about being interrupted. "Hello?"

"Ms. Merrick? This is Allen over at Frenksel Automotive. I'm just calling to inform you that we've had a chance to look over your car."

"Oh. Well, that was fast. I knew the sheriff was having it yanked from the river. Any idea what caused my brakes to crap out?"

Behind me, Jax's shadow moved a bit closer. I could feel him standing close and it was giving me chills.

"Yes. We know exactly why your brakes didn't work. Ms. Merrick…it looks as though they were cut."

Chapter Seven

Jax

This was against the rules. Don't get involved.

And yet as she ended the call, I opened my damn mouth.

"Cut? What the hell is going on?" It wasn't eavesdropping. The guy on the other end of the line was practically yelling. I would have heard the call even without the demonic boost. "Why would someone cut your brakes?"

She tried to cover it up, but it was impossible to hide. At least, from me. A quick nibble at the left corner of her bottom lip and an overexaggerated roll of her brown eyes. That, and the hint of gray smoke that rose from her shoulders. "They're wrong. Obviously. Why the hell would someone *cut* my brakes? Everyone loves me. You, on the other hand…"

She was lying. The taste of fear, sickly sweet and thick in the air, was all around. This wasn't random and she knew it.

"Apparently, they love you so much it hurts," I said

coolly.

"Now look who's funnier." She flashed a thin smile. It bothered me that she thought she could pass it off as real. I'd been gone a few years, but I could see through her. Always could. Shit like that didn't change.

"Seriously, Sammy. What's this all about? First you leave school, now someone tries to put you at the bottom of the river? Who'd you piss off?" There. Another opening for her to come clean.

She crossed her arms and glared, the expression sexy as all hell. The right-hand corner of her lip quirked. Eyes narrow and focused. Head tilted sideways. Hair falling across her eyes. "If—and that's a *huge* if—the brakes were cut, it was probably a mistake. Maybe they got the wrong car."

"Yeah. Because that kind of shit happens all the time in Harlow." Think snails. Open-heart surgery. Naked dudes. Anything other than the way she looked and the sound of her voice. It was derailing my focus. "If I hadn't been in the car, you wouldn't be here right now."

I thought back to the night I'd left. The one and only time we'd kissed. A real kiss—not the too-brief brush in the car at the bottom of the river. Soft lips. Warm skin. The scent of honeysuckle all around. The feeling of contentment quickly overshadowed by something dark and poisonous.

"Oh, that's right." She smacked her head, pulling me from the memory. The gray mist faded as she glanced back toward the building. "You saved me." Another step closer. I found it impossible to look away. "And why do you even care? This is none of your business."

I bit down hard on the inside of my cheek. Only Sam could make me this particular shade of pissed off. "I was in the car, too. Whoever your friendly would-be murderer is, he almost offed me, as well. Technically I have a right to kick someone's ass."

She blinked, genuinely surprised. "You have the right?" She was standing so close. All I'd have to do was move my hand an inch—maybe two—and I could touch her. The thought pulled unwanted reactions from my body. "You—" She shook her head, backing away slowly toward the building.

I should have seen it coming.

In a single, fluent move, Sam pivoted and reached for the container of dirty water. Bucket in hand, she moved back toward me. "*You have the right?*"

She wouldn't dare... "I know what you're thinking, Sammy. Don't."

She grinned. A wicked smile that did fucked-up things to my brain. The way her bottom lip protruded just a hair. Eyes narrow. Cheekbones sharp. Samantha Merrick was the picture of perfection—even if she *was* contemplating assault with a stinky weapon.

"Wanna know what else you have a *right* to?"

Unfortunately there was only one thing on my mind at that particular moment, and the words came out before I could stop them. "Well, since I saved your life, I think I probably deserve a kiss. At the very least. *With* tongue."

She froze for a second, face paling. Oh. Yeah. Stumped her good. It didn't last, though. She closed the distance between us and leaned close, stopping mere inches from me. The hand holding the bucket fell to her side.

"Jax..." The sound of my name on her lips had a powerful effect on not only me, but the demon. As she nuzzled my ear and ran a finger up the other side of my neck, the demon rumbled and the scene around me changed. Another flash, this one unlike anything the thing had shown me before.

Sam was beneath me, breathing hard and biting down on her lower lip. She arched her back and moaned, exposing herself to me, and my real-time pulse spiked. The vision wasn't real, but was wreaking havoc on my body all the same. It was impossible not to see her like that, willing and vulnerable, and not have a physical reaction.

There was a surge of amusement from the demon. It enjoyed the way this made me feel. Hungry and furious. Starving to touch her, while at the same time, so terrified of hurting her more than I already had. The flash continued, and I watched, unable to block it out, as I lowered my lips to the hollow of her throat. I worked my way down, dipping between her breasts and nipping at the skin along the way, drawing shocked little noises from Sam's lips.

The flash ended, leaving me hard and hot, and for a second, I forgot to breathe.

"You really want a kiss? How about a wet one?" The heat from her breath lingered for a moment, followed by a stream of tepid, foul-smelling water as it rained over my head and ran down my shoulders.

I stumbled away and flicked the excess water from my arms. In a way, I was thankful. While not as good as a cold shower, it helped get the situation back under control. Unfortunately, it also made the demon furious. It pushed, but I gritted my teeth and stuffed it down. With an irritated sigh, I met her gaze and held it. "Are we even now?"

"Not a chance." She let the empty bucket fall to the sidewalk and rubbed her hands down the sides of her jeans. "But who cares, right? You're leaving again anyway." Sam turned on her heel and strode to the door. A quick glance over her shoulder, and she was gone.

It was plain to see by the swirling colors above her head that she wanted me to stay despite how I'd left her behind. That alone should have lit a California wildfire under my ass. But something was wrong. Sam was in trouble — whether she knew it or not.

An hour ago, I'd been ready to leave. I'd come to the club to say good-bye once and for all, determined to put Harlow, and her, in the past for good. Now I had no choice. I had to stay — at least until I made sure she wouldn't have any more "car trouble."

I'd gone back to Rick's for a dry shirt. At least, that's what I told myself. What was supposed to be a ten-minute stopover ended up being three beers for me and two hours' worth of bullshitting. I probably would have stayed longer, but Rick was exhausted, and I knew I was pushing my luck. I gathered my coat and was almost out the door when Chase came in.

"My jaw is fine. Thanks for asking."

I stopped halfway across the living room. Turning around was a bad call, but I did it anyway. "You shouldn't be here."

"I told him that," Rick called from the other room. A series of coughs followed.

Chase leaned against the doorframe and grinned. Not a care in the world. That always bugged me. Easy and smooth. The guy never stressed over anything. "Why? Because you'll kick my ass?"

Fists tight, I took a step closer. It was a dangerous move considering the way the demon inside raged, but I couldn't help it. "It's a miracle you're not in traction after what I walked into yesterday."

My brother was the only human whose emotions I couldn't see. We'd written it off as the curse—technically he was part of it, the Abel to my Cain—but it still bugged me. There had never been a problem seeing Rick's colors. He frowned. "I got a little carried away trying to prove a point."

"What fucking point? All the other girls in the world and you pick Sammy?"

Chase sighed and grabbed a baseball from the table. He'd won the game with it in tenth grade, and Rick had it mounted. "The *point* is, that even when I push your buttons, you can hold it together. If anything was going to set your dial to meltdown, that would have been the thing to do it. It was one little punch, man. I'm fine. Besides, I was a little jealous."

Had everyone in this town lost their goddamned minds? "Jealous? Of the snarling monster living in my head?"

Chase tossed me the ball and sank onto the couch, the same one Rick had when we'd first moved in with him. Shit brown with pale-yellow pinstriping. "She's always been all about you. Never looked twice at me. Even after all this time."

"And that drives you crazy, doesn't it?" I seethed.

Chase threw his hands up. "No arguments here, man. It *did* drive me nuts. I don't get the appeal. You're so dark and broody. I'm fun and charming."

"And a prick that'll fuck anything that walks." I added, throwing the ball back with more force than necessary.

"Is it my fault chicks find me irresistible? They always have." He rolled the ball between his hands, then tossed it back.

"The girls you got, I never wanted."

"And the one you got, I did."

There was no point in talking about it. If Sam found out the truth she'd be horrified—and who could blame her? I was a monster unworthy of love and compassion. Someone like her deserved to live in the light. Not stay hidden away in the dark. "Sam and I have no future together. Do whatever the fuck you want."

"Since you don't want her, maybe I *will* take a swing." Chase shrugged. "Nothing serious. I have to admit, I'm really curious what she'd feel like underneath me."

The demon's rage ignited, mingling with my own emotion and making everything hazy. I threw the ball, this time with enough force to embed it in the wall right beside Chase's head. "I'll fucking kill—"

Chase jumped off the couch, taking several of the cushions with him, and threw up his hands again. "Relax, man. I'm just kidding. You know how I love to tweak you. But obviously you have an issue that needs resolving."

The ache intensified, mouth going dry. Limit. Being here, listening to my brother's voice, was testing my limit. The demon, sensing a crack in restraint, tried pushing itself to the surface, but I kept it down. Barely. "Could we drop the Sam thing?"

Chase took a step closer. "Look, I'm sorry. Rick said you didn't want me here, and I get it, but I haven't seen you in three years. You could have at least called once in a while to let me know you were still alive."

"No," I said coolly. I'd felt the demon's animosity toward him in the past, but since coming home, it seemed to have intensified tenfold. What used to be an itch to punch Chase in the face had turned into something just short of need. "The sound of your voice makes me sick. I want to physically rip you to shreds each time you open your goddamned trap. You've always been careless, but are you suicidal, too?"

"I know what you're thinking—"

The demon roared. I felt it as clearly as the breath moving through my lungs. The internal tremor rocked me to the core and everything momentarily went black. Deep breath. I'd worked for years on keeping the thing controlled in stressful situations. If he wasn't careful, my brother was going to undo all that progress in a single afternoon. "If you knew what I was thinking, you'd be running right now."

Chase had the intelligence to at least look worried. He was hovering in the doorway just out of reach. "You can't leave town, Jax. Not yet. It's Samantha. *She* needs your help."

"She doesn't need anything from me except distance."

"At least hear me out, okay?"

Maybe he knew something about what was going on. Something that Sam wasn't telling me. "Talk fast."

"About a month ago Samantha came back home. One day she's going to Huntington, staying on campus, the next she shows up on my doorstep asking me to help her find an apartment in town."

"And your point?"

"My point is, this is Samantha we're talking about. She couldn't get away from this place fast enough, and now she's back out of the blue?" Chase folded his arms. "I think something happened at school."

"What could have happened?" The question was for my brother's benefit. I already knew the answer. She'd been attacked. I'd gotten there just in time to scare the bastard off. Unfortunately, I hadn't gotten a good look at the guy. It would have given me great pleasure to give him an up close and personal introduction to the demon.

Chase frowned. "No clue. She won't say."

"Maybe because it's none of your damn business what she does?"

Expression darkening, any caution my brother felt drained away, and in a bold move, he stepped closer. "Lemme guess. She lied to you, didn't she?"

She had, but I'd seen through it.

Chase grinned. The smug satisfaction in his expression made me—not the demon—want to smash his face into the wall. "Well, maybe in her eyes it was a lie of omission. That car going into the river wasn't the first *accident* she's had since coming back home."

"What the fuck are you talking about?" Was there a connection? Had the person who attacked her at school made other attempts?

"Ask her. You're the only one who has any hope of getting the truth. She pretty much brushes everyone else off."

"You ask her. You've been here with her all this time." The demon was getting antsy. Hands gripping the doorframe opposite my brother, I growled, "And you two seem pretty fucking cozy."

"Get over it already," Chase snapped. He took a deep breath, and his expression cooled a little. "I know this is hard for you, but I'm just asking you to stay for a few days. Just find out what's going on."

The demon flooded my mind with images of bodies washed in blood and screaming in pain. One body particular—Chase's—made me sick, but at the same time, filled me with a twisted sense of satisfaction. I couldn't take it anymore. "You need to leave."

"What about—"

"Get out!" The scream tore from my throat like a weapon, leaving me edgy and raw. Beyond the front door, a dog started barking and a car alarm blared to life. "I don't trust myself to keep it away. Go. Before. I. Tear. You. Apart."

My brother sighed and backed away. "You're here. I'm here. Like I said before, you haven't done any real damage, man. You had the strength to walk away at McCarthy's. You don't give yourself enough credit."

I braced both hands against the doorframe, gripping the wood until my fingernails dented the surface. "And you're giving me too much."

Chapter Eight

Sam

Not bad. I smoothed the skirt and examined my reflection in the mirror. A black lace mini paired with a deep-burgundy bustier. I'd never worn anything like it, but tonight's festivities called for something a little more dangerous than the usual jeans and Viking logo black tank. A little self-conscious and a lot exposed, when this was all over, Martin better be giving me a damn raise. To combat the drop-off in business due to the Gentleman Stalker, he'd decided to make Fridays theme night. The theme? Gothic hotties.

I fluffed my hair and slipped into the pair of boots I'd worn on Halloween two years ago. The skirt was a little short for my taste and my makeup was heavier than normal. Awesome. I looked like a Gothic hooker. If I managed to get through the shift without breaking an ankle, the night would be a raging success.

Calling in sick had crossed my mind, but other than the fact that I had less than twelve dollars in my bank account and rent was due in two weeks, it was actually good I was working tonight. The busier I stayed, the less chance that my mind would wander. Denial was my best friend. Always had been.

I'd been fine before getting the call from the car place. Cut brakes were not an accident, and that shot my theory to shit, bringing up a ton of other, scarier, possibilities. Last week I'd nearly been run down crossing the street on the way to the library. A few nights ago, there was an attempted mugging on the way out to the car after work. Bad driver. A shitty part of town. An old clunker...

But it wasn't about an old clunker anymore. It was about brakes.

That had been *cut.*

My accident hadn't been an accident.

I pulled the rental car into the lot behind the Viking. The club, housed in the old Kmart warehouse, was wild on its quiet nights. I could only imagine what kind of a crowd Martin's theme night would bring. Resigned, I slipped in through the back door.

A slender black woman with a thick Southern accent and warm smile slapped the bar and let out a hoot the moment I walked through the door. Virginia Pells—Gin to most people—was a thirty-year-old who looked like she was twenty, acted like she was sixteen, and dated men in their fifties. She was a kind soul who, unlike most of the people working for the Viking, had gone out of her way to befriend me. "Hell musta froze over because look who just walked in five minutes early." She let out a whistle. "And damn girl, you look hot."

"I feel ridiculous," I responded, peeling off my coat. Tossing it on a hook behind the bar, I immediately tugged at the skirt. The damn thing was so short that one wrong move and the entire club would be seeing London and France. "Thought you were off tonight?"

Gin gave an enthusiastic shake of her head. Long bleached-blond dreadlocks whipped back and forth. "And miss this mess? Not a chance, baby. Not a chance." She backed away from the bar and I got a good look at her. Gin normally went heavy on the eye makeup, but tonight she was rocking a look straight from the movie *The Crow*. Skin-tight leather pants and bloodred thigh-high boots paired with a bright-red bra that she'd covered with a black mesh shirt. "So spill. I heard the evil Flynn boy was back in town. Say it ain't so."

I rolled my eyes. Christ. Had Aunt Kelly started a phone chain or something? It wasn't fair that everyone labeled Jax the bad one. Half the things he'd been blamed for when we were younger were Chase's doing. "He's not evil. He just has issues with authority."

Gin winked. "The way I heard it, you both do."

She had a point. Jax and I had gotten into a lot of hot water when we were younger. Everything from breaking into the high school for a midnight swim, to stealing the Harlow PD sign. I wasn't as wild as I used to be, but I had my moments.

The buzzer rang to signal that the doors were about to

open, thankfully sparing me from further talk about Jax. All he'd done by blowing in and out of town was stir up the muck that lived inside my head and my heart, and the sooner I could put it all behind me, the better.

As the doors opened and the people began filing in, grinding to the already-pumping music and laughing like they hadn't a care in the world, I decided to let it go. What was done was done and he wasn't coming back.

There was nothing here worth staying for.

Those were his exact words.

I glanced down at the small digital clock resting on the shelf just beneath the bar. One a.m. and I'd been hit on, spit on, and grabbed, and narrowly avoided being puked on. All in all, it had been an uneventful night as far as shifts at the Viking went. Still though, it'd been a long day and I was ready to crash.

College hadn't been the right place for me, and I was no closer to figuring out what I wanted to do with the rest of my life than I had been the day I graduated from high school. Now here I was, dressed like an emo version of a sorority girl, slinging brew instead of drinking it. Not exactly how I'd envisioned my first steps into adulthood. On top of all that, I was the target of a brake-cutting, shadow-jumping lunatic who apparently had a hard-on for me. Yeah. So far being a grown-up was awesome.

A glance in both directions told me no one was looking, so I poured myself a shot and downed it fast. At nineteen, I was allowed to work at the bar, but had been warned that if one sip passed my underage lips, my ass was fired.

It was like Gin said. I had an issue with authority. Besides, my nerves were fried.

By one thirty, the club started winding down. Theme night had been a huge success—which sucked. That meant Martin would do it again. Hell, he'd probably try to do it every night. Apparently an excuse to leave the house in a costume trumped a serial killer on the loose.

"I gotta say, Sammy… That is definitely a *good* look for you."

I froze and begged myself not to turn. Once I looked into those eyes it would all be over. He'd have me eating out of his hand. Barking like a dog. Purring like a fucking kitten. Dignity would be a thing of the past. Shit… Drink.

I needed another drink.

Back to the bar, shot glass poised at my bottom lip, an inexplicable nervous twitch ran through my body. I tilted the cup back and swallowed, cringing as the liquid burned my throat, then poured another and did the same. With a deep breath, I faced him. "See now, I'd love to say this is a good surprise, but, ya know… You're kinda like herpes. Totally unwanted."

"You're comparing me to an STD?"

I put my elbows on the bar, leaning forward just a bit, then realized what I was doing. OhMyGod, I'd just unintentionally flashed him. Stupid low-cut top. I straightened and pulled the soft material higher. "Yeah. I think so."

He straightened as well, meeting me a little more than halfway. His gaze traveled over my body, grin appreciative. "I think you have the wrong Flynn. Besides, we both know you're excited to see me, *Samantha*."

Tingles. I got tingles every time he spoke my full name. He always managed to make it sound so sultry. That single word uttered from those perfect lips had the ability to turn me into a pile of goo. He knew it, too. Made sure to drop his voice an octave or two whenever he said it.

He shifted to the right, revealing part of what looked like a black tribal tattoo. The itch to see the rest of it, to know where it ended, was driving me nuts. No matter how I tried, I couldn't drag my gaze from his arms. His strong, toned arms... "Back for another bucket of puke?"

"I owe you for that."

"I know." I pushed off the bar and started wiping down the counters. "How about you run away again. That'll teach me."

"Sam," Martin slammed a hand down against the bar to get my attention. "Start restocking. Gillian can watch things here."

Yeah. And Gillian could use her padded *personality* to steal my tips, too.

Grumbling, I turned away from Jax and headed for the corner of the room. The only storage was in the basement and I hated going down there. Normally, I would have argued to have someone else do it, but with Jax standing there, I wanted to stand around and talk to him—which made me itch to get away.

I was almost to the door when I realized I had company. Seriously. This day couldn't get any worse. "Stalking me? Really?" As if I didn't have enough of that crap going on already?

He shrugged and held the door open wide. "We were talking. I figured we could walk *and* talk."

"We weren't talking, Jax. You were talking—I'm convinced it's because you love the sound of your own voice. I was trying to walk away." I gestured to the steps, then started down them, holding tight to the railing so I didn't end up in a heap at the bottom. "Exhibit A."

He wasn't deterred. "I wanted to give you a chance to apologize."

Apologize? Was he kidding? I opened my mouth, and then closed it. No. This is what he wanted. To get me going. Instead of answering, I went down to the bottom and made my way through the narrow aisles toward the liquor storage as though he wasn't there.

"Nothing fancy," he continued. "A simple 'I'm sorry and want to make it up to you' works for me."

I couldn't keep my mouth closed any longer. Reaching the end of the row, I turned on my heel and pinned him with my most intimidating glare. "What the hell are you doing, Jax?"

He stopped a few feet away. "Waiting for my apology?"

"Try waiting for rabid monkeys to fly sideways out of my ass," I snapped. "I mean, here. What are you doing *here*? You skipped town with no notice three years ago, then you pop back for no reason. You say you're leaving, yet here you are."

He stepped closer. "In a rush to get rid of me?"

I wasn't. But I was. And then I wasn't. There it was again. That damn indecision. "Matter of fact, I am." I backed up until I hit the shelf where the club stored its extra vodka. A loud rattle and several clinking bottles, and one zoomed from the top, past my right side. It happened so fast. One second Jax was in front of me, the next he was on my right side, a bottle of vodka clutched in his hand inches from the ground.

He straightened and handed over the bottle. "There. I saved you from having to explain why you broke a bottle. I think I deserve a thank-you."

The air caught in my throat. There was a mischievous tilt to his lips, but also a stark seriousness in his eyes. I hated how it made me feel. Comforted by the familiarity of it, while at the same time, betrayed because he'd left me behind.

Jax was the one who, up until the night he disappeared, had always been there for me. He brought me back to life after my parents died, the only person who'd been able to reach into the darkness and yank me out.

Our relationship had been the most natural thing in the world. Like breathing or the rotation of the planet. We were made for each other, two halves of the same whole. It'd never occurred to me that we wouldn't end up together. Then he found the courage to tell me he felt the same way, and was gone the next day.

I needed to say something witty to break the tension. "If you're going to try negotiating another kiss you're out of luck."

A wicked smile crept across his face and suddenly it was impossible to concentrate. The basement, normally so much colder than the main floor of the club, felt like Texas in July. My clothes, the ones that only a moment ago felt too revealing, were constricting and in the way. He leaned across and took the bottle, making a move to put it back on the shelf. On the way up, his arm grazed my cheek, the sleeve riding up so that it was skin on skin, and a tiny gasp slipped from my lips. He stretched farther, like he was trying to reach the next shelf, letting his free hand skim up my bare arm and past my shoulder. The touch was so light, barely there, yet the most incredibly electric thing I'd ever experienced. It left me burning and desperate, on the verge of dragging him close and begging him to put his hands all over my body.

When he was done, he paused by my ear, warm breath caressing my cheek, and whispered, "If I *want* a kiss, trust me, I'll *get* one."

If the reaction from his body pressed close against me was any indication, then he *did* want that kiss. And more.

When he finally pulled away, the expression on his face had morphed from jovial to serious. "What I want is for you to tell me the truth. What happened at Huntington?"

An icy wave of panic rolled over me. Admitting it happened, out loud, scared me nearly as much as the actual attack had. If I didn't speak about it, then I could pretend it wasn't real. Even though a masochistic part of me wanted him to keep going, to push past and claim my personal space as his own, my breath faltered and the walls sprang up.

A million retorts bubbled to the surface and I bit down hard on my tongue to keep from saying something I'd regret. We stood there, eye to eye, neither of us willing to budge. The air cooled and fire between us fizzled, and all the rejection I felt when he turned his back and left came rushing to the surface again. "This should really go without saying, but why the hell do you care?"

"Because I know there's something going on and I'm worried."

"If you were so concerned about me then you should have stuck around." The bitterness in my voice grated. "Can't just walk back into my life and plant yourself in the center again."

I pushed him, but he wouldn't budge. It only made me angrier. More helpless. There was too much of that in my life right now. The shitty job. The lack of direction. The overdue bills piling up. I was giving inches and life was taking miles. I'd reached the breaking point. An explosion had been building for some time now, and how poetic was it that Jax was conveniently standing right here?

"What you did was *selfish*. Whatever your issues were, it was easier to run away than stay here and face them. A coward," I breathed. "You're a damn coward."

"You don't know what the fuck you're talking about," he snapped, then softened just a bit. "I didn't just decide to leave on a whim. I had a damn good reason. And it really pisses me off that you could even think it was a careless, spur-of-the-moment choice and that it didn't rip me the fuck apart." He grabbed the shelf on either side of my head and leaned close again. "Just tell me what the hell happened at Huntington."

"No."

"Yes," he growled, then took a deep breath. "You need to tell someone, Sammy. For your own sanity."

"I was attacked." The words spilled out before I could stop them. It was him. The cosmic pull he had on every part of me. Mind, body, and soul.

My heart pounded, a thundering echo inside my chest, and a rush of anger crashed over me. It chased away the hurt and replaced it with pure rage. That he'd gotten what he wanted. That I'd had to say it out loud. That I, in some small way, blamed him for the whole thing. It was completely irrational, but I couldn't push the feelings aside.

I braced my hands against his chest and gave a good

shove, this time putting some solid distance between us. *Do. Not. Cry.* "Someone attacked me on my way home from a party one night and I couldn't take it. I ran away. Are you happy now? You know the truth. Do you feel better?"

For the longest moment he said nothing. He was staring at me with the strangest expression. Not anger or confusion. Not pain or regret. It was like he was concentrating. I could see him breathing. The steady, slightly quickened rise and fall of his chest as he inhaled and exhaled, and then, the flexing of his right hand. I was just about to scream at him again when he finally spoke.

"No," he said, almost too low for me to hear. "I don't feel better."

A tickle in my belly. That sinking feeling that comes when you say or do something that can't be taken back. More than embarrassment. Mortification. Heat flamed to life in my cheeks, and I knotted both fists tight, determined not to lose it in front of him again. While saying it out loud lifted the two-ton weight that had been crushing me, it also let that raw, wounded part of my soul spill out.

I wanted to stop at that, but the words just kept coming. "I left a party. Halfway home, someone came up behind me… He tried to wrestle me into the shadows and everything got dark really fast. I don't remember much. Whoever it was covered my mouth with a rag…I dunno…" I'd gone to the police. They'd taken a statement and made a promise to look into it. Miraculously, I hadn't been badly hurt so it wasn't a priority.

The whole situation was eerily familiar. A fuzzy memory, one from the night my parents were killed, lurked just beneath the surface, but I couldn't grab it. Being attacked must have stirred things up. "I think — I think someone scared the guy off."

Jax nodded. He was too quiet and it was making me nervous. When he spoke again, there was a feral intensity to his voice that scared me. "You remember anything else? Weight, height, hair color? Any defining characteristics?"

I didn't want to talk about this. Not with him. Not with anyone. But there was no way he'd let it go.

"His voice was muffled and gravelly. I remember thinking it sounded wrong somehow. Fake, almost. Like one of those prank voice boxes, ya know?" That voice was the star of my recent nightmares, telling me to stop struggling. To give in. It was the sound that woke me in a cold sweat, sometimes screaming until my throat was raw. "I'd been drinking at the party and I'd had a huge fight with Aaron, this guy I went out with once. He got grabby and I decked him. Everyone at the party saw it go down. That's a big part of why the cops dismissed the whole thing. A domestic dispute, they called it — but that's crap. Aaron had been drinking, same as me. The guy who jumped me didn't smell like alcohol."

He didn't respond, so I continued, too afraid of letting the silence float between us.

"I left school a few days later. I couldn't concentrate. I kept looking over my shoulder. Waiting for someone to break down my door in the middle of the night. I kept thinking..." That history was repeating itself. And it was, right? The attack, the accidents, the car... Those were connected in some way. I wanted to tell him. To throw myself into his arms and let him help me carry the weight like he used to. But that time had passed. "I kept thinking I was insane. I just couldn't handle it."

"Sammy, this is nothing—"

"Martin is probably ready to shit rocks," I said, gathering several bottles from the shelf before I lost my nerve and spilled it all. There was no way I'd let him finish that sentence. Already, a familiar stinging sensation in the corners of my eyes told me enough was enough. He made a move to take some of the bottles from me, but I jerked away, refusing his help. When I looked at him again, I had my game face on. This Sam could take on the world all by herself. She didn't need anyone. She didn't need Jax.

"Let me help you. Please."

I was pretty sure he wasn't talking about the armful of bottles. "It's all good. *I'm* good. I make really great money here and I was going to have issues paying next semester's tuition anyway. I would have had to drop out. Whoever this wacko was, he did me a favor."

With that, I made my way back out to the floor, hoping to God he'd finally take the hint and just move on with his life.

Because that's what I needed to do.

Chapter Nine

Jax

Fifteen minutes passed before I could even think about leaving the basement. The anger raging inside, provoking the demon, was borderline nuclear. I thought getting her to admit what happened out loud would help, but the truth was, it made things worse. For both of us.

The night on campus that Sam was attacked was the first time in years that I'd been so physically close to her. The demon went nuts, and once I was sure she was safe, I freaked and ran for the town line.

After hearing that the brakes had been cut, and seeing her reaction tonight, I was positive these accidents were connected. I imagined finding the bastard and tearing him apart, tiny piece by tiny piece. Not that this was the first time it'd crossed my mind. For days after the attack, I'd thought of nothing more. But in the end, I'd walked away, sure that there was no way to find the person responsible. The demon flashed images of a faceless man, beaten and broken a thousand different ways.

Something needed to be done.

When I was sure I had my anger in check, I left the cellar and surveyed the main room. Sam was back at the bar, fake smile firmly in place. Her colors were a mix of gray and red, but also the deep blue of sadness. It hurt to see her in pain, but in a twisted way, it was easier. Knowing that I'd caused that pain would make it easier to leave. Justified.

She was talking to a black woman with blond dreadlocks, and a tall man who kept stealing subtle glances down her low-cut shirt. If he didn't back the fuck off soon, there was a good chance I'd cross the room and kick his teeth in.

From the smell of it, the club was mostly human, although there was a faint trace of a demon or two. Each one had its own unique scent. A slight variation of sulfur and what I found similar to burning motor oil. It wasn't surprising to find some here.

I hovered by a table on the other end of the room. The place was almost empty and they were bound to boot me any minute. Still, I couldn't tear my eyes away from Sam. The distinct swirl of gray that surrounded her was like a black cloud hanging over her head. I could taste it from across the club, the sticky sweetness of her fear.

How many nights had I woken to find her sitting on the balcony outside her room in the middle of the night when we were younger. Nightmares. They were always the same — someone attacking her. We sat across from each other for hours, until the sun came up. Sometimes we talked. Other times we just watched the stars. Now, if I was right, she was reliving that nightmare in a very real way.

People were heading for the door in groups. Two of the three bars had closed, Sam's being one of them, and I watched from across the room as she gathered the garbage and headed for the exit. If I had any hope of ending this, I'd need details about the person who'd attacked her. She had to have seen something. Heard or smelled something. Even the smallest detail could be important. Just a few more questions and I'd leave her alone. If I could track the guy down and finish him off, I could be on my way and done with Harlow in a day or two tops.

She slipped out the door right before I reached it, and when I stepped into the cool night air, she was already flipping open the Dumpster lid. I was about to call out to her, but the sound of an engine roaring to life, followed by bright lights flooding the narrow alley, stopped me cold. Sam didn't turn around. She never had the chance. The engine revved twice, then squealing tires filled the air as the car shot forward.

I crashed into her a second before the car collided with the corner of Dumpster—right where she'd been standing— and continued on without slowing. The clatter it made was drowned out by Sam's startled gasp and her almost-deafening heartbeat as I crushed her to the brick wall.

My own heart thundered. She was so close. I could smell the night on her—the smoke and alcohol from the club— but also a scent that was all Sam. Sweet and distinct. It took a second to get the words out since the inside of my mouth was suddenly like the damn Sahara, but I finally backed away several inches and asked, "Are you okay?"

She shook her head. Not back and forth or up and down,

but more in a circular motion. "Yes… No. Sort of." A shaky sigh escaped her lips. "Wow. Someone needs to learn how to drive. That guy—"

"Someone just tried to run you down, Sammy," I barked before she could get any further. She wasn't glossing over it this time. "*On purpose*. I know about the other stuff that's been going on, so don't try to bullshit me."

She kept her eyes down and said nothing.

"I'm never going to buy this shit you're selling. Just let me help you. Please."

Sam lifted her head. For a second she didn't say anything, but it was all there in her eyes. Pain. Betrayal. Sadness. Even without the dizzying mix of color swirling around her shoulders it was obvious. "It isn't your problem. Remember?" she asked quietly. She made a move to walk away, but hesitated, gaze lifting to meet mine. "I don't get it, Jax. One minute we're standing in the woods and you're spilling your guts and spouting shit about it being you and me against the world. You kiss the crap out of me, then the next morning I'm waking up to Rick at our front door telling us you've left home." She ran both hands through her long hair, then clapped her hands once. The sound echoed in the alleyway. "Boom. Just like that. No note. No phone call. No explanation. Not even to me."

"I did what I had to do," I said. "I know that doesn't make a lot of sense, and that you don't understand, but I did what I did for you."

"*For me*?"

"I don't expect you to for—"

She hit me. Fist tight, Sam punched me in the jaw. The blow didn't hurt. In fact, it felt good. Justified. I deserved it and then some. This was her chance to let it out.

"How *dare* you say it was for me," she cried, shoving me hard in the chest. The waves of gray and blue turned red, swirling like a tornado. "It was for you. For your own selfish reasons." She shoved harder, and the demon grew restless, excited by her outrage. "But whatever your reasons were, they were all for you and no one else."

Maybe it was the demon, and maybe it was just my own temper, but I couldn't stop myself. When she raised her hand to push me again, I caught it and held tight. Pushing her back, I said, "I'm not going to say this again, so listen carefully. There are things you don't know—" She opened her mouth to interrupt, but I clamped a hand across. Always talking. Always interrupting. "Things you'll *never* know. But it killed me to leave and if you think I haven't felt guilty about it every fucking day since, you're delusional."

She pried my hand lose and laughed. A broken, painful sound that touched me in places I didn't want to go. "Guilty? Good. You should feel guilty. I would have never been on that sidewalk—at that stupid college—if you hadn't left me behind. You don't care about anyone—"

I grabbed her by the shoulders and forced her back to the wall again. "Enough!"

She stared, shocked.

"Like it or not, I did what I did because I had to. Not because I *wanted* to." What the hell was it about this girl? She was a magnetic pull that seemed to suck away all common sense. Before I knew what I was doing, I brushed my thumb lightly across her cheek to wipe away a single tear.

She closed her eyes for a second, holding her breath and staying absolutely still. When she opened them, a lot of the red smoke dissipated. "Did you know? That night you left, when you kissed me, that it was good-bye?"

Fuck. Her words were like a scythe cutting me in half. If I'd known, I never would have kissed her. "No. It wasn't supposed to be a kiss good-bye. It wasn't supposed to be the end. I wanted it to be the beginning."

"But it *was* the end, right?"

There were a million ways I wanted to respond. All variations of *hell, no.* "Right."

By the subtle nod of her head, I could tell she'd expected as much, but the pain was still there. In her eyes and in her colors. Deep blue. In the way her breath hitched and her eyes glistened. Sam took a deep breath. "Then do it."

"Huh?"

She pushed against me, stopping a few inches from my lips. "Kiss me good-bye."

My gaze dropped to her mouth, lips ruby-tinted and inviting. Shit…

Inside, the demon rumbled, but instead of the usual images it fed me—blood, violence, and rage—it showed something else. A flash of the kiss the night I left. Then, another of the one at the bottom of the lake. It wanted me to kiss Sam. The want fanned into something stronger. Need. It *needed* me to kiss Sam.

So I did.

It wasn't a slow, sweet kiss. It was the dive-right-in-before-you-lose-your-fucking-nerve kind. Arms winding around her waist, I pulled her close and covered her mouth with mine. Soft, warm, and eager, she tasted faintly of vodka and cherries. It was sensation overload. A veritable shock to my system. I was a lightning rod in a hurricane. Pushed to the brink, but happy, because it's where I was meant to be. Always riding the line between pleasure and pain.

This was need. A primal, dark, animalistic force that screamed in every one of my limbs. Being here with her now, after having been away for so long, made me desperate to take as much of her as I could. Devour what I could get and savor it.

I ground my hips against her, groaning into her mouth when the sensation threatened to send me crashing over the edge. She gasped and pushed back, riding the high as eagerly as I was. There was nothing gentle here. Nothing chaste. The moment was about something forbidden and raw. The curse had taken my life from me, but I wasn't the only one. It destroyed everyone it touched. Breaking and shattering until there was nothing left but emptiness and anger.

Sam's fingers clutched my shoulders, digging into skin like she was trying to keep me there forever. The energy radiating from her was a humming vibration setting every part of my body on fire. I tasted her sadness and regret, and the pain she'd felt for every day I'd been gone. Breathing deep, I took it in, giving the thing inside what it craved and easing some of my pain. It drove the demon crazy. The monster scratched and writhed to get a bigger taste. I pushed it back.

She couldn't feel the emotion like I could, but I wanted to make sure she understood what I was unable to put into words.

That I missed her.

My lips moved with hers as I roughly grabbed either side of her face. Sliding my hands back, my fingers tangled through her long hair, then settled to cradle the back of her head to keep it away from the brick wall. A contented sigh rose in her throat at the contact. It was the most fragile, delicate sound I'd ever heard and it drove me crazy.

That she was the single most important thing to me...

She deepened the kiss, rising up onto her toes and licking at my bottom lip. Her cheeks were warm and wet, tears falling freely now. The debris of the broken past between us momentarily washed away.

That everything I was doing was to keep her safe...

We were approaching the danger zone. The demon, restless and itching for the surface, pushed harder. It flashed a succession of images, all variations of Sam, naked beneath me and moaning my name. Breath ragged, I grabbed her arms and pinned them above her head.

"Oh my—" Her voice cut off as she arched violently into me, ending in a desperate whimper that almost made me come right then and there. The fire blazed between us, raw and dangerous, and it was only when my fingers moved to slip beneath her skirt and remove the satiny barrier between us that I was able to stop and pull away.

The ache that had plagued me for the better part of the day was quickly building toward blinding pressure. Pressure that would only be released by feeding the demon. I needed more than the tiny bits of the anger, lust, and sadness I'd pulled from her. I needed something bigger. Something darker.

Sam stared. From the thick mist of orange lust swirling around her head and shoulders, it seemed like she'd push forward again, but to my relief—and disappointment—she didn't. The spark in her eyes dimmed, and she moved sideways along the wall and toward the door, breath coming in jagged, uneven pulls.

When she spoke, her voice was low and sad. The anger was gone, replaced by nothing short of devastation. Despite the fact that we'd both wanted it, that kiss had been a mistake. As big a mistake as the one in the woods three years ago. "Now *that* was a good-bye."

Fuck. I'd come out here to get closer to finding out who was trying to run her down, and instead I'd driven the space between us wider.

"Have a nice life, Jax." She slipped back into the club, and even though every instinct screamed for me to follow, the thing inside prevented it. I was on fire. The demon's need left me an exposed nerve, raw and bleeding. Taking from her had only further ignited the monster's hunger. If I didn't feed it something violent soon, it would take matters into its own hands. Or, rather, *my* hands.

I stumbled around the back corner of the building. Kissing Sam made the demon hungrier. My elation at being so close to her was a drain on the thing. I'd known better, and yet I'd done it anyway. Now someone else had to pay the price. Violence. The demon would take what it needed from some poor bastard and leave me stuffing back the guilt.

Sucking in a breath, I held it, trying to zero in on the strongest source of emotion. There was a banquet of lust and greed in the area, still lingering around the club, but something else caught my attention. A sweet scent that made the demon go wild with anticipation. It was coming from the east side of the building.

Twelve feet. Nine feet. Six. Four...

In the alley around the club, two men stood over another. The one on the ground was curled in a ball, unmoving, as his attackers kicked him and laughed. The demon rumbled, flashing nondescript images of blood and gore. This was the part I hated. It was also the part that the sickest side of me loved. Letting the hunger propel me, I started down the alley.

"What the fuck do you want, man?" the taller of the two snapped as I approached. The man squared his shoulders and puffed out his chest in an attempt to scare me off. Silly human. Arrogance rolled off the man in thick yellow waves. They mingled with the crimson ones, swirling together just above his head in an intoxicating combination that had the demon inside going crazy.

"This ain't your concern. Move it along," the other snapped. He, at least, had the intelligence to back away. The waves wafting from him were gray in color and reeked of fear.

I stopped a few feet away. The demon's excitement hummed through my body as it flashed another image. Bloody and broken men.

Satisfaction—and a temporary peace—was within my grasp, but a sound shattered my concentration, forcing me to stop shy of following through. A far-off noise. The softest whisper of a plea for help. *Sam.*

I whirled around toward the club and held my breath, listening for the direction it'd come from. She was nowhere near the building; the sound echoed north slightly. The woods. She was in the woods.

The prey, so close at hand, was forgotten. The noise my boots made as they pounded the asphalt echoed like a bullhorn inside my head. Back around the building. Through the parking lot and across the street. A horn blared, bright lights zooming toward me. I jumped, kicking my feet up and pivoting so that my hip skimmed the hood. I landed gracefully on the other side, clearing traffic, as another sound came, this one from deeper in the woods. A single name called in desperation.

My name.

I followed the sound she made, stomping through the branches and dead leaves, and caught up to her as she changed direction, moving toward the cliffs. The wind kicked up, carrying the unexpected scent of sulfur. *Demons*? Two of them. And Sam.

One turned, wearing the guise of a tall man, letting go of her and stepping into my path, as the other continued. Blinded by anger, I collided with the other demon, sending us both careering into a nearby pine. We crashed into the trunk with jarring force.

I recovered, backing away as the other demon did the same. Stocky with a buzz cut, its individual smell was more potent than others I'd come across. More vile. It coated the back of my throat like foul syrup, nearly kicking in my gag reflex.

It smiled and snapped its teeth. In a voice that held the slightest rasp, it said, "Pathetic thing. You don't possess the strength to take what's not yours."

The demon inside me scrambled with nearly blinding force to take control, and it was only as I lunged forward, aiming for the enemy's neck, that it calmed a little. Normally I would have dragged it out, let the thing inside savor the violence, but there was no time to lose. A quick jab, and the other demon clutched its throat and went down hard, sputtering and gasping for air. I didn't wait to finish it off.

The other one—also a demon from the smell of it—was just approaching the cliff with Sam when I caught up to them. The blond's voice was cold and his eyes dead. "Turn around and walk back the way you came."

"Jax…?" Sam's voice didn't wobble. She didn't cower or cry. She was scared. Terrified. I could see my own emotion too, crimson rage leaking all around, calling to the demon. It bled into the air, haze drifting around my head like a miasma.

The demon moved. A twitch, really. But it was enough to spur me into action. Pushing forward, I sprinted toward them. Toward the edge of the cliff.

I was a foot away when the other demon brought its elbow back. It connected with Sam's shoulder, sending her off balance.

She tumbled over the edge.

I jumped.

Chapter Ten

Sam

I saw Jax surge forward just before the entire world tipped backward and the solid ground beneath my feet disappeared. A valiant, although pointless, last-ditch effort to save me. My heartbeat thundered as I braced myself for the inevitable, taking comfort that there was little chance I'd drown in the waters below. The jagged edge of the cliff would get me long before I reached the bottom, breaking my body like a child's toy.

A scream caught in my throat. The impact came—but there was no pain. One second I was watching the ground zoom steadily closer, icy wind biting at my exposed skin, the next everything shifted and I was staring up at the sky through a mass of tangled hair. Warm, solid arms enveloped me and a familiar scent—mint and leather—filled my nose as I plummeted.

"It's going to be all right."

It was going to be all right? *Jax?* A new kind of panic exploded in my chest. I'd seen him jump forward, but never imagined—

"Deep breath," he yelled over the sound of the wind whipping past us.

Numb, I obeyed, and sucked in a lungful of cold air.

The noise was like a car backfiring. One second the clear night sky loomed overhead, the next everything had a filmy sheen. Jax took the brunt of the impact, but I still felt the jar and the sting of the icy water. Disoriented, I flailed, kicking hard in hopes of breaking the surface. *Air. Can't breathe!* Every muscle stung. From the frigid temperature or the impact, I didn't know. Didn't care, either. All that mattered was air. Precious, glorious, *necessary* air.

But as hard as I kicked and as much as I flailed, my head couldn't find the surface. The burning in my chest became too much, and instinctually, I opened my mouth to suck in a lungful of air. Of course, I got water instead.

Everything grew dark. I was vaguely aware that I'd stopped kicking. My brain raged at my body as the pounding of my heart throbbed in every limb, and echoed in my ears. *Fight!*

It was too late. The darkness closed around me.

I was dead.

Taking a deep breath, I cringed. Okay, not dead. Death wasn't supposed to be painful. Or cold. Struggling onto my knees, I braced both hands against the dew-wet grass as a series of body-racking coughs tore from my throat. I was sore and soaked and freezing—but I was alive...despite someone's increasingly enthusiastic efforts to change that.

As reality crept back, I found myself getting numb. I went over the cliff just as Jax—

Jax.

It wasn't my imagination. He'd jumped, too. Wrapped himself around me, making sure he hit the water first. Frantic, I whirled around and scanned the area, sure I'd find him floating facedown in the water. But other than an occasional ripple from the increasing breeze, the surface of the water was still—and empty.

A knot formed in my chest as I squinted against the darkness, trying to see across to the other bank. He must have pulled himself from the water farther down. There was no need to panic just because I didn't see him. That didn't mean... A shiver ran through me. Something rustled and I jumped, whirling around fast enough to make myself dizzy.

Jax. He was crouched against a nearby tree.

I stumbled to my feet, almost toppling over as the heels of my boots sank into the soft earth. My legs felt rubbery, and the jolt of adrenaline that had kicked in during the fall still lingered, making every movement feel twitchy and sharp. "Jax, how—"

That was as far as I got. A low rumble filled the air and he drew himself up. Dark hair fell across his forehead, the strands dripping.

Jax let out a roar that was nothing short of animal. I jumped at the sound, about to take a step away, and noticed a dark smear across the side of his face. Blood. I reached out, but he flinched and the hair in his face fluttered back.

Time stopped. Something hazy nipped at my subconscious, drawing attention to his eyes. As the moon peeked out from behind the clouds, I got a good look at his face and gasped. His eyes, no longer the comforting gray I loved, were black. Solid black. No. It just looked that way. A trick played in the absence of light. "Jax?" I tried again.

He stepped away from the tree, head tilting to the left. Then, the right. No answer.

"Please," I begged. "Are you all right?"

Nothing. The silence was driving me crazy, and as he started toward me, I had to force myself to stand still. This was Jax, but for some reason, a little voice inside my head was telling me to run.

He stopped in front of me, so close, and in a deeper than normal voice, said, "Samantha Merrick."

My full name. "Jax, you're scaring me." I pointed at the rocks. "What just happened—we—"

"You are a strange creature." He ran a finger across my cheek, letting it linger at the corner of my mouth. "Your place in his life confounds me."

Creature? "My place in whose life?" I backed away a step, half expecting him to follow. He didn't. "What are you talking about?"

No answer.

That was my breaking point. He'd obviously gone into some kind of shock. I tried to grab his hand, but he jerked away. "NO!" A harsh, angry sound filled the air, and he jumped forward, knocking me hard to the ground. When I turned back, he was gone.

I started walking. The wind kicked up and the breeze against my still-damp skin made me shiver. I was numb and in need of hot coffee and a place to curl up and pretend this past month had never happened. Was one of the men who pushed me from the cliff tonight the same one who attacked me on campus? I was lucky Jax had been there…

He'd saved my life again. This time by jumping from the cliff and somehow shielding me from the fall. He must have dragged my sorry, waterlogged ass from the river as well. Then he snarled and ran away.

Snarled? Really?

Jax could explain away the car with fact. I'd done some research. Once the car filled with water, it would have been easier to get out

But the fall? How had he done it? There was no way to brush it aside. He'd taken the brunt of what'd been, essentially, a thirty-foot nosedive, and walked away?

Run away, actually.

That was impossible. He should be dead. We both should. And then there was the way he acted after I woke up. The animal-like growl. The odd words. The way he'd pushed me to the ground hard enough to knock a tooth loose?

He'd already admitted that there was something he couldn't—*wouldn't*—tell me. I had a feeling it had to do with why he'd left home, as well as how he was able to save me twice from situations no one should have survived. He was hiding something, and I intended to find out what it was.

After trekking through the woods, soaking wet and freezing, I finally managed to make it back to town. My keys were gone. I'd been clutching them when the men grabbed me on the way to the car, and must have dropped them somewhere along the way. I tried retracing my steps, but gave up. There was no way in hell I was going back to that cliff, and the chances of seeing anything in the dark, even with a full moon, were slim. I might have been able to use my cell as a flashlight, but that was gone, too. Probably at the bottom of the river with the fish. It made calling for a ride impossible. That left no other choice but to walk. Through the woods. At night. After being pushed from a cliff to my death.

I was having a really shitty week.

A horn honked, pulling me from the crazy sludge that was my thoughts. I'd hit a pay phone and called Chase to pick me up two blocks from the club. I'd been careful, passing by the lot to check on Jax's car. It was still there, parked a few spots down from the rental, so wherever he'd run off to, it'd been on foot.

"Um," Chase's eyes skimmed my body from top to bottom as I pulled open the car door. "Do I want to ask why you look like a sexy drowned rat?"

I wrung out the edge of my skirt before sliding into the passenger's seat. We hadn't been alone since he'd kissed me at McCarthy's and I was feeling a little awkward despite the fact that I knew the whole thing had been staged, but I couldn't help feeling a bit used.

"I lost my damn keys at the club." I shrugged and gestured to my wet clothes. "And this... Would you believe a sudden downpour?"

He shook his head and pulled away from the curb once the door was closed. Four blocks later, he spoke again. "I thought tonight was your night off? And why are you dressed like that—not that I'm complaining."

"Theme night," I said with a weary sigh, and fastened the seat belt. People thought I drove fast, but anyone who'd ever been in a car with Chase would surely dub me the queen of safety. Heedless of speed limits and stop signs, he had more traffic infractions than I could count. It blew my mind that he still had a license.

"Well, I *like* theme night." He waggled his brows and pulled the car into a spot at the front of my building. When I didn't respond, he frowned and shifted around to face me. "You okay, Samantha?"

My hand hovered over the door handle. The words formed, and slipped to the tip of my tongue, but I couldn't force them past my lips.

If I confessed what happened at the cliff, Chase would tell me I imagined the whole incident and was suffering from some weird kind of post-traumatic stress thing. No. This was something best kept to myself for now. "Yeah," I said, forcing a smile. "Been a long day, that's all."

I made a move to open the door, but he grabbed my hand. "I'm really worried about you." The look in his eyes made my breath catch. A fierce seriousness that almost bordered on possessive. But it was there and gone too fast to be sure. "If you get yourself killed, how will I see if we're compatible?"

Thankfully, serious never lasted long with Chase.

He leaned forward like he was going to kiss me. I threw up my hands. "No way. *Don't* go there." I pulled away and swung my foot from the car.

Chase fell back against the seat, frowning. "Stop." He sighed. "Please."

I don't know why, but I did. Maybe it was his tone. Three parts apologetic and one part commanding.

"You're seriously bludgeoning my ego here." His lips slipped into a grin. "Usually I'm fairly irresistible. I'm even thinking about having my tongue insured."

I didn't know whether to be upset or angry. "Where is this coming from? That kiss at the diner was a joke. For Jax's benefit. Right…?"

"It's my brother, isn't it?" Something dark settled on his face and he narrowed his eyes. One of the biggest differences between the Flynn boys was temperament. Jax was always dark and sarcastic. Chase, on the other hand, bounced back and forth on the tip of a pin. One second he was laughing, the next he was spitting poison. I was used to it, but it still unnerved me sometimes.

I wanted to deny it, but the words stuck in my throat. Why did he even need to ask? He watched us growing up. A thing like that didn't just go away. It was sad, and probably a little pathetic, but even if Jax never came around, he'd always be the one.

Chase sighed and pounded a fist against the dash as some of the tension left his body. "I'm not into you. Not really." He threw up his hands. "Not that you're not amazing or anything. I just—I know you and Jax have some pretty intense, screwed-up history. I thought maybe…" He twisted back so he was staring out the window. His right hand tapped the wheel to an uneven rhythm as he let his head tilt back against the seat. "I hate myself—like, *really* hate myself—for saying this, but he's got…problems. I've seen firsthand what he's capable of when he's angry. It's not pretty."

A small part of me wondered if any part of what he was saying came from real concern or was strictly out of jealousy. Because that's what this was. Jealousy. He wanted me because his brother was back in town. That was it. When Jax was gone again, things would go back to normal. He'd done it when we were young, too. Vied for my attention, then as soon as he got it and Jax wasn't looking, he was off and running after some new, shiny thing.

I couldn't help the defensive chill that crept into my voice. "You forget that we grew up together. I know all about his issues."

"No. I really don't think you do." When he turned I could see it. Plain as pie, in his eyes. Sadness and something else. A secret. There was definitely something he wasn't saying, and a part of him seemed...happy about it? No. That couldn't be right. Chase could be a bastard, but he wasn't outwardly cruel.

"Maybe not, but maybe I don't need to." I thought of all the rumors flying around town. Rumors I knew for a fact were 100 percent bullshit. Everything from blaming him for the fire that burned down the Harlow mall several years ago—when he wasn't even here—to insane whispers that he was the Gentleman Stalker. "I know you love your brother, Chase, but sometimes I think you're just as blind as the rest of the town."

That seemed to surprise him. He pulled back, brows high, and shook his head. "What's that supposed to mean?"

"Everyone has Jax pegged as the bastard while you walk around with your head held high." I could see the hurt in his eyes and that wasn't my intention, but he needed a dose of truth. Maybe it was the recent brushes with death, but it felt like the truth didn't get enough attention around here and it pissed me off. I reached around and popped open the door. "You're not a bad guy, but you're not perfect. Just like Jax isn't a perfect guy. Maybe he just needs the people he loves to have some faith in him."

Chapter Eleven

Jax

I strode down Sixth Street, coat blowing behind in the gusty wind. I was doing my best to ignore the painful pressure in my muscles and the ache that came with it. When the demon didn't get what it wanted, it made things difficult. When the need became too much, usually I'd stalk the streets looking for a fight. I kept to the seedier parts of town, which generally made it easy to find some deserving bastard to unload on.

Unfortunately, Harlow was a small place. Everyone knew everyone else. I wasn't eager to go kicking the crap out of people. I'd been taking little bits from random sources. A portion of anger here, a nibble of sadness there. Soon though, the demon wouldn't give me any choice. The longer I went without feeding it, the stronger it got. Backward if you asked me. The damn thing should get weaker when denied its twisted little snack.

I'd barely roughed up the demon on the cliff, and never even got to take a swing at the other—not that I had any idea what would have happened. I'd never fed on another demon before. Didn't even know if it was possible.

The sooner I got this wrapped up the better. Being in such close proximity to Chase was bad for *everyone's* health.

Then there was Sam. While the demon forced gruesome scenes on repeat inside my head, I could only focus on her. On what had happened tonight.

On what I'd done.

The demon had never spoken to anyone while in control. Tonight, watching it approach her, hearing it say her name, terrified me. How the fuck was I going to explain everything?

After I left home Sam moved on with her life. School, a job, other boyfriends. It was hard to watch—and I did—but it was the only way to keep her safe from my world. I kept tabs on her every step of the way, dropping in and secretly stealing glimpses just to be sure she was safe and happy. I'd always felt like a bastard for doing it. Like some sick creeper stalking the one thing I knew I could never have. Until the night of the party.

Really, after what happened to her parents, her reaction of leaving school after the attack was understandable. They were killed in a home invasion. She'd seen the whole thing from the closet in her parent's bedroom. The kicker was, it had been the bastard's second attempt. The first time, Mr. Merrick was able to scare him off and call the police. The second time around, he hadn't been so lucky.

Now with multiple attempts on her own life I couldn't imagine what Sam was going through. And she didn't even know the half of it. The demons on the cliff had thrown me. Was the person who attacked her at school a demon? I wasn't sure how I could have missed it. I'd been right there and would have smelled the thing on her for sure.

In places like the club it was much harder to zero in on a specific source. All those people crammed into one place was like a traffic jam of emotion, all knotted together. But out in the open air, it'd be hard to miss. Still, it was the only explanation.

Demons didn't mix well with humans. There was little chance that a human stalker had contracted demonic hit men to off a single girl. Most people had no idea they even existed. I'd been so preoccupied with the attack that the fact it'd been perpetrated by a demon had totally slipped past me. That was the only other possibility.

The big question now was, could I take care of it without having to tell Sam the truth? Like the rest of the world, she had no idea these things existed. I wanted to keep it that way.

I rounded the final corner and the Viking came into sight. The club was closed, but the small dive bar across the street was still kicking. It was a smaller hunting area than I normally liked, but time was running out. A deep breath told me that while it wouldn't satisfy the demon completely, or take away the pain, I'd find exactly what I needed to maintain control.

The place was small and run-down. There were several people at the counter, and a few more scattered around the room at tables. At the bar, a girl shrieked, the sound almost entirely drowned out by the pumping music coming from various speakers on the walls. She yelled at the bartender for a refill, holding up her empty glass when it became obvious that he couldn't hear her.

It didn't take long to find a target. In fact, I found the *perfect* target. The demon that pushed Sam over the edge was seated at a table in the corner with a few of the bouncers from the club laughing and doing shots and carrying on. Other than the brief scuffle at the cliff, I'd never fought another demon. I had no idea what to expect—but I was eager to find out.

I settled at the bar and waited. Patience wasn't a virtue me or my demon possessed, but in this case it was worth the effort. It took a while, but after six shots, the bastard headed for the restroom.

The demon writhed beneath my skin as I stood and made my way into the hall. Starving. It was starving. The sudden severity scared the shit out of me. What if this had nothing to do with Chase or Sam? What if, as I got older, the demon's hunger grew? I consoled myself by sticking to people who hurt others. Drug dealers, child molesters, men who beat their wives... The black stains on society had sustained the demon all this time.

But no matter how much they deserved what they got, or how the darkest parts of me enjoyed it, in the end a part of me died each time. The thought of having to up the numbers made me sick.

Fingers itching to feel the monster's bones break, I slipped through the bathroom door. The satisfying snap, crackle, and pop as things were crushed was always music to my ears, and would calm my nerves.

Directly across from the entrance, cloaked in a haze of orange and yellow and wobbling at the urinal, was my prey. I locked the door behind me, and probably should have checked to make sure we were alone, but the sight of the thing sent my demon into a frenzy, which only aggravated my own hatred. It had tried to hurt Sam.

I stalked forward and grabbed a handful of the demon's hair. The bastard flinched, surprised, as I ripped it away from the dirty porcelain and heaved its body across to the other side of the room. A feral sound, followed by a spike of potent, sweet-smelling crimson smoke. The enemy crashed into the row of sinks on the other side of the room, ripping one off the wall on the way to the floor.

It took an enormous amount of self-restraint—on my part and the demon's—but I waited for it to pick itself up before striking again. I wanted a fight. I needed a challenge. Destroying the fucker while he was down would offer neither.

"You," the demon snarled, as it climbed to its feet. The thing spit a mouthful of blood and wiped the tip of its chin with the back of its hand. Crimson puffs rose in the air, and sent the thing inside me into a crazed fit. "I saw you go over the cliff with that bitch."

"Guess you saw wrong."

"Guess so." With a dark chuckle, it grabbed the porcelain sink from the floor and heaved it at my head. I jumped to the left and then ducked fast to avoid the shattered pieces that rocketed through the small room like miniature bullets, then lunged forward and slammed my opponent's head into the mirror. The glass shattered. Tiny pieces coated in blood fell to the floor with soft plinking sounds and scattered across the room to mingle with the broken porcelain.

From the first time I'd done something horrible to appease the demon, I imagined a switch in my head. I told myself that when hungry enough, the demon simply flipped it, turning me into a darker, crueler version of myself. Someone who caused others pain to end his own. Someone who had absolutely no control. That switch flipped, but this time, it was me who did it. I was in total control.

It teetered back and caught itself on the edge of the remaining sink, hesitating for only a moment before whipping out a blade and brandishing it with a wicked smile.

I hadn't dealt with a lot of demons, and before coming back to Harlow, hadn't tangled with any, but a knife? What the fuck was that all about?

It lunged for me. I pivoted, dodging the blade, and brought my elbow down in an attempt to ground my opponent. The other demon danced away with time to spare and brought the blade down across my forearm in a long, clean slice. I didn't feel it. It could have been adrenaline, or maybe because my demon lingered close to the surface, but it must have been deep. There was nothing for a moment, then a sea of red flowed freely.

Normally the sight of a wound excited the thing inside, but for some reason, this time the injury enraged it. It flashed an image of Sam's face, then another, as she fell from the cliff. The terror that hit me in those last moments rushed back, and ducking another blow, I grabbed the bastard's forearm and twisted until it was on its knees.

Gritting my teeth against the urge to snap its neck, I growled, "Was it you that attacked her at Huntington? Why?"

No answer.

My grip tightened. "Did you follow her here?"

This time the demon snarled, shaking its head violently

from side to side.

Another flash of pictures through my head, these back-dropped by fire and black smoke. On the ground were bodies. Hundreds of bodies. Broken bones and twisted limbs. And blood... More blood than I'd ever seen before. Since coming back to town, the images the demon showed me had become more violent, but this was the worst yet. I couldn't place the scene, but it was unlike anything I'd ever witnessed. A charred landscape with bold, fiery clouds overhead. "Did you?" I yelled, shaking off the vision.

Another twist of his arm. A loud snap. A howl of pain. Closing its eyes, the other demon relented. "Tonight was the first night I laid eyes on the human."

"So someone told you to come to the club tonight?" I asked, leaning close to his ear. "Who was it? Human or demon?"

The demon didn't answer the question. Instead, it pulled its lips back and snarled.

"If you're not the one who wants her dead, then tell me who is." Another twist. Another crack. "Someone *told* you to do it. *Who*?"

"Kill me," it spat. "I will not betray my kind."

I laughed. No? We'd just see about that. Grabbing its right hand, I wrapped my fingers around the demon's thumb and yanked back hard. The sounds it made—blissfully cracking bone and an otherworldly scream—was like a serenade to my ears. Thick gray smoke rose from its shoulders, filling the room. My demon sucked in the fear greedily, causing the pain to ebb and giving me a renewed sense of energy.

"Release me!" it bellowed as I bent back another finger. Thank God for the music outside. The last thing I needed was someone calling the police.

"Care to try again?"

"I am a soldier. You cannot break me."

I grabbed yet another finger and snapped it back. "Hear that? Sure as hell sounds like breaking to me."

It let out an anguished roar.

"I can make this drag on forever. I've got nothing but time." I yanked back on another digit. "Ten fingers. Ten toes. Two arms and legs... This could get interesting."

"Giving you what you want will change nothing. It will *stop* nothing."

"Why don't you let me be the judge." I gave in to the demon just a bit, digging my fingers into the bastard's flesh until I felt the skin give. He tried to scream, but I clamped a hand across his mouth to keep him silent. I moved my hand. "You're a soldier. A soldier for what?"

"If I tell you he'll kill me," it rasped, breathless and afraid.

I chuckled. The sound was dark and dangerous and a little comforting. This was who I was. This was my life. I bent low and whispered in the demon's ear. "I'm the one you need to worry about. What he'll do to you would be merciful compared to what I'll do if you don't tell me what I want to know."

A frantic nod. "I don't have a human name—only an address. Fifty-fifth and Aberdeen. Number 882."

Its fear wafted up to meet me. It drifted all around, permeating the air and filling the monster inside. I savored the feeling—a twisted euphoria I loved and despised—as a shudder of contentment ran through my body. This was huge. I knew there wouldn't always be a demon on hand to feed on—before this all went down, I'd only ever run into two or three in passing—but knowing I had the option to feed on them eased some of my guilt.

"Please, man. I told you what you wanted. Let me go."

Let him go?

"Okay." A single, tight-fisted blow to the man's jaw. I let his body fall to the floor. I left him alive because the risk of someone recognizing me, then finding the body, was too great. Time to pay Sam's stalker a visit.

As I approached the door of the apartment, my cell rang. Sam again. She'd called four times now. I killed the ringer and stuffed the phone back into my pocket. The demon flashed an image of danger. Something about this place made it nervous and even though I hated the thing, it had never steered me wrong before. Letting the demon rise closer to the surface, I listened at the door, allowing it to heighten my senses. There was a strange smell coming from inside. Something faint that, without the demon's help, I'd never have picked up. A fetid scent mixed with something spicy. Something rotting. There was someone inside the apartment—but they weren't alive.

Grabbing the handle, I gave a single twist. The knob rattled, then fell to the ground with a clatter. With one last look down the hall to be sure there were no prying eyes, I retrieved the knob and slipped inside.

The smell that hit me upon entering was ten times more potent than in the hall. Hand clamped tight across my nose and mouth, I moved past the entryway and into the living room. The building itself was nice—not swag really, but certainly not the run-down shitholes I'd been living in over the last few years. There was a mirrored ceiling and two matching walls, in addition to glass end tables and a large, empty floor-to-ceiling fish tank. An assortment of architecture magazines fanned across the coffee table, while paintings of uniquely shaped buildings adorned the walls. It looked like the kind of place I'd expect Chase to live. A bachelor pad designed with homemade porn movies in mind.

Other than the furniture, there wasn't much else in the apartment. In fact, there was nothing. I pulled open several of the kitchen cabinets and drawers to find them bare. There were two used wineglasses on the counter sitting next to an empty bottle, but when I opened the fridge, it was just like the rest of the apartment. Nothing. On closer inspection, all the shelves in the living room were empty. There wasn't even a television.

I moved through the place, randomly opening closet doors and drawers, and following the strange smell. Each step toward the back of the apartment brought me closer to the source. When I reached the end of the hall and rounded the corner on what appeared to be the master bedroom, I stopped to take a deep breath. Yeah. It was definitely strongest in here.

I walked to the closet and pulled open the door. It was the only thing in the apartment, other than the wineglasses, that appeared to have been used. At first, everything looked normal. A row of shoes. From brand-new sneakers to shiny dress loafers—all obviously never worn and strictly for show. The clothing rod was strung with hangers draped by suits, most still with the tags attached, several pairs of jeans, and a leather jacket. There were boxes stacked neatly on the top shelf, but when I reached for one, I found it empty. They all were.

My nose itched and my eyes watered as I fought against my gag reflex. The longer I stayed here, the more the smell bothered me. With the demon so close to the surface, everything was amped. I tried pushing it back to dull my senses, but it wouldn't be moved.

I gave up and held my breath, bending down to push aside the shoes. The floor beneath them was a slight shade darker than the rest of the closet. It paid off. There was a trap door hidden in the floor. It didn't take much to pry it open because there was no lock, which struck me as odd. Beyond the door was a narrow set of concrete stairs leading into blackness.

Leading into death.

The scent of sulfur permeated the air. I couldn't discern how many, but there were multiple variations. This place didn't belong to one demon. It belonged to several.

I climbed down one step at a time, readying myself for anything.

It looked just like any other storage space. Rows of boxes, a few pieces of old furniture… And three women. All naked.

All dead.

I'd seen a lot of bloodshed in my life. Hell, I'd been the cause of most of it, but what I found at the bottom of those stairs was enough to turn my stomach five times over. They were stacked on top of each other. Piled like garbage in various states of decay.

Next to them was a pile of hair. No. Not hair. Entire

scalps. Demon trophies. I let out a breath and sucked another in, holding it. I was a monster in every sense of the word, but this... I backed away slowly, unable to tear my eyes from the gruesome sight. Even my own demon, who was usually excited by the sight and smell of death, was quiet.

I started backing toward the staircase, eager to get out into the fresh air, but something on the table in the corner caught my eye. A small bracelet. It was a tiny red-and-black dream catcher attached to a double black leather band. There were two small charms. Leaves.

I remembered the first time I'd seen it. I was fourteen and at the county fair. The woman at the booth explained how dream catchers were believed to siphon the bad dreams away. It'd been the perfect gift for Sam.

She'd been wearing it the night I left town. When I arrived home a few days ago, I noticed its absence, but simply assumed Sam removed it when I never came home. But obviously I'd been wrong. She must have been wearing it the night she was attacked on the Huntington campus.

I'd missed it. The attacker on campus *had* been a demon. But why? It made no sense. What could demons possibly want with Sam?

Chapter Twelve

Sam

Pacing. A nervous habit that drove Aunt Kelly nuts, I couldn't stop doing it. From the kitchen to the front door. Front door to bedroom. Bedroom back to kitchen again. Pretty soon there would be a rut in the floor a mile deep. I'd tried Jax's cell phone five times since Chase dropped me off but there was no answer. It was almost 6:00 a.m.

The weight of what had happened last night—or, what almost happened—was starting to settle, and if I stopped moving, I was sure I'd go into shock. It made sense to think the person who attacked me would want to silence me if he thought there was a chance I saw his face. Had he dragged in a friend to help?

I stopped in the middle of the living room and let out a scream of frustration. Childish? Sure. But it helped. At least, a little.

Grabbing my coat, I headed toward the door. Pacing the room wasn't going to get me anywhere. I needed to find out who this wacko was. Maybe one of the security cameras at the club had gotten the license plate of the car by the Dumpster. Or maybe someone had seen something funny while my car was parked out in front of McCarthy's the other day. Big-girl boots on and laced, I reached for the door, determined to get some answers.

"Sammy," Jax said as I threw it open.

"Holy crap!" I jumped back, startled. I was relieved to see him, thankful that he was here and in one piece. Not that I let that show. "Oh my God. Skulking on the other side of my door? A little freaky don't you think? Even for you…"

He pushed past without waiting for an invitation. "I don't skulk." Turning, he winked. I hated it, but despite the fact that it'd been the night from hell, the quirk of his lip and curve of his cheek sent my heartbeat racing. "I loom. Much sexier, don't ya think?"

I closed the door and backed into the living room. "You also jump from cliffs." As soon as the words left my mouth, I regretted them. I was going to get to the bottom of it, but I'd planned on using a bit more tact than that. Grilling him for answers was the best way to get none.

His expression darkened and he drew himself up, a hulking, broad-shouldered figure looming against the pale violet walls of the apartment. Beautiful and dangerous. Along with cocky, and arrogant…

"Jump from cliffs? You sure you didn't slip in a drink or three back at that club?"

I had done a few shots—my main excuse for asking for that kiss—but I was stone-cold sober by the time we ended up over that cliff. "I had four shots between getting to work, being assaulted by your tongue, and getting heaved over the cliff."

He stepped closer, right eyebrow rising slightly above the left. Just like when we were younger, the expression never failed to send a spike of fire shooting through my veins. "Assaulted by my tongue? As I remember it, you asked for it…" Straightening, he added, "You went over the side and were lucky enough to end up in the water instead of smeared across the rocks. I made it down to the bank and pulled you out. End of story."

"I—you—that is *not* what happened!" I yanked off the jacket and pushed forward, jabbing a finger at his chest and refusing to be sidetracked by the ripple of muscle on the other side of the fabric. Muscles that were so close… Flattening my hand, I savored the feeling beneath my palm. His heartbeat thumped. A steady rhythm that seemed to be increasing—much like my own. The urge to slip my fingers beneath the material and revel in his warmth was like an itch I needed to scratch. My breath caught. Butterflies roared to life in the pit of my stomach, and even though there were more important things to focus on right now, my limbs just wouldn't respond. "I know what I saw."

That whole refusing-to-be-sidetracked part didn't work out so well. "What you saw?" He pushed against my hand. "Tell me, what did you see?"

Heat rushed to my cheeks and I knew damn well I was as red as holly berries. I swallowed. "I saw—"

He leaned to whisper in my ear. "Seesaw. That's what you're doing here, Sammy." The tip of his nose brushed against the edge of my ear and I bit down on my tongue to keep from gasping. Tiny licks of flame fanned to life in my belly and drifted lower, refusing to be pushed aside.

I knew him too well not to know what was going on. When he didn't want to talk about something, he'd do whatever was necessary to derail the conversation. I turned away. There was a lump forming in my throat, and when I tried to speak, the words came out soft and cracked. I needed distance. "Back away, please."

His lips were still at my ear, breath like the heat rising from a sultry summer sidewalk to melt my brain. "Are you sure?"

No. "Yes," I said, before the heat between us tripped me up. I sucked in a deep breath and gently pushed him farther away, determined to get the conversation, and my mind, back on track. There was something I needed to get out. "Thank you."

"For what?"

"You saved my life, Jax."

His grin faded, lips twisting into a cruel smirk. He advanced, causing me to back away. "You wanna make me out to be some kind of hero. Trust me, Sammy. That's *not* what I am."

Why couldn't he just accept my damn gratitude? "You're—"

He kept coming. With each step, his voice grew darker. "You're wrong. About what you *think* you saw—and about what you think I am." A laugh. Not a giddy, happy sound, but something broken and pained. "I'm a thing. A *bastard*. I don't care about anything."

I stopped backing away and stood my ground, pinning him with my best *I-call-bullshit* stare. "You're lying."

He shook his head. "I'm not. Yeah, I pulled you out of

the water. But I did it for my own selfish reasons."

"Really?" I forced out a laugh and folded my arms. His words were designed with a single purpose. To make me angry. To make me hate him. Sidetracking me hadn't worked, so now he'd moved on to pissing me off. When the world pushed too close, he pushed back. It was just what he did. "And what selfish reasons would those be?"

He closed the distance between us and leaned in close, breath puffing out across my cheek. For the longest moment he stayed there refusing to move or speak. Just...watching. I'd seen it a thousand times before. When he was on the verge of losing his temper, or when he was trying to keep his emotions in check to keep the world where it belonged—on the outside.

I used to be the one person who had the ability to crack his shell. The one person he'd let see beyond the broken casing and into his mind. But not this time. This time he kept me out, clinging to his cruel mask, giving me nothing.

When he moved, he brought his lips to my ear and whispered, "I saw an opportunity. I was hoping you'd be thankful I dragged you from the river." He pulled away and ran a hand up my bare arm, lingering at my collarbone. With a single finger, he traced the line all the way around to the curve of my breast, letting it still for a moment at the cleft of my cleavage. "Maybe offer a proper thank-you. We never did get the chance to give each other a test drive when we were younger. Not too late."

The words fell from his mouth and oozed into the air, turning to vile poison as they drifted to my ears. I opened my mouth, then closed it, horrified. I had nothing, so I slapped him.

The sound was like a rocket in the silence of the room, and when I looked in his eyes, there was a twinge of justification. *Shit.* I'd reacted exactly how he'd wanted me to. Exactly how he would have expected anyone else to.

Jax leaned in again. "Come on, I look just like your boyfriend. How much of a stretch would it be? One good fuck and I'll be able to put you and this whole place behind me. Who knows—you might actually like it. Or is that what you're afraid of?"

Every syllable dripped venom. Too much venom. Jax had anger issues. Authority issues. He had issues with his issues. But one thing he wasn't, no matter how hard he tried to convince me—and everyone else around us—was cruel.

I'd seen it too many times. Tiny glimpses of who he really was. When he thought no one else was watching. I'd never deny that Jax Flynn had a dark streak that rivaled the starless night sky, but he also had a bright streak. One I'd been witness to on many occasions.

It took several tries, but I finally managed to find my voice. I was angry at him for leaving. That would always hurt. But it was plain to see he was in pain. Lashing out to push me away. "He's not my—"

A knock on the front door stopped me midsentence.

I tried to slip out from between Jax and the wall, but he grabbed my arm. The expression on his face was a mix of anger and desire that gave me both chills and goose bumps. "Don't. We need to finish this."

I didn't understand what he meant and wasn't sure I wanted to know. The knock came again, this time more urgent. "I don't know what happened to you while you were gone, Jax, or why you want so badly for me to hate you, but

I don't. And I won't. No matter what you say, and how hard you try to make me believe you're the bastard of the century. I am, however, going to see who's at the door."

"No," he growled, tightening his grip. "You're not." His fingers twitched, and he inhaled deeply, eyes growing wide.

I was about to suggest he shove the bossy crap up his ass sideways, but splinters of wood exploded inward, showering the entire room in debris. Jax yelled—I couldn't quite make it out—right as a dark blur of a thing knocked me sideways. The entire world spun, and I landed hard on the floor in front of the couch. I scrambled to my feet a second before Jax launched himself at the intruder.

The man, completely bald with an athletic build and dark sunglasses, laughed as Jax's fist connected with the side of his head. They tumbled to the floor, trading blows in a flurry of grunts and snarls. In the mayhem of it all, the man's glasses were knocked from his face and I found myself rooted in place. Black. His eyes were black. The room began to spin.

"Get—out, Sammy," Jax growled, pulling me from the haze and gaining the upper hand against the intruder. He rolled his weight on top of the other man, fingers wrapping tight around his throat. It looked like he had it under control—until Black Eyes bucked once and threw Jax off balance. He teetered, but recovered quickly and jumped with stunning grace to his feet.

It was like watching a perfectly choreographed scene. Deadly, but beautiful. They traded blows, each ducking and twisting with the elegance of an experienced dancer. I wanted to run, but found it hard to tear my eyes away from it all.

The man with the black eyes threw a powerful right hook. Jax dodged it with time to spare, but in the process, backed up too far. His heel caught on my laundry basket, and gravity sent him to the ground.

He tried to jump to his feet, but Black Eyes was too fast, shoe coming down hard in the center of Jax's chest. The crunch the impact made chilled me to the core.

Laughing, the man kicked out again, this time at Jax's head. I flinched as his head rocked to the right, eyes rolling back, and then fluttering closed. "Pathetic. The Son of Cain falls so easily." The man bent closer, hand poised to deliver what I feared was the final blow.

"No!" I screamed.

A second later, those freaky black-as-night peepers were glaring at me.

"Shit!"

Jax was conscious and trying to move, but he didn't get more than a few feet before falling back to the floor again, sputtering to catch his breath.

"Pretty little thing," the man drawled as he cornered me. His voice rasped like a lifetime smoker with an odd gravelly twang. There was something so familiar about him. Not the man specifically, but his voice. The eyes... I'd seen them before—and not at the bottom of the cliff when I thought Jax's eyes looked strange. Another time. Something else... "I can't kill *him*, but I'll enjoy feasting on *your* bones."

"I have some ribs in the freezer. I bet you'd like munching those bones a hell of a lot more than mine." I babbled, inching away as panic threatened to overtake me. The blood rushed in my ears as my heart drummed in my chest. Heart attack. I was going to have a heart attack.

Unwanted memories of the night my parents were murdered pushed their way to the surface despite my most valiant efforts to tamp them down. An almost inhuman voice. Strange inky eyes. Everything was jumbled, pictures popping in and out of my mind in random order.

I'd seen the whole thing. Watched from a louvered closet door. The man who broke into our home murdered my father first, then tortured and killed my mother. I was too small at the time—too young—to do anything.

The man snarled, drops of foamy white spittle flying from his lips as he crouched down, readying to attack.

I dropped to my knees as he charged, ducking behind the small DVD case I'd found at a garage sale a few weeks ago. He crashed into the case, scattering the discs in every direction. I stumbled to my feet, grabbed a handful, and started chucking them at his head. Not the most badass weapon in an arsenal, but improvising was a way of life.

The man batted them away, cackling. "Your fear is delectable. I wonder," he whispered, pushing forward as he diverted the last DVD-turned-missile. Hot, fetid air puffed across my face and I did my best not to gag. "What can I do to turn your fear into terror?"

I gasped and tried to pull away, but he was too strong. Screwing up the last reserves of courage, I asked, "What the hell are you?"

He leaned closer and with a grin I'd never, ever forget, said, "I'm a thing of nightmares."

Not happening. This was not happening. Another nightmare.

That was the answer. I was trapped in a nightmare. How else could I explain the fact that history was about to repeat itself? I'd escaped my parents' fatal home invasion only to go down in one of my own. That was cruel, even by fate's standards.

The man chuckled, obviously thrilled by my response, and leaned in for what I assumed would be the kill, but something stopped him.

"Back away."

His eyes widened and he turned slowly toward the sound of a new voice. Behind us, Jax had climbed to his feet.

He didn't appear to be in distress over his injuries any longer. Standing tall, he approached slowly, stiff and angry. His eyes now matched the man's—the color of night—and his voice was much deeper than it should have been. More like how it had sounded at the bottom of the cliff. His lips peeled into a smile fit for a madman. Dangerous and un-hinged. "Now."

The intruder backed away. "Son of Cain—"

"My name is Azirak." A low, primal growl followed, and I backed away as well. He turned, and to me said, "Samantha Merrick." And that was it. Nothing less. Nothing more.

Jax—or Azirak—refocused on the enemy, and took a step closer. The bald guy, who a minute ago was ready to kill me, was now on the verge of pissing himself. He backed away, then snapped his teeth twice in Jax's—Azirak's—di-rection. A strange language spilled from his lips. When he finished, he turned to me with a wicked grin and said, "I'll see you again, pretty thing."

The window behind us exploded as he crashed through.

Chapter Thirteen

Jax

Until I knew exactly why these demons wanted Sam dead, and how much they knew about her, staying at her apartment wasn't an option. I'd brought us to the hourly motel by the highway on the outer edge of town.

I shifted, twisting my body toward the door. I hated being here with her right now. So soon after reclaiming control from the demon. From *Azirak*... The thing inside had a name. Funny, how all this time I'd never given it any thought.

After I fell, it had forced its way into the driver's seat to deal with the other demon. When the bastard fled, to my surprise, the demon—*Azirak*—willingly relinquished its hold, but it still squirmed, hungry and desperate for violence.

Too bad. Feeding wasn't an option just yet. I needed to help Sam. My priority was keeping her safe and getting to the bottom of this mess. Demons. For some reason, demons were hunting her. Demons that knew what I was. More specifically, *who* I was.

We'd been in the motel room almost an hour and she still hadn't said a word. She sat in the chair by the door, tense and watching me as though any moment I'd sprout a tail and horns. Thick gray tendrils rising to mingle with black—confusion—was the only evidence I needed. She was in shock.

The silence tore at me. If she was going to scream or cry, or cast me off as the disgusting thing that I was, it needed to be now. "Say something, Sammy. Please."

"Something," she mumbled absently, fiddling with the hem of her shirt without looking away.

"I'm serious." I crossed the room and knelt in front of her chair. It was impossible to miss the way she tensed, shrinking away as though I might try to take a bite out of her. I adjusted, rocking back a few inches to give her some room. "You're worrying me."

That got her attention. She rose from the seat and moved closer to the door. "*I'm* worrying *you*? Really?"

I stood. This was better. A fight I knew how to deal with. "You know what—"

She held a hand up. Some of the fear in the room dissipated and I fought a grin as the gray quickly turned to all crimson. How many girls—hell, people—would hold their shit together after what had just happened? Sam was strong, but it wasn't until that moment that I realized how strong. She called herself a coward, so ashamed of her darkest fears, but obviously she didn't see things clearly.

"I'm going to ask questions. You're going to answer. We clear?"

I nodded. The truth. It was something I feared and

revered. On one hand, it might make her stay away. That's what I wanted. To shield her from the thing that lived inside of me. On the other hand, even though it was selfish and irresponsible, I wanted to find some way to keep her in my life. That alone proved what a bastard I was. If I cared about her at all, I'd never look back.

"That man that attacked us—his eyes were—" She took in a shaky breath as a spike of fear rose from her shoulders. Not a clouded smoky gray, but a dark ash color. Terror. "Was he human?"

Again, she caught me off guard me. Here Sam was pulling the short straw of crazy—and doing it with a straight face. "No."

If the answer surprised her, it didn't show. In fact, she seemed oddly vindicated. "If he wasn't human, what was he?"

"A demon," I said without hesitation. There was no point in sugar coating things. Sam was a big girl and she was in over her head. It was only fair to let her know how far. The quicker she accepted it, the easier it would be to get to the bottom of this shit.

"A demon," she repeated, starting to pace. The set of her shoulders turned rigid and worry creased her forehead. "You're saying that man—"

"It wasn't a man, Sammy. It wasn't a *he*. *It* was a demon."

She stopped pacing and whirled on me. "This is insane…"

Might as well let her have all of it. "It's all connected. I think the attack at your apartment, and all the others, were related to what happened on the Huntington campus. You're under attack, but I don't believe it's just one person."

She froze, her expression a mix of bewilderment and

fear. "You just— A demon— No. Just, no. You can't possibly know that for sure!"

"I do—"

"*You're* insane."

Time for blow number two. I reached into the pocket of my coat and pulled out the bracelet I'd taken from the demon's apartment. Setting it down on the table, I took a step away. "You lost that the night you were attacked, didn't you?"

Six deep breaths. I watched the rise and fall of her chest, and the flutter of her eyes as she pinched the bridge of her nose. The ashen cloud swirled frantically above her head. She crossed the room and stopped a few feet from the table, eyes glued to the delicate red-and-black leather jewelry on its surface. Picking up the bracelet, Sam held it as though at any moment it might come alive and take a chunk out of her. "I—where did you find this?"

"I think it was the apartment of the one who attacked you on campus. Or, at least, it was staying there. I picked up more than one scent."

Sam was pale. She backed away from the table and sank onto the bed. "How did you find *that*?"

"It doesn't matter. What matters is, we've got a big problem. The one who attacked you wants you dead, Sammy. I don't know who, and I can't figure out why, but I know what we're up against, and it's not pretty."

"What we're up against? You mean the men who tried to throw me off the cliff? Is it the mob or something?"

I knew Sam's breaking point, and it was obvious she was closing in on it, but I needed to tell her the truth. "They were demons. Same as the thing that broke into your apartment.

The attack at Huntington, the cliff, and I'm willing to bet my right hand, all the others, too."

"Demons," she repeated. "You're telling me demons are after me. Trying to kill me. That right?"

"I know this is hard to accept, but—"

"No. No. This is easy. All makes tons of sense. Demons. Demons want me dead." She rolled her eyes and ran both hands through her hair, pausing for a moment to tug at the roots. A nervous habit. With a determined nod, she stood. "Let's go."

"Go? Go where?"

Her eyes were wide. "The *police*. These bastards tried to kill me. The cops need to know about that. You said you know where one of them lives. They can pick him up."

"Sammy, you're forgetting an important fact."

She just stared at me.

"The man that attacked you wasn't a man. It was a demon. Going to the cops won't do anything. Something tells me the government hasn't started issuing demon-hunting tools to the local police."

"Forgetting for a second that I'm actually going to ask this out loud, why would a demon—I'm sorry, demons, plural—attack me?"

"I really don't know. Most feed on pain and violence, but there's plenty of that to go around. There's no reason to hunt any one particular human to get it." I hesitated. "Honestly, I'm really not sure what we're up against. When I was at the apartment I found three other bodies."

She paled by the minute. "Bodies—"

"They'd been there a while."

"As in, dead? *Corpses*?"

"Yes." I frowned.

"So, I have an entire *demon army* after me?"

Motherfucker…

The demon in the bathroom of the dive bar said something about being a soldier. "We'll figure this out. I promise."

She squared her shoulders and said, "And you? You seem to know a hell of a lot about this shit. That thing called you Son of Cain. And your eyes…" Some of her color returned. "Next you'll tell me you're some kind of chosen, once-in-a-generation demon slayer? Is that right?"

I waggled my eyebrows. Inappropriate timing? Yep. But I wanted to lighten the mood. Besides, she brought it out in me. "Would you think it was sexy if I said yes?"

"Yeah. You're a regular Buffy—or would it be Angel?"

"Angel was a pussy. I'd be more of a Spike. He was a true badass." I sighed and nudged her back. "The truth is…" God. Did I really want to go through with this? Lay all my cards on the table and hope it didn't scare the shit out of her? Once I went through that door there was no turning back.

"Jax?"

I squeezed my eyes closed and silently counted to ten, before opening them and turning to face her. I needed to see her reaction. "I'm one, too. A demon—partially, anyway." Azirak stirred, fighting for control. "I'm cursed. I've got this thing living inside me. Azirak. This—"

Sam fell back against the wall and slid to the floor. The expression on her face nearly broke me in two. Fear and pain, mingling with the almost bitter taste of betrayal, filled the small room.

"This isn't happening." She let her head fall between her

knees and covered the top of it with her arms. "I'm asleep. Having another nightmare."

I stayed where I was even though every impulse screamed to gather her into my arms and hold her until this all went away. In another lifetime, maybe that would be possible. In this one? It was nothing more than a fantasy getting in the way of the cold, hard truth. "I wish that's what this was. I wish I could tell you that you'll wake up tomorrow and it'll all be a dream, but it's not. This is some serious shit, Sammy, and for whatever reason, you're stuck in the middle of it."

She uncurled, shaking her head from side to side slowly. "His eyes," she whispered. Her face paled. "I couldn't figure it out at the time. Why they looked so familiar."

"Familiar? What are you talking about?"

She didn't look up at me. "I buried the memory when we buried my parents." Her gaze rose to meet mine. There were tears in her eyes. "It's all real."

"Sammy, what memory?"

"My parents. The man that killed them—"

I took a step toward her but she flinched and I froze. She couldn't mean... "Are you saying a demon killed your parents?"

She nodded. "Yes." Then a second later, shook her head. "No—I think so? I'm not sure what I'm saying because what I'm saying is *insane*. But I remember his eyes. They were the same bottomless void."

It all made sense. For her to have believed what I told her about a demon, there had to be a reason. "Sammy—"

"I was knocked over the edge. You jumped and grabbed me and broke my fall. A fall that should have killed us both. And the car. At the bottom of the river. I would have drowned. And your eyes…" There was so much pain in her expression. A flicker of betrayal and a ton of hurt mixed with a hint of fear. "You're like the others? A demon?"

Something inside me shattered. She was looking at me like I was responsible for the most horrific moments of her life. It was worse than any hunger pang the demon could inflict. "I am a demon," I said softly. "But like I said, it's not the same. I'm more…complicated."

"Tell me," she said. The gray smoke around her head lightened, but didn't dissipate. "Explain to me how you're different from that black-eyed thing that just tried to kill me. Please," she begged. "Tell me how you're different from the monster that killed my parents."

The desperation in her voice swept me away and the words came before I could give them any thought. "I could break you. Snap your bones like they were nothing more than twigs. Hell, part of me wants to because it's what the thing inside me feeds on. Fear. Anger. Rage. Violence… Those are the only things that keep it calm. Under control." I stepped close to her, and when she didn't pull away, bent low and cupped the side of her face, letting my thumb trail lightly along her bottom lip. "But I won't. That's the difference between that thing and me, Sammy. I won't hurt you. I would never hurt you."

Except I had. Hurt her. I'd hurt her in ways I could never take back. The gray around her darkened until it was solid black. Confusion. She let her head fall forward into her hands. "I need to think."

"What you need is to pay attention. These things slaughter people for food *and* fun. They're ruthless and without conscience and there is nowhere on this earth you can go to run from them if they want you dead." Although the revelation about how her parents really died was raw and I hated glossing over it, there was no time to break down now. This was bigger than just a single demon.

She didn't move. Didn't pick her head up or budge from the floor. It almost looked like she'd stopped breathing. A moment later, she lifted her gaze to meet mine. "Fine. Show me."

"Show you?"

Sam uncurled and stood, squaring her shoulders and taking a step toward me. "Your demonic powers. Show me what you can do."

"You want me to— How am I supposed to do that?"

More of the gray faded. "Should be easy. Smite something. Pull a rabbit out of a hat."

"*Smite something?* I'm not God, Sammy."

She waved offhandedly and stood, coming several steps closer. "Whatever. I'm sure there's something impressive in your demon arsenal."

"It doesn't work that way. This thing inside me? It's dangerous. I can't drag it out to do magic tricks."

She eyed me. "You just told me you *weren't* dangerous. Make up your mind."

Shit. Everything with her was so much fucking harder. Twisted in a way I couldn't possibly unravel. "I'm not dangerous. Not to you."

"But you *are* dangerous? To *other* people?"

I wasn't sure how to answer. Now that she might be on the verge of turning away for good, the truth burned a hole in my gut. But other than the demonic secret I'd kept, I'd never lied to Sam. "Yes," I said. "Sometimes I'm dangerous to other people."

She pushed past me and bolted out the door. I didn't stop her. She needed to be alone to process all this shit? Fine. I'd give her the illusion of being alone. Grabbing my coat, I slipped from the room, locking the door behind me.

Chapter Fourteen

Sam

By now, someone had to have seen the broken window and called the landlord. The only reason the old man agreed to rent to me was because I swore I'd be no trouble. Forget wild parties. Having a guy show up and attack me, then bust up the place, defined trouble.

So instead of going home, I took a cab to Kelly's. My aunt had left this morning for some weeklong bingo retreat, so I had the house to myself. I kicked off my shoes, curled into a ball on the couch, and closed my eyes.

Bad idea.

My father's death had been quick. A broken neck. But my mother's death... The man—*the demon*—had played with her. The sick sounds of pleasure, laughing in amusement as my mother begged for mercy, were impossible to tune out. I'd heard everything. Seen everything. It was all coming back.

My strange attacker. My parents' killer. Jax…

And what about Jax?

Demons were all bad guys, right? That's what folklore and religion said. They went around causing chaos. Eating babies, stealing virgins, murdering parents. The look in Jax's eyes when he faced that other demon had been deadly. Rage so primal that it gave me chills. But he wasn't evil. He couldn't be. All he'd ever done was take care of me. When I was at my worst, he pulled me from the darkness. Time and time again, Jax had been there.

Answers. I needed answers.

But where did you go to research demons? Asking Jax was out of the question — for now. Then I knew. Who was the best person to ask about the devil?

God.

It was close to 9:00 a.m. by the time I reached Saint Vincent's church. Double mocha latte in hand, I climbed the narrow stairs and pushed through the ornate double doors as a knot formed in my stomach. The cavernous room was empty, lit with a thousand tiny candles along either side. The rows of polished pews sat like soldiers, lined up and waiting. It hadn't changed at all.

The floor was carpeted, but I still heard each step as my feet carried me farther inside. *Clomp. Clomp. Clomp.* It'd been thirteen years since I'd been in this church. Thirteen years, three months, twelve days. Not a day went by that I didn't think about it. The day they put my parents in the ground.

The memories flooded back despite my best efforts to shelve them. Sitting in the front row with Aunt Kelly, staring at the two large boxes containing my parents' bodies. The kind but scripted words the priest spoke as half the town looked on. The white and blue flowers covering every inch of the altar. My first glimpse of Chase and Jax, who'd been seated beside Rick several pews behind.

"Can I help you?" A man's voice broke the spell.

I turned, thankful. Memories of that day only led to thinking about the events that made it necessary. There'd been more than enough of that today. Coming down the aisle toward me was a tall, white-haired priest. "I, ah, was hoping I could talk to someone."

The priest smiled and gestured toward the confessional at the back of the room. "Confession starts in an hour, but I have a few moments if you'd like to beat the rush." He winked. "It gets crazy in here. Yesterday we had to pull apart two elderly women."

Huh. A priest with a sense of humor. That would definitely help.

"No, nothing like that. I actually had some questions."

He stepped back and slid into the nearest pew, sliding down to make room. "Oh?"

I followed suit and took a deep breath. "Demons."

"Ah. We all have our demons. Drugs, violence, sex—"

"Um, no." God, I felt like a moron. "I mean, like, real demons."

His expression changed. "I see."

I wanted to run from the building and never look back, but I needed answers. "Are they real? Demons, I mean."

His right eye twitched, and it was plain to see he was trying to cover up a smile. "Do you believe yourself possessed?"

Okay. Now he was making fun of me. "Of course not." I shifted in the seat. What I needed was an excuse. "I'm an intern over at the *Harlow Journal*," I lied. "I'm helping with some research."

His eyebrows rose. "On demons?"

"There's this whole demon worship thing going around some of the college campuses along the Eastern Seaboard. I'm trying to get some basic information about lore and stuff."

He thought about it for a moment, and just when I was sure he'd dismiss me as a liar, he frowned and said, "As sure as there is a God in heaven, there are demons. Yes. I believe them to be real."

"And they're all evil, right?"

He leaned back in the pew. "Evil is a relative term. Are people truly evil?"

"Um, is that a trick question?"

He smiled. "There's no handbook. Much of these things go on faith. I don't believe there is black or white, only shades of gray. Demons exist to tempt us into evil. Angels exist to tempt us into good. Who's to say the right angel couldn't tempt a demon? Or vice versa? I believe they're the subtle whispers we hear in our daily battles with morality. "

"So they're not fanged, drooling monsters?"

He glanced over his shoulder, then turned back to me. "Not all of my brethren would agree with my beliefs, but no. I don't think so. In fact, it's my opinion that you wouldn't even realize if you walked into one on the street."

"So you think they're here. Out there walking around?"

He hesitated, then sighed. "There are many stories, mythology if you will, depicting the path of demonkind after

God cast them from heaven. Some believe they reigned in hell, while others insist they were cursed to walk the earth for all eternity." The priest leaned back, a mischievous look in his eyes. "I met a man once who insisted he was one of the first cast aside, and sat in place of honor in hell, at Lucifer's right hand. Whether it was true or not is a mystery, but he spun an intriguing tale."

I bent closer. Now we were getting to the good stuff. "What did he say?"

"He told of a great, bloody war that raged over centuries, slowly tearing hell apart. Lucifer grew tired of his children misbehaving, and like God, cast them out. It is said that they were banished here, forced to live as mortals, stripped of their heritage and forced to sustain themselves on their rage."

"What about a specific demon. The Son of Cain?"

The priest's brow furrowed for a moment. "I don't know of a demon by that name. Do you mean Cain and Abel?"

I shook my head. "I'm not sure? Is there some kind of myth connecting them to a demon?"

"Cain was the firstborn son of Adam and Eve. He grew jealous of his younger brother, Abel, and in a fit of rage, murdered him. The act brought true violence into the world. He was the first murder. There are rumors that Cain's bloodline was marked by God as punishment for soiling his creation. Some being cursed to carry an unspeakable evil throughout the ages."

"So then the descendants of Cain are demons?"

The priest smiled. "I think it's a metaphor for the anger and jealousy in all humans rather than a literal meaning."

Or, it could be the tall, dark guy I'd loved since childhood was an actual, honest-to-God demon, just like he said...

Chapter Fifteen

Jax

I watched Sam leave the church. Judging by the stiff set of her shoulders and the grim expression that weighed her mouth down at the corners, she didn't get the answers she wanted.

I followed as she made her way down Topper Avenue, staying far enough behind so I wouldn't be spotted. Coffee. A magazine. She even stopped to look in several of the storefronts. Things I knew she had no interest in. Barbet's Baby Emporium. Fisher's Pet Shop. She was stalling.

Sam stopped in front of Hellman's Fine Jewelry. It was now or fucking never. I stepped from the shadows and came up behind her, and peered into the window. "Way too high-maintenance for you." She was looking at a pair of white diamond earrings with a weird little squiggle thing on the bottom. "Plus, they're so bland. Diamonds? You're more of an emerald kind of girl."

"Stalking is a crime, you know." She turned from the window and started walking again. There was a chill in her voice that stung. I understood, but it still hurt.

Screw it. At least she was talking to me. That had to be a good sign. No rushing off screaming at the top of her lungs. "Depends. Demons stalk. It's generally what we do."

Sam didn't stop, but her entire body tensed. Okay. Might be a good idea to ease up on the jokes.

"I know you're probably—"

That time she froze. After pulling me off the street and into a side alley, she poked me hard in the chest. "You *know*? Somehow I doubt you *know* anything going on inside my head."

I folded my arms and leaned back against the brick building. "Then tell me."

She backed off, then collapsed against the brick wall beside me. "I—I'm not even sure what to say. I have so many questions. Questions that I don't think I even want answers to."

"Then don't ask." I shrugged, trying to keep it casual.

"What?"

"Don't ask the questions. Think the worst of me and leave it at that—because I promise you, most of the horrible things going through your mind right now are true. But you have to trust me so we can beat this thing. Demons don't stop, Sammy. We need to find out why this is happening and end it, or it's going to end you."

Her eyes went wide. "And *how* do we do that?"

"I don't have it with me, but I *am* a card-carrying member of the evil-infested. Like I said, the cops are out of the question. They wouldn't have the first clue how to deal with this. I do." The lie tasted bitter. I had no clue what to do, but it worked. A thin line of pink rose through the gray and twirled around her shoulders. Hope.

Part of me was elated at the possibility that she'd be able to see past my darkness, while another part was terrified of what that could mean for her. What I was would only drag her down. "It's okay you hate me for leaving…for what I *am*…but you have to know deep down inside that if I'd known you were in danger, I would never have left you."

"How do I know I can trust you not to feed me to your demon buddies?"

"Demons don't have buddies. Plus, I know who really stole Officer Davies's patrol car in ninth grade." I leaned closer. Close enough to smell the raspberry scent of her shampoo. After all these years, she still used the same brand. It brought a rush of memories, both good and bad, that left me reeling. "I never told. I think that makes me trustworthy."

A flush rose in her cheeks and she backed away. "Fine. Then how do we deal with this?"

"First we need to find out the identity of the demon. One of them, at least. On the inside it's a monster, but on the outside, it looks, walks, and talks human. More than likely, it's got a job and a home. Relationships. We need to track it down. We can't stop it if we don't know where to find them or why they're even after you."

"You said you'd been to its apartment, right? There must be something in there. Something with a name on it."

I shook my head. "Nope. I looked. It's full of furniture, new clothes, and corpses. Everything else is empty. It's like the place is for show or something. I don't believe it actually lives there."

"Doesn't matter. There still has to be a name on the rental agreement."

Sam seemed to have calmed a little during the ride to the demon's apartment complex. Her colors showed more confusion than fear, and she wasn't avoiding my gaze anymore. Even talked a little.

She folded her arms, glaring at the door. "So how are we going to do this? The sign on the door says they're not back until two. We just stand here and wait?"

We were outside the rental office. Inside, the demon stirred, remembering the last time I'd been there. "They're not going to just tell us the name of the person renting that apartment. I suggest a little breaking and entering. We have less than an hour before they get back."

She broke into a grin. "I like where this conversation is heading. May I?"

I stepped aside and gestured to the door. "Go for it."

Sam knelt in front of the lock and pulled a small, silver pick from her pocket. It took her twelve seconds. Maybe fifteen. She had the door open and was standing in front of me wearing the same grin I saw most nights in my dreams. Mischievous and sexy as all hell. "Shall we?"

I scanned the hallway, listening carefully. Once I was sure the coast was clear, I slipped into the office, fighting back the spike of desire as I brushed against Sam on the way in. The demon felt it, too. It flashed images of the kiss outside the club, urging me to do it again. When I didn't act, the demon rumbled, angry, and a twinge at the base of my neck trailed up toward my temple, then bloomed into pins and needles and spread throughout my body. Next came the flash.

Sam stood in front of me, eyes wide and mouth slightly agape. There was fear in her eyes, but also fire. Fire that, despite the rage building inside me, spread throughout my entire body like a match set to dry leaves. I tried to shut out the scene, to force myself back to the here and now, but the demon was determined. Almost happy. I could feel the thing's pleasure and knew it salivated at the building mix of lust and anger.

Sam took a step back as I stalked forward. A starving lion cornering prey. That's what this was. Primal and dark and on the verge of sending me over the edge. Four steps from where I stood to the tree, I watched as vision-me in the demon's scenario lunged for Sam.

I gripped two fistfuls of her shirt, and with a single flick of my wrists, tore the material down the center exposing a wash of cream-colored skin with just the smallest hint of a flush. The remnants of the shirt fell to the ground, and something roared inside. A feeling that tugged against the very thing that kept the demon in check. It bowed and twisted, and in the sickest parts of my soul, I wanted this to be real. To be something more than the monster's sick way of communicating.

I shoved her hard into the tree and she gasped on impact. There might have even been the hint of a protest, but the words were stolen as I claimed her mouth with savage force.

It was nothing more than a flash.

The same kind of illusion the demon had tormented

me with my entire life, but it felt different somehow. Maybe because it was playing out a scenario that I wanted more than anything else. A twisted fantasy that the darkest parts of me wanted to be real. The one thing I wanted.

Sam.

The sensation was electric. I was, in reality, nowhere near her, yet I could feel her lips on mine. Her small body beneath me. The tremble of her chest as I crushed her to the tree and the sharpness of the bark as it bit into our flesh. My body reacted, a tightening in my belly drifting lower and fanning into an all-consuming fire.

A soft noise escaped her lips, driving the demon—driving *me*—straight into madness. Fingers knotted through her long hair, pulling and tugging to bring her closer. When that didn't quench the fire, I gripped her shoulders, yanking her from the tree, and forcing her hard to the floor. She laughed, throwing her head back and baring her neck to me. A tearing sound filled the clearing, and a barrage of warmth exploded beneath my fingers as the material between us was no longer a hindrance.

It broke me.

A roar tore from my throat and the flash ended, leaving me breathless and burning like a supernova.

"Jax?"

There she was. Still standing a few feet in front of me, just inside the office door. I tried to stop myself, but I was under her spell. As in the flash, it took four long steps to get from where I stood to her. I backed her against the wall, stopping just short of crushing my lips against hers.

"Jax?" she asked again, but this time the tone was different. Breathless and hopeful.

Excited.

It was enough to snap me back to reality. "We need to move quickly." I shook my head to clear the muck and stepped away from her. Control. "Um, the filing cabinet," I said, pointing to the large set of drawers on the other side of the office. "Start there. The apartment number is 882."

She went right to work, while I kept to the far end of the room, doing my best to keep Azirak under control. It probably wouldn't be helpful if I jumped her right here in the office, but I got the impression that the demon wanted it.

As badly as I did.

Chapter Sixteen

Sam

Keeping quiet siphoned every bit of self-restraint I had. Questions. There were so many. I wanted to know the details behind Jax's demonic side despite the possible answers, because crazy or not, I still wanted him same as always. But first we had to deal with the threat to my life. After that was handled, there'd be time to ask questions. Time to crumble and mourn the death of my parents again. And if he was still determined to run, I'd get him to change his mind.

Several subtle glances told me he was on the other side of the office, riffling through a pile of papers on the manager's desk. Every once in a while he'd pick his head up and catch me watching him. Each time, chills raced down my spine, and my heart went into overdrive. How the hell was it that a single glimpse could do that? It was like he devoured me with every glance.

"Got it," Jax exclaimed. He snatched a paper from the filing cabinet on his side of the room and waved it back and forth. "The file says the apartment is rented to Bob Dowdy. There's another address in this file for him, too. We can check it out."

"Bob Dowdy," I said, rolling the name around in my mouth. I closed the filing cabinet and climbed to my feet. "The demon's name is *Bob*?"

His right eyebrow rose slightly above the left and he set the folder back into the drawer where he'd gotten it. "Were you hoping for a Lucifer? Maybe a Damien?"

"Smart-ass." I rolled my eyes. "Does the name sound familiar?"

"Why would it?"

I shrugged. "I dunno. Don't you guys, like, all know each other or something?"

"There's no club, Sammy. We don't meet once a year at a convention for the demonic." He stuffed the paper into his back pocket and hitched his thumb toward the door. "Let's go see what we can dig up on this thing."

I nodded and reached for the handle, giving it a quick turn. Nothing happened. "Um… It's stuck."

"Stuck?" He moved to nudge me aside, but stopped when I turned at the same moment, putting our faces inches from each other.

"Go ahead. Do your thing," I said.

"My *thing*?"

We didn't have all day, but the way he said it woke the butterflies in my belly. The manager would be back soon, but reality be damned, I wanted him to kiss me again. "Yes. Your thing. Your demon thing. I want you to open the door."

Actually, I wanted him to throw me over his shoulder and head for the desk on the other side of the room, but since that was less likely than a two-headed panda wearing a top hat and singing show tunes, I'd settle for getting the hell out of here.

He stepped closer. "Using my *demon thing*. Is that right?"

I swallowed and tapped the door, forcing myself to breathe. "We don't have all day, Jax. Get to it."

Jax took a deep breath and let his eyes flutter closed for a second. When he opened them, there was a wicked smile on his lips. With one hand braced against the door, he leaned in and whispered, "I could open the door, but you'd much rather I kiss you, right?"

I nodded. It was all I could manage.

"Even though I'm a demon?"

His voice was like melted chocolate. Rich and soothing. It didn't matter to me in that moment that he was a demon. It wouldn't matter, I realized, in *any* moment, because he was Jax. And he was what I'd always wanted.

"I would wreck you, Sammy. Make you scream for hours and hours until your voice is gone and you don't remember your own name. Is that what you want?"

My mouth was dry. Legs mushy. Heart on overload. Again, all I could do was nod.

He pulled away, smile gone. At first he looked confused. Brows furrowed and lips pursed. Then he just looked indifferent. A rush of cold replaced the spot he'd been and I shivered. "Tell me," he said, voice icy and low. "How does it feel to want?"

The chill turned into a glacial freeze. My heart, seconds ago banging like a woodpecker gone postal, was now dead.

Words. They were just meaningless words meant to push me away. Still, it hurt. "Fuck you," I said, backing away.

He laughed, but there was something off about it. It was forced. "No—" Jax turned away from me to stare at the door. "Do you smell that?"

"Smell what?" I snapped. "The odor of asshole? As a matter of fact, I—"

He clamped his hand across my mouth and leaned closer to the door. The urge to bite his hand came—and went. Pissing off a demon, no matter how big a dick he was, probably wasn't the path to a long life.

"Gasoline," he said, voice hushed. "I smell gasoline."

I pried his hand away from my face. "You're crazy." But no sooner did I get the words out than the smell filled my nose, followed by a rush of clear liquid from under the door. It crept across the tile floor, filling the spaces between and rolling over the grout like a mini tidal wave.

Jax reached for the handle again, but halted midway. Without a word, he pivoted, hand shooting out in a blur, and knocked me back as a rush of flame spilled in from under the door.

"Shit." I gasped, backing toward the window. Fumbling with the lock, I threw it open and looked down. We were on the fourth floor. The office was in the back of the building and faced nothing more than an empty lot. There was no help in sight.

With the help of the gasoline, the fire spread quickly, catching the numerous stacks of papers strewn around the room. The temperature rose as thick gray smoke billowed into the air. A series of body-racking coughs doubled me over and I gasped for air.

"Do you still have an issue with heights?" Jax asked, taking my arm and dragging me closer to the window.

I glanced over my shoulder. "If I say yes, will that change anything?"

"Nope," he said, maneuvering a leg over the sill.

"Then fair warning," I said, letting him tug me closer. "I may puke on you."

"Noted."

I stepped out onto the thin ledge as Jax inched closer to the fire escape ladder a few feet away. I made the mistake of peeking down. It was quick—nothing more than a flicker—but it was enough. Vertigo hit with a vengeance. The fire wouldn't get me. The fall from the ledge wouldn't, either. But that sudden stop at the bottom? Yeah. That'd do it right.

Jax wrapped his right hand around the far side of the ladder and stepped onto the rung. He climbed down a few bars, and with his left hand, waved me over. "Okay. Come here." He patted the second rung from the top and said, "Step right on this one. Don't worry. I won't let you fall."

I did as told, and rung by rung, we descended the ladder until there was blissfully solid earth beneath my feet. I would have dropped and kissed the ground, too, if it weren't for the fire engine and four police cars that came rocketing into the lot.

The Harlow Police Station was, unfortunately, a place I knew well. Jax and I had our fair share of trouble as kids. No formal charges had ever been filed, but any time anything went wrong in town they looked to Jax first. Granted sometimes he *was* the culprit, but nine times out of ten, it was just simple minds and the overinflated rumor mill of a small town.

I got into nearly as much trouble, but that, too, was Jax's fault if you asked, well, anyone. Everyone blamed him for dragging me along as though I had no mind of my own. Then, after he'd left town, they explained my delinquent behavior as acting out as a result of the *horrible tragedy* I'd suffered at such an early age, and of course, added in that Jax must have messed with my head. That had always pissed me off. The truth was, I'd been a juvenile delinquent all on my own.

Frank Spencer was the police chief now. He'd been a close friend of my mother's, and had always looked out for me. I knew he felt bad. The entire Harlow Police Department did. They'd never caught the man—*thing*, I knew now—that murdered my parents. It was one of the town's only unsolved crimes.

Frank, a short, stocky man with a scant patch of thinning brown hair and a crooked grin, slid into the seat across from me wearing his standard frown. The poor guy had to get out more. He always looked like he was having a bad day. Pasty and irritable, he never smiled. "You want to tell me what the hell you were doing in that office, kid?"

They'd separated Jax and me the moment we got to the station. I knew the drill. I sighed. "Would you believe we were on a scavenger hunt?"

Frank rolled his eyes. "This is serious, Sam. You're over eighteen now and that means criminal charges. You were just caught breaking and entering, and are suspected of possible arson. Give me something. Please."

"Arson?" I balked. "Because we tried to set ourselves

on fire?"

"So you're saying you didn't set the fire?"

"I didn't set the fire."

Frank slid a pen and note pad across the table. Tapping it twice, he asked, "Did Flynn set the fire?"

"No!"

"Why do I find that hard to believe?" As a patrolman, Frank had pulled Jax over shortly after he'd gotten his license. Jax thought it'd be funny to roll his window down a few inches, order a burger and fries, then roll up the glass and flip the man off. Needless to say, there was no love lost between the two.

"He didn't do it. Neither of us did."

Frank sighed. He leaned back in the chair and kicked both feet onto the tabletop. A watery memory fought its way to the surface. Frank, at my parents' house, doing the same thing on my mother's coffee table. She'd hit him with a rolled-up newspaper. "I see your choice in companionship hasn't improved since we last saw each other. I'd hate to have to haul you in when he goes down—because we all know he will. You're just starting to get your life together."

I was over eighteen, so they wouldn't call my aunt, but Frank wouldn't just let me walk out of that office without some kind of explanation. So I gave him one. The real one. "I was searching for information on someone who rents an apartment in that building. Me. My idea. My reason. Jax was helping me."

"So he came back to town to help you break into an apartment office building?" Frank snorted. "And who were you digging for information on? And why?"

"I wanted to find the man who attacked me at school," I

said. Did it without a warble, too. "You can call the Huntington police if you don't believe me. It's the truth. Some guy
attacked me."

Whatever he expected me to say, that wasn't it. Frank's
demeanor changed instantly, going from hard-ass cop to
concerned family friend. "Sam, if something happened, you
can't take matters into your own hands. You need to let the
proper authorities handle this. Does this have something to
do with your car ending up in the river?"

"I think so. Yeah."

He scribbled notes on the pad. I tried to see what he
was writing, but Frank kept the pad tilted up, away from my
prying eyes. "What makes you think this person—who did
you say it was?—is the one who attacked you? Did you see
his face?"

"I did some digging. That's all I can tell you. His name
is Bob Dowdy."

All the color drained from Frank's face. "When did you
say the attack occurred? You went to Huntington, right?"

"Last month," I said. "And, yeah. Why?"

"I don't know where you kids are getting your information from, but you're wrong about Dowdy." He leaned
in, hesitating for a moment before blowing out a loud sigh.
"Bob Dowdy was a person of interest in several cases involving local missing girls, but he was found murdered. He
couldn't have been the one who attacked you. He's been
dead for months."

Chapter Seventeen

Jax

When Spencer brought Sam out of the interrogation room, I was relieved to see the man didn't look angry. It shouldn't have surprised me. The guy had a soft spot for her—which had helped get her out of a lot of the trouble *I'd* gotten her into over the years.

He walked her across the room and pointed to the chair across from his desk, next to mine. "Sit."

Silently, Sam did as instructed.

"How long are you in town, Flynn?" he asked, taking the seat behind his desk. "And how many more times do you expect to visit my station?"

"I'm only passing through. Don't worry. Your women and children are safe."

"Somehow I doubt that," he mumbled.

I was about to make a smart-ass comment, but something

about Sam caught my attention. She was leaning forward in her seat, subtly craning her neck to see onto the top of Spencer's desk. I followed her gaze. There was a file with Dowdy's name on the front.

"I don't want Sam anywhere near you when you go down—because we both know you will. Your kind always does."

Sam wanted that file. Only to get it, she'd need some help. "When I go down? Had that same talk with Lucy, did ya? I hear she goes down all the time."

Spencer's face turned a pretty awesome shade of red. The last I'd heard, he and his daughter, Lucy, hadn't spoken in years. She was currently the main act over at the Double Trouble, Harlow's premier adult entertainment venue.

Sam's face got white as snow. Obviously the last thing she wanted right now was a throw-down between Harlow's police chief and a cocky demon with an extreme attitude problem. Too bad, because she was about to get it.

"I gotta take a leak," I added just as Spencer's face reached critical mass. He was cruising for a heart attack if he didn't calm down. Nudging Sam's foot with my boot to get her attention, I gave a subtle nod toward the desk. Even if she didn't manage to get the file, the whole thing was worth the grin she gave me.

"Sorry. No bathroom on the premises."

I stood and met the older man's eyes with a challenge. "I passed a bathroom on the way in here."

"Out of order."

"The hell is it is," I shot back.

I took two steps and stopped in front of the large potted fern in the corner of Frank's office. "Your choice. You cough up the key, or I water your plant."

Frank stood, forgetting about Sam. The expression on his face was nothing short of joy. "You whip it out and I'll toss your ass in jail."

I couldn't be sure, but when the sound of my zipper filled the small room, I thought I heard Sam groan.

We'd set up in the back corner of Jill's diner on the edge of town. Sam was spread out on the other end of the table, trying to drown the ice in her soda. When she thought I wasn't watching, she'd glance up and stare at me like she was trying to see into my brain. I wished she'd stop. There were waves of black and dark blue swirling around her head. It made the demon twitchy, while at the same time made me want to apologize for being such a dick right before the fire broke out. "Sammy?"

She hadn't said more than ten words—none of them relevant—since we'd left the police station, and was staring at the file we'd taken. When the cop hauled me away, Sam snagged it. Eventually he'd notice it was gone and considering our combined history, put two and two together, but there'd be no way to prove it. "Are you going to tell me what happened? What did Spencer say?"

She sighed, and without looking up, said, "It wasn't Bob Dowdy."

"Huh?"

"The guy that attacked me. It wasn't him. Dowdy isn't the demon."

"But the apartment? I don't get it."

"Dowdy has been dead for months. Cops found him facedown in a gutter on Hooker Avenue. They searched his house and that apartment. You said you found bodies there? Well, someone put them there recently, because they weren't there when the cops went in."

"Wait, why did the cops go in?"

"The police have been keeping it pretty hush-hush, but I guess they had him figured for that Gentleman Stalker."

Shit. Now we were back to square one. "The demons must have killed Dowdy and taken the apartment. Please tell me you didn't tell Spencer about the bodies..."

"No way. I'll make an anonymous tip. If he finds out either of us was actually in the apartment, his head will implode."

"But you told him about being attacked at Huntington?"

She lifted her gaze from the file, unapologetic. "I had no choice. I had to give him something. He's not stupid, and if this thing really is taking girls, then it needs to be stopped."

"We went over this before. The cops can't stop it."

"Why?" Defiance bloomed in her expression. She leaned back in the seat and folded her arms. "If the cops were unable to deal with a demon, then how were they able to keep you locked up for the afternoon?"

"Are you seriously asking me this? What should I have done, busted my way out the front door?" I snorted loudly, causing the people two tables over to glance our way, irritated. In a foul mood already—the damn demon was hungry again—I smiled politely and proceeded to flip them off. "I couldn't have done it anyway. I don't have a *demonic arsenal*, as you put it. I'm a little stronger, tougher, and faster, and have a lot more attitude than the average Joe. That's it. Far as I can tell, other demons are pretty much the same."

As I spoke, Azirak shifted and squirmed. It flashed another one of the battlefield scenes. Fire and brimstone and piles of bones in a battlefield so high, they reached up into the clouds. The flash was so intense that I could smell the smoke. Burning flesh and otherworldly screams echoed in my ears, making me feel like I was right there in the middle of the field.

"Jax?" Sam's voice, and the warmth of her hand resting atop mine, pulled me from the scene.

"Sorry. The demon was showing me something." Deep breath. A cold sweat broke out at the base of my neck.

Knowing Sam, she wanted to ask questions, but thankfully, she bent over the file.

I needed something to take my mind off the images. Tapping the table, I said, "Lemme see the folder for a sec."

Sam slid the papers across the table. On the outside, I was calm. Inside though, Azirak churned, encouraging the bubble of fear and unease that brewed. I opened the folder. First page. A girl seven months ago in Farmersville. She was cute. Long brown hair and dark eyes. No known family, but a friend had reported her missing. I'd passed through town around that time on my way to check on Rick and Sam. I'd rented a room for two weeks before moving on. I vaguely remembered hearing something on the local news about the search.

I flipped the page. Two weeks later, a girl went missing from Hempstead Township. Again, I'd been in town around the time.

In fact, I'd been in all the towns. The list went on and on. The dates and locations matched my travels.

"Jax?" Sam asked, worry tainting her voice.

I swallowed, unable to answer. Another page. Another girl.

"Jax, you're freaking me out here."

I was freaking myself out. All those girls. All those towns. The air around me bled gray, my own fear nearly choking me.

When I found my voice again, I faced Sam and pushed the file back across the table. "Listen to me carefully, Sammy. I want you to get up and walk out that door. Go anyplace other than Kelly's. Go someplace where I won't find you."

I thought I'd made myself clear, yet Sam was still sitting across from me, looking like I'd lost my mind. Waves of black rose from her shoulders.

"Did you hear me? Get *out*!" I couldn't help raising my voice.

She sighed and began gathering the papers in no particular rush. When everything was collected in a neat pile, she stuffed them back into the envelope and stood. "Well?"

"Well, what?" I snapped.

"Are you ready?"

"Was I speaking another language? Was it confusing that I wanted you to leave *without me*?"

"Nope. Crystal. Not doing it though."

Fuck. She was going to make me spit it out. "I think this all has something to do with me."

"You? How could—"

I flipped the file around and slid it back across the table, tapping the top page. "I was there. In the same city at the same time each and every one of these girls went missing."

Leaning back, eyes wide—Sam laughed. Not a sexy giggle or an amused chuckle, but an all-out snorting chortle.

I couldn't decide if I should be worried about her sanity—or furious because she wasn't taking this seriously. "Since when does cold-blooded murder tickle your funny bone?"

She pulled it together, grabbing the edge of the table to steady herself. "I'm—I'm sorry, but you? Never."

Sam held up a hand, then reached across and pulled me from the seat. Stunned by her reaction to my confession, I let her drag me to the door.

"I didn't mean I was the one who attacked you. I mean, it's too much of a coincidence that I was in each one of those towns at the time."

"So you think this demon is, what, out to frame you?"

That wasn't what I thought—was it? No. If there was some kind of warrant for me, Spencer would have been more than happy to lock my ass away. "I'm not sure. I just know that everywhere I am, it seems a girl disappears."

Sam herded us through the door and onto the sidewalk. Once outside, I pulled away.

"If that's the truth, then it's really good news."

"How is that *good news*?"

She was grinning. "Because then we know who his next target is. You can protect me."

Sam had blinders on when it came to me. I'd told her the truth. She'd seen the demon. I'd been a dick. Treated her like shit. I'd even tried—and failed—to scare her. What more could I possibly do?

Try harder.

Snatching her wrist, I turned and dragged her into the alleyway across from the diner. She stumbled twice, tripping, but I didn't slow down. Once we were concealed in the shadows, I shoved her against the building.

"You think this is a game? I told you, I'm a monster."

"Right," she said, nodding. There wasn't even the small-est hint of gray swirling above her head and it pissed me off. "A vicious monster. One that's sticking around to protect me?"

"You need me to spell it out for you? Okay. I've ripped people to shreds, one limb at a time. *Slowly.* I've made them suffer, taking joy in their pain and agony." I pulled away so I could see her expression.

"Whatever you've done, it's because of the demon," she insisted.

Inside, Azirak swirled, amused. Funny. The thing thought this was funny—and it was right. "You want to believe it, but the truth is, I *like* it. I like the feeling of holding someone's world between the tips of my fingers. Playing judge, jury, and executioner." I was disgusting. "Hearing them scream… Rage and violence are my life—and I like it that way."

For a second I was sure I'd gotten the message across. Sam's eyes were wide, and with the demon's help, I heard her pulse race. But it wasn't gray waves of fear rising from her body—they were crimson. She was pissed.

She shoved me hard and I didn't resist—only she wasn't doing it to get me away from her. Hands flat against my chest, Sam pushed me across the alley and into the adjacent building, standing on her toes so that we were face-to-face. The waves of red receded, and she took a step away.

I didn't dare move. Didn't dare breathe.

In a move I never saw coming, she reached out and cupped the side of my face. The gentleness of the touch was like a jolt of electricity. Sharp and painful. My mind raged to pull away, but Azirak, despite its mounting hunger, encouraged me to stay where I was. It was intrigued by Sam's actions. Confused, but interested.

"For the first time since we met the day of my parents' funeral, I can't figure you out." Her fingers trailed, warm and soft, down the side of my face, stopping to rest at the base of my neck. "I don't know if it's me you're trying to convince — or yourself."

"You —"

She pulled my head down so our foreheads met, and whispered, "I wish you could see yourself the way I see you. You are not a perfect man, Jax Flynn, but you are *not* a monster. You've done what you needed to survive, but I refuse to believe that true evil is within your range." She pulled away and tilted my head up a few inches so that we were face-to-face again. "Maybe — just maybe — you have some connection to the thing that's doing all this. But that doesn't make it your fault. Like you said, we'll figure it out and we'll stop it. Together."

I ripped the folder from her fingers and propelled her away. Waving it, I said, "Didn't you notice anything about these victims, Sammy?"

Hesitant, she rolled her eyes and took the file back, leafing through. "They're all girls?"

"They're all girls with *brown hair* and *brown* eyes." I took the folder back again. "They're all girls who are about five foot three and weigh about a buck twenty. No real family."

She wasn't getting it.

"They're *you*, Sammy. Each one of these girls resembles you."

I watched it happen. The moment she realized I was

right. A puff of gray wafted from her shoulders and her skin visibly paled. But it didn't last. Sam took a deep breath and looked away from the folder. "Even if you're right, that doesn't make this your fault," she repeated.

And with those words, she leaned forward, rose onto her toes, and brushed her lips to mine. So brief. So painful. Azirak went crazy, urging me to push against her and make us one. It wanted her as much as I did and that terrified me more than any lapse in control ever had.

"We can do this," she said.

But I wasn't as optimistic. This demon was essentially following me. Killing girls wherever I went.

Girls who looked like Sam.

Chapter Eighteen

Sam

Jax's footsteps echoed against the floorboards above the living room as I paced the floor. He must have been worried that the demon would attack Rick, because he insisted on stopping off to check on his uncle. He'd asked me to wait outside, but I hadn't seen Rick in so long.

"Do you ever listen?" Jax growled, coming down two steps at a time. "Outside means not in the building last I checked."

"Next you'll try slapping a collar on me and commanding I bark like a dog," I said. It was the perfect opening for a Jax-like retort, but he didn't answer. He didn't even snicker. I looked around the room. "So where's Rick? I wanted to say hi."

"He's upstairs. Sleeping."

"Sleeping?" I said. "In the middle of the afternoon?"

He didn't answer.

"Jax?" I tried again.

"He's sick," Jax said after a moment. "Cancer. That's why I came back to Harlow. He doesn't have much time left."

Everything started to spin. "Sick— How—? Kelly never said a word. Chase either."

"He asked them not to. It happened really fast. He went downhill quickly. Didn't want anyone to know."

I blinked. I didn't know what to say. Rick Flynn was family. "I... I'm sorry, Jax."

"He doesn't want your pity," he said coolly. "Neither do I."

"I know."

"Then forget I said anything."

I stared. Forget? Was he crazy? "I can't just—"

He was in front of me, face so close that I could feel the heat radiating from his skin. "You have more important things to worry about. You need to learn what it's like to deal with a demon."

One second he was burning for me like a California wildfire, the next he was trying to cram an iceberg the size of Texas between us. The back-and-forth of his mood was making me dizzy. "What does that mean?"

"It means," he said, eyes narrowing to thin slits, "maybe you need to see the truth firsthand. Maybe then you'll keep your pathetic human ass away from me."

He wanted me to be afraid of him. The big bad demon next door. Hah, right. I'd seen him puke all over himself after eating too many Atomic Dogs at the fair. Watched him rescue a litter of kittens from a partially submerged storm drain on prom night. And knew all about his annoying obsession with old John Belushi films. Once you see someone recite every line from *The Blues Brothers* wearing a hat and shades, it was impossible to view him as an emotion-sucking, flesh-eating demon hell-bent on terror and destruction.

But as sure of him as I was, I didn't need the attitude. I leaned in a little closer, catching him off guard. "You didn't think my ass was that pathetic when you were staring at it before."

"I wasn't—" His eyes went wide, and he mumbled something too low for me to hear. Fist curling tight, he smashed it into the wall by the door, sending me about a foot off the ground. Tiny bits of paint and plaster rained down, scattering on the floor at our feet. "This mess is your fault."

"My fault?" I snapped. "While I don't for a second believe any of this is *your* fault, I sure as hell don't blame myself, either."

When Jax turned back around, I was barely able to hold back a gasp. While not completely blackened like they'd been in my apartment, his eyes were rimmed with black. The demon.

"It—I—" Something furious sparked behind Jax's eyes, but he stepped back and took a deep breath. "You need to *see* what I am."

We'd borrowed Rick's car and were sitting, parked around the corner of Harbor Street and Forty-Fifth Avenue. I didn't come down this way if I could help it. Hell, the cops didn't even come down this way. Every week there was something in the paper about a murder, and there wasn't any street corner you could hit without seeing either a hooker, a drug dealer, or gang-style graffiti.

"Why are we here, Jax?"

"Because you need to understand what I am, Sammy. You need to see it firsthand."

"And we're going to do that inside Rick's car?"

"We're waiting for something."

"That's not too cryptic. Any chance you're going to tell me what?"

No answer.

A few moments passed. When it was obvious he had no plans to talk, I took matters into my own hands. The silence was too much. "This is why you left? This thing inside you?"

"Yes," he responded without turning away from the window. "The members of my family are the cursed descendants of Cain. Sometimes the male children are born with a demon attached to their soul."

"Sometimes?"

Jax's posture relaxed just a bit and he turned to me. Now, eyes their normal shade of gray, he seemed to be more himself. Guarded, not cruel. Angry, not vicious. "Sometimes it will skip several generations. The last person on record to have been born infested was my great-grandfather."

My next question had been burning a hole in my mouth, and I was proud of myself for keeping it bottled up until now. "What about Chase? You guys are twins. Does he…?"

"Have a demon?" The light in his eyes changed. It became darker. Angrier and more like the Jax I'd seen before we came down here. "No. I was the *lucky one*."

"Is that why you two fought so much as kids? Because you got stuck with it and he didn't?"

He thought about it, picking at a loose thread on the steering wheel leather. "I guess a small part of me resented his freedom. The curse means having to live with a demon whispering in your ear all the time. There's a lot of suicide in my family tree… But the thing with Chase and me? The animosity? That's mostly the demon."

"How do you mean?"

"It hates him." He shook his head. "The things it wants me to do to him. The things it shows me… Part of the curse, I suppose. Cain killed his brother, Abel. Guess history is doomed to repeat itself."

I squeezed his hand. "But you resist. You're stronger than that thing inside you, Jax. It's why no matter what you say or show me, I know you'd never hurt me."

"I'm not stronger," he said. The agony in his voice made my heart squeeze. "It's why I have to stay away. When I'm not near him, it's easier. Quieter. When he's standing in front of me — I want to give in to the demon. It shows pictures of Chase lying broken and bleeding by my hand, and you want to know something, Sammy? I like it.

"As a kid, I used to make excuses. Blame the dark thoughts and short fuse on the demon, but as I got older, I realized that was bullshit. It's not all because of the curse, it's just me. Who I am. And who I am will always have this little voice in my head that whispers, as long as Chase is alive, I'm no good. I'm ruined."

"You're not ruined," I insisted, angry. Jax was messed up, and yes, he'd probably done things I couldn't even comprehend to survive, but he was still *Jax*. And that meant that I'd do whatever was necessary to save him from himself. Just like he'd done for me as a child. Just like we'd been doing for each other most of our lives. "And I'm going to prove it. Have a little faith."

A bitter laugh escaped his lips. "How are you going to accomplish that?" He twisted in the seat. "And faith? I prefer reality," he said. "You can't save me, Sammy. You want to save everyone—but you can't."

"I do not," I responded.

"Sure you do. You've always interfered in Chase's relationships, nudging him toward who you thought were the *good ones* and talking him away from the ones you deemed unworthy. Teachers, friends, family—everyone. I'm not judging. It's just who you are, and I get it, but it's not always possible. Not with me. Not anymore."

Heat flamed to life in my cheeks. He was right, of course—even if his observation was worded callously. I tried to save everyone. It was because of my parents. I hadn't been able to save them. It was crazy. There was nothing I could have possibly done to change the outcome of that horrible night. But as I got older, I saw it. There was always someone to save. Rick, when Jax left home. Kelly, when Uncle Ken left her for a younger woman. Chase. Jax… Everyone. Everyone but myself.

But this was different.

"I know I can't save you from the curse." I kept my voice even. "But I believe I can save you from yourself." I reached across the car and slid my hand through his hair, wrapping it around to the back of his head.

Jax closed his eyes and sighed.

The sound was warm, running through my body like liquid heat, and gave me the courage to do something bold. Twisting, I pulled his head close, guiding his lips to mine.

Surprisingly, I met with no restraint.

His teeth grazed my bottom lip, tongue slipping between to give him unrestricted access. Our position was awkward, both twisted sideways and leaning forward, but it didn't take away from the rush. In the back of my head, a small voice chided me for this. Anyone could walk right over and pull up a chair. The problem was, I didn't give a damn. And neither did he.

One minute his hands were idle. The left still on the steering wheel and the right at his side. The next, he was dragging me across the car, hefting me onto his lap so that there was no space between us—which wasn't hard because there wasn't a lot of wiggle room in a Toyota.

Mint and leather filled the small space, taking me back to the night of our first kiss. Just like then, I lost myself. The warmth of his body pressed against mine. The sound of his breath, quickened and raw. The way his arms wound tight around me like he'd never let go. The way his lips moved with mine was symmetry in its most basic form. It was all perfection.

"This was worth waiting for," he whispered into my mouth. He ran his tongue along my upper lip, tasting it, then captured the bottom one, drawing it into his mouth before letting go. He pulled back and watched me for a minute, the heat in his eyes blazing. His pointer finger traced across my cheek, lingering at the corner of my mouth before he bent forward and kissed me again.

That's when things got intense.

I tilted my head back as he trailed a line of scorching kisses along my chin and down the left side of my neck, pausing at the collar of my T-shirt with a frustrated growl.

Beneath me, his hips lifted. The friction sent tingles so exquisite, I couldn't help the low moan that escaped my lips. He chuckled. "That sound… Again." He breathed the words into the hollow of my neck. Each syllable was like a flamethrower held close to the flesh. "Do it again."

He didn't need to ask. The second his teeth grazed the soft skin above my collarbone, I let out another soft whimper.

"Perfect."

His voice, so deep and dark and full of promise, was enough to bring me close to the brink. Leaning closer, I tried to reclaim his lips, but Jax wasn't interested in my mouth. Not right then. With his left hand, he grabbed a handful of my hair and tugged. Not with enough force to be painful, but hard enough to prove he meant business. He ran his tongue from just below my ear, down to the corner of my collarbone. The trail it left was volcanic, igniting every inch of my body, turning me into a single raw nerve.

I threw my arms around him, desperate to pull him close. If not for the fact that he was so much taller and had the seat pushed all the way back, there wouldn't be room between us. He resisted with another chuckle and lifted his hips again, and I pressed harder against him, the feel of our bodies so close it stole my breath.

It had the same effect on Jax. He gasped, pushing me back against the steering wheel. When I tried to lean forward, though, he held me there, arms locked tight and eyes stormy with need. His breathing was heavy and he seemed so conflicted.

Something over my shoulder seemed to catch his attention.

"It's showtime," he rasped.

Chapter Nineteen

Jax

The demon raged inside. When I saw the target pass by, a man in his late thirties sporting dark sweatpants and a bright-blue hoodie, I was tempted to ignore him. Despite the reason I'd brought Sam out here. Despite of what common sense was telling me. Despite the pain I was in...

The definition of stupid was doing something even though you knew the outcome would be unpleasant. I'd kissed Sam twice since coming back to town. Each time it happened, things got worse. The demon seemed hungrier. Angrier. The pain was sharper. Still, I was almost willing to ignore it all and continue kissing her—even though Calvin Gutierrez had just walked by.

In the dark hours of the early morning, I'd stopped here to feed the demon, sure I could find some poor bastard deserving a good ass-kicking. What I found was Calvin

Gutierrez beating the shit out of some girl in the alley be-hind the liquor store on Eighth. I would have gone for him then, but I'd hesitated and the opportunity was lost. But I hadn't forgotten about him. A little digging and some Inter-net research, and I had all the information needed to nail the bastard.

I was out of the car and around the front before Sam even opened the door. "Jax?" she called. I ignored her. The best thing I could do right now was tune her out. Even if I *was* having second thoughts about showing her this side of my life, the demon was too far gone to care. It needed to feed. Really feed.

Now.

Sam called to me again, but her voice was far away and tinny. Ahead, Gutierrez leaned casually against the corner of the liquor store talking to a heavyset man. There was a quick exchange—a wad of bills passed off in return for a small white bag—and the other man was gone. I quickly took his place.

"Hey man," Gutierrez said with a nod. "You wanna—"

I grabbed the corners of the bastard's hoodie and hauled him into the shadows of the alley. Azirak roared with excite-ment, soaking in the man's surprise and fear. The emotion seeped into the air around us, sinking into my skin and slip-ping down my throat as I breathed.

I pushed him up against the wall, pinning him there by jamming an elbow up against his throat. The first blow was about to hit when footsteps pounded the pavement at the mouth of the alley.

"Jax! What the hell are you doing?"

I inhaled again, savoring the sweet scent of the man's

fear, and without looking at Sam, said, "This is what I am." I brought my head forward, bashing it hard against Gutierrez's. I felt the vibration, and heard the mingled screams of both Calvin and Sam as they begged me to stop.

But it was too late. The demon had gotten a taste, and it wouldn't let go now. Not until sated. This is what it craved. The little portions I took from random people here and there allowed me to function, but this was what the demon thrived on. True violence.

"You think that I'm worth saving?" I yanked my prey away from the wall, spinning hard and letting go. Gutierrez stumbled back, landing between two garbage pails. They clattered and fell to the ground, spilling trash all around. "You think I'm a *good man*?"

I hauled Gutierrez off the ground and shook him hard. "What—" the man mumbled. "What did I do to you?"

"This *isn't* who you are," Sam insisted. She inched closer, standing at the mouth of the alley. Even with the sick, delectable smell wafting all around, I still sensed her there. But it didn't matter. There was no turning back.

As the demon fed, the poisonous emotion seeping in, a twisted feeling of euphoria filled me. A detached, weightless sensation that made me feel like I was bulletproof. I pushed Gutierrez back against the wall again, grabbing hold of a fistful of his hair. Once. Twice. Three times. I slammed his head into the brick. "Does this feel familiar?" I whispered in the man's ear. He was barely conscious. "Do you remember doing this to that girl a few days ago?"

"Stop!" Sam screamed. A second later, she was dragging me away. Gutierrez slid down the wall and crumbled into a heap. I resisted the urge to spit on him. People like him were garbage. Gutierrez was just like me. He fed on the misery of others. His nose was bleeding. So was his head, and both his top and bottom lip were split with a nasty-looking gash, but he was still alive. Still breathing. But I'd taken what I needed. For now.

Reality would set in soon. It always did. The amped, contented feeling never lasted long. But at that moment, I reveled in the mist of my prey's emotions. Pain. Suffering. Fear. They fed the demon and eased my pain and that was all that mattered. Those first few moments after a feed were blissful. They were the only ones that brought any semblance of peace. There was no pain and no itching hunger creeping out from the darkest corners of my subconscious. There was only satisfaction.

"The corner of Eighth and Broadway," I heard Sam say. When I turned, she was on my cell phone. It brought the world crashing back down, and with it, the demon's rage.

Before I could stop myself, I ripped the phone from her hands. She gasped. "What the hell—"

"What the fuck do you think you're doing?" I advanced, and for the first time, Sam actually looked scared. Tufts of gray rose around her shoulders and swirled above her head.

"I didn't give my name. I had to call an ambulance. That poor guy is—"

"Is still alive," I snapped. "And unfortunately he'll continue to live, which is more than he deserves. And that *poor guy* beat some girl the other day. I'm sure he's beaten others, too."

"It doesn't matter what he did, Jax. You're not God. You're not judge and jury. You don't get to decide what he deserves."

Azirak was amused by Sam's words, and I, still feeding off the demon's high, couldn't help smiling. I didn't know where the words came from, but somehow I knew they were true. "But I am. I'm this world's judge, jury, and executioner."

In the distance, sirens wailed, and Sam paled. She grabbed my hand, flinching for just a second. "We need to go."

I looked down. The front of my shirt was splattered with red. Same with my forearms and hands. "I'm—" That tiny switch inside, the one that shut down my humanity and set the demon free, flipped back. Guilt flooded in and a rush of cold came over me. The broken bones, the echo of screams inside my head, the blood... This part I hated. The guilt. Not because of what I'd done—but because of how I'd felt while doing it. Invigorated and enthusiastic. I didn't like feeding the demon. I *loved* it. And Sam had seen the whole thing.

She tugged on my arm and I followed, lost in a haze. The movement of my legs and the warmth of her touch barely registered, along with the feel of her hand slipping into my front pocket in search of the keys. Like a child, I allowed her to stuff me into the passenger seat, and was vaguely aware of the squealing sound the tires made against the pavement as she peeled away from the curb.

We drove for several miles. I wasn't paying attention to the direction. North. South. It didn't matter. I was too busy staring at my hands. Hands that were covered in blood and to blame for the pain and suffering of so many. I'd lost count. Until February in my eighteenth year, I'd kept a running total. The number of poor bastards who had been unfortunate enough to wander into my path. They were the horrible and the violent. Sick and twisted... But they were humans whom, as Sam pointed out, I had no right to judge.

"Pull over," I said, looking up from my bloodstained hands.

"Pull over? Where?"

"Now," I snapped. The sound rattled around in the small space, making Sam flinch. The car listed hard to the left and stopped a few seconds later. I couldn't get out fast enough. Air. I needed air. I stumbled several feet from the door, doubling over and bracing myself against a nearby pine tree. My pulse thundered as the blood rushed through my veins.

Sam came around the front. "Jax?"

"I liked it, Sammy," I said with as much control as I could muster. Turning to face her now wasn't an option. "It made me *happy*. I took more pleasure than you can possible imagine from making him bleed."

She didn't answer right away, and when she did, her tone wasn't sharp or disgusted like it should have been. It was soothing. *Forgiving*. "Funny. You don't look very happy right now."

I straightened and pushed off the tree. A single step and I sank to my knees.

The blood on my hands would wash away but I would always see it. Each time I closed my eyes, the world turned red. How many nights had I sat in roach-infested motels, staring at a blade and wishing to hell that I had the strength to end it all? Most committed suicide long before they reached their twenties. They'd done the honorable thing. Spared the world from their particular flavor of madness and horror.

I was a fucking coward.

Too afraid to leave this life behind for fear of what the next held. After everything I'd done, there was no eternal peace waiting on the other side. "When I left, I made a choice to continue living—even though I knew what that would mean for others. You were right. I'm selfish, and this is the price I have to pay. There's no happiness out there for me, Sammy. No redemption. Only endless blood and violence."

Sam didn't say a word as she came around to stand in front of me. The sun was going down and the broken beam of light that shone through the trees was so bright, that it illuminated the outline of her body, making her look like angel.

An angel standing over the devil awaiting judgment.

"I don't believe that, Jax. I don't believe that there's anyone who can't be saved." She pulled me close, cradling my head against her belly. "You can be saved. I can save you."

"This asshole behind us is getting on my nerves," Sam mumbled.

It was starting to get dark and we were almost back to town. She'd been complaining about the car behind us for the past ten minutes. I glanced over my shoulder. "Pull to the side and let him pass."

"I'm going over the speed limit. There's no reason for him to be on my ass."

I checked the speedometer—she was going almost seventy—and peered into the passenger's side mirror, squinting against the glare from the other car's headlights. It was too close to see the plate number, but it looked like a New York plate. I was about to suggest turning at the intersection ahead when the car lurched forward.

"What the hell?" Sam cried. "Did he just hit us?"

This time when I glanced into the side-view mirror, I saw the car swerve around to the left. The engine revved and the car shot forward. "Shit. What the fuck is it with you and cars?" I was never getting into a vehicle with this girl again.

She never got the chance to respond. The other car hit us again, this time on the driver's side. The car veered uncontrollably to the right. Dirt and gravel kicked up, spraying everywhere. I turned to check on her as soon as we stopped moving, but my door swung open.

"Out," a deep voice commanded.

A demon's voice.

My demon was surprisingly quiet. Normally when I was in danger, it grew active and unsettled, flashing its two cents in the form of gory, unwanted pictures. This time however, it had nothing to say. Typical. The fucking thing was in the way until I actually needed it. I did as instructed and Sam followed suit on the driver's side of the car as three demons watched.

One of them stepped forward. It was one of the demons who'd been at the cliff. Not the one who'd sent her over, but the one I downed first. It ignored me and turned to Sam. "You weren't supposed to be a problem anymore—yet, here you are."

"Well, that's me," she said with an uneasy grin. "Trouble."

Another one, shorter than the first, chuckled. It stepped forward, grabbing Sam's chin and licking its lips. "Aren't you delicious?"

There was no thought involved. There was Sam, and there was the bastard's hands on her. I leaped forward with the intention of snapping every bone in the thing's arm, but instead of the satisfying sound of crunching and an agonized howl, I got a mouthful of dirt. The demon standing to my left had swept the back of my knees. "Stay down," it growled. "Or we'll destroy her while you watch."

I could take one for sure—probably two—but three? It was possible. There was too great a risk of Sam getting hurt in the cross fire. Gritting my teeth, I remained on the ground, but stayed ready to act.

The one from the cliff chuckled. It stepped around the car and came to stand in front of me. "I owe you," it said. "You attacked me when I was weak. Before I'd fed."

"We could feed from her," the third said. It stepped forward, long black coat swishing as it moved, and ran a finger along Sam's arm, from shoulder to elbow. The demon brought the finger to its nose and inhaled. "I bet she'd be mighty tasty. Smell that fear. Just a touch of resilience and a boatload of sex. That's my kind of meal."

The short one snorted in disgust. It wrinkled its nose and stepped away. "She's demon touched. She's already been tasted. I prefer my food fresh."

"I don't know. Looks like she'd leave a bad taste." the one standing behind me chuckled. "I'm not picky, though."

The one from the cliff growled. His stance and the way the others kept looking back to him, almost as if for approval, meant he was the one in charge. "She's not to be touched."

"I don't see what the big deal is," the reprimanded demon griped. "She's as good as dead. Zenak insists she's trouble for his boy. Stupid to waste such a perfectly fine meal."

Trouble for his boy... I'd heard of demon hierarchy, but had no idea how it worked. These demons must report to the demon that attacked Sam.

"But she's full of such decadent emotions," the one

behind me said. "We could each take one little taste. It wouldn't kill her. Not if we were careful."

The short one let out a snort. "You? Careful? That's rich."

"This coming from the demon who plays with his food for weeks before chowing down good and proper."

Listening to them talk about Sam seemed to wake my own demon. The thing inside stirred, spewing scene after scene of carnage. One by one they would fall by my hand. Broken, bloody, and cold. And while I hated to agree with anything it wanted, this time we were in sync. The only problem was Sam. How to get her out without her getting cut down in the cross fire.

Azirak flashed more images, growing impatient. Me bringing swift death to everything my fingers touched. Showered in their blood and grinning like a kid at the candy store, I stood over their corpses, breathing deeply as their life force slipped into the ether.

No. Not me. Azirak. The demon wanted me to hand over control. There was no trust between us, but I had enough common sense to recognize the situation for what it was. With Azirak in control, I'd have more of an edge.

Still, I was worried about Sam. The demon, sensing my hesitation, flashed an image of her face surrounded by soft light and flowers. Happy.

I thought back to the way it'd pushed me to kiss her. How it spoke to her in the woods at the bottom of the cliff. It wasn't intrigued by Sam.

It *cared* about her.

My hesitation dissipated. I let myself fade, giving the demon the reins. The transition was smoother than usual. Like simply stepping aside on a crowded sidewalk to make room for someone else. For the first time, I felt everything as though I was still in control. The movement beneath my feet as the demon started to react. The electric sense of excitement bubbling in my chest. Maybe because, for the first time, we wanted the same thing. We were the same instrument in a task we both believed in.

I became a vessel of destruction. And even though it was still bound by the limitations of a human body, the swath of chaos Azirak cut was nothing short of devastating. It flew across the hood of the car, mowing down first the demon that laid its hand on Sam's arm. The enemy bared its teeth, hunched and ready to pounce, but Azirak was much too fast. A powerful uppercut to the jaw and the thing flew backward. My own body followed the momentum of the blow and we landed together in a heap. Fingers I vaguely recognized reached for an enemy throat. The skin tore easily, flecks of red exploding in every direction. The entire thing took no more than five seconds. Six at best.

Time for the next.

By the time Azirak tore through them, all three were dead, nothing more than piles of skin and gore, and Sam had fallen to her knees. Her eyes were wide and fixed on the first demon to go down. The one that had touched her.

At the sight of her, the demon relinquished control and I fell to my knees in front of her. "Sammy? Can you hear me?"

She nodded, silent. I reached across to take her hand, moving slowly because I was afraid to spook her. When my fingers wrapped around hers, she blinked and turned. "We're okay," she said. Her voice was shaky, and she was crying.

"We're okay," I confirmed, helping her off the dew-wet grass. "Let's get you home."

Chapter Twenty

Sam

"Are you *sure* you're okay?" It was the fifth time he'd asked, and even though I kept insisting everything was fine, I wasn't so sure. I sat curled on Kelly's couch with a lukewarm cup of coffee. It didn't smell the least bit inviting, but holding it was keeping my hands from shaking.

Chase had left me four messages, worried after dropping me off at the apartment last night. He apologized multiple times about the almost-kiss and begged me to return his call. I left him a voice mail to let him know I'd be staying at Kelly's, warned him I was pissed about the information he'd kept from me about Rick, and settled down to let everything sink in.

The things I'd seen today would stay with me for the rest of my life. Jax's expression as he hit that man in the alley. Over and over. Then, the contrast of revulsion mixed with remorse and agony when we stopped by the side of the road. As for the rest, I refused to think about him tearing apart those other men. *Demons.* Not men. Still, it didn't make the carnage any easier to watch. It didn't matter what they were on the inside. On the outside, they looked like people.

"I'm okay. Today's just been..." I shrugged. "Hard. Today's been hard."

"I'm sorry," he said, stalking the room from end to end. He'd been jittery since we'd left the field. Twitching and energized like someone had plugged him into an outlet. "I tried so hard to keep you away from this part of my life, and in the end, you ended up in deeper."

I set down the cup and grabbed hold of his hand as he passed. "Sorry? You saved my life, Jax. This thing that attacked me at school isn't going to give up. The car, the cliff, tonight in that field... You made me see the truth. You had my back. Just like always, you had my back..."

The truth about him had thrown me for a loop, but in the end, it didn't change a damn thing. I wasn't sure what kind of person that made me, and I didn't care. He might be a demon, at least in part, but he was still the same Jax I'd known my whole life. It hurt when he left, but I *did* understand it now. He was still the same infuriating, cocky shithead I loved. The one I'd always love.

"I shouldn't be here." He looked like he wanted to turn and run, but surprised me by coming closer.

"Because you're dangerous? Didn't you hear me? You saved my life. For a guy who's all supercharged and shit, you don't have a firm grip on reality, do you?"

He was quiet for a moment. When he did speak, his voice was low and deadly. "Do you think it's the best idea to piss off a hungry demon?"

I ignored him. "Explain to me how you're dangerous." I stood and took another step—the last step—until we were nose to nose. He'd washed away the blood and gore and was standing in front of me as though at any moment he'd bolt. "Is it because you saved my life at the bottom of the river? Or maybe it was because you propelled yourself from the top of a cliff to keep me from getting crushed or drowning. Is *that* how you're dangerous?"

He made a noise deep in his throat and tried to back away, but I held tight to his wrist.

"Oh. I know. It's because you charged a group of demons who were probably going to kill me in some horrible, Hollywood-worthy epic way, and again, saved my life."

"I want you to hate me," he said, voice dropping to barely a whisper. "In fact, I *need* you to."

So much pain, and all I wanted was to take it away. He'd always been my rock, but I realized in that moment, he was just as fragile as me. "I would do anything for you, Jax—except that. Not ever. I can't."

"I can't control this thing inside me." His eyes were on mine, but it was almost like he was staring straight through. He brought his hand up, twisting it to the light as a tremor went through him. No hint of the fight remained, but it was like he was staring down at the most vile thing on earth. "I'm covered in blood. My entire life is covered in blood…"

I took his hand and yanked it from the light. Without commenting, I swept my fingers across his cheek and down the line of his jaw. The muscles tightened beneath my touch.

He pulled away and took a step back. "Either you're too stupid to see the truth, or you have a death wish. The demon inside? I need to feed in order to retain any kind of control." He stepped forward, drawing himself up. "Did you *see* how I fed it, Sammy? I inflict pain and misery and violence. I induce fear and rage until there's nothing else left."

I stood my ground, refusing to let him see that his words had an effect. "I'm not going to pretend I know what it's like to be you, or that what I saw tonight wasn't scary as hell. I won't stand here and tell you that it's okay or that I understand what's going on. I do have faith in you, though. I know the truth, Jax, and I'm not disgusted or angry." I looked him in the eye. "I'm not afraid of you."

"You should be. Azi—I—we—I shouldn't stay. That's why I need you to be stronger. I need you to hate me. Tell me to get the fuck out."

I'd only seen him like this once before. When he was fourteen and I was thirteen. Two of the guidance counselors at school had accused him of lighting the locker room on fire. Jax insisted he didn't do it, even providing an ironclad alibi, but they didn't care. He was just the easiest to blame.

He took their punishment and accepted blame in the same angry silence people later came to expect from him, but that night he'd broken down. I remembered his voice, so close to breaking. So full of pain. So lost…

"It's okay."

He shook his head and stumbled away, strands of dark-brown hair whipping back and forth in his eyes. "It's not. I shouldn't be around you for so many reasons, but ever since I killed those fuckers in the field, my head's been full. Buzzing. Like white noise with a kick." His head rose and his eyes met mine. "I've tried to push you out of my head and out of my life but you just won't fucking let go!"

He sank to the rug like a stone, head falling forward into his hands as another shudder went through him. I followed him down, urging his face up. "It's okay," I repeated.

"Killing those things did something to me. I've never killed another demon before. They gave me something extra. Something I don't normally get from just kicking the shit out of a human." He didn't look away.

The torment in his expression was like a vise around my chest, squeezing all the air and leaving nothing but pain.

"It's like the most amazing high," he said, his eyes wide. "And I know it's wrong, but it makes me feel like maybe I could… Just once…"

And he was on me. Warmth engulfed every inch of my body as his large frame covered me. His hands were everywhere. Calloused palms and needy fingers slipping beneath the hem of my shirt and into the waist of my jeans. Rough nails scraping bare skin hard enough to send a jolt of excitement, but not enough to draw blood.

Somewhere in the back of my mind I knew I should put an end to this, at least until things were squared away. But the memory of that earth-shattering kiss in the car earlier was too strong. I wanted to feel that way again. To capture the spark between us and lock it away, safe, from the mess that had taken over our lives.

A trail of volcanic kisses, from the base of my chin and down to my collarbone, stole the thought from my mind. There was so much passion. So much need. This was more than desire. This was a connection. Something we desperately needed right now.

"So perfect," Jax mumbled into the hollow of my throat. The slightest pinch as his teeth grazed the skin, and I couldn't help the small noise that escaped my lips. It was more surprise than anything else, but it froze Jax in place. A moment later, a chill rushed the room as I found myself alone on the floor.

He watched me for a second from across the room, the light from the window casting an eerie shadow across his face. In that moment he truly looked demonic. Demonic, but beautiful. Dark and dangerous and breakable all at the same time. "This is—shit. I have to leave."

I jumped to my feet and crossed the room to where he stood, lingering at the base of the hallway. When he didn't come closer, I reached for him. "Jax, wait."

"You don't know what you're doing," he growled. There was a flash of black before he closed his eyes. When he opened them, they were normal again.

I shoved him across the hall and into the adjacent wall. "I think I do."

Slipping my fingers under the shoulders of his trench coat, I slid the heavy material off. It fell to the floor with an audible *plop*. Still, he tried to pull away. I wouldn't let him.

Tracing patterns across his chest, the hard muscle beneath my fingers trembled, our skin separated by nothing more than thin cotton. With a groan, he wound his fingers, shaking with need, into the material of my shirt. His head tilted back against the wall, eyes closed, as his breath quickened.

"Don't," he hissed. But it was halfhearted. His hands were moving across my back, tugging at the fabric of my shirt, the conflict in his voice leaning toward acceptance. And finally, surrender. "Fuck…"

Jax's fingers scraped against skin as he dragged me closer. A wave of need washed over me, and I held on tight, desperate for him to see this through. I brought my lips to his ear, begging softly, "Please don't stop this time."

He growled and tensed. "Don't push me, Sammy. This isn't what you want."

His voice changed. Lower and laced with an edge of danger, it only made me want to nudge him more. We'd never gone this far and it was something I'd thought about nearly every day since that night in the woods. My lips rose with a defiant smile. "It's *exactly* what I want."

I pulled back and saw him break. Like a piece of glass shattering into a million tiny pieces. His stony resolve gone, he crushed his lips to mine again, but it wasn't the same as before. It was harsh. Violent.

A second later he shoved me away and the sound that filled the air caused my heart to shudder.

Chapter Twenty-One

Jax

I ignored the demon and did my best to focus on Sam. She was standing in front of me, pale, as the waves of orange lust bled slowly into gray. The noise. It hadn't come from her—it'd come from me.

Sam, whose beautiful, creamy white skin would look so lovely covered in red. Next came the images. Sam, lying broken and bloody on the floor. Her eyes wide open and unseeing. Stomach torn open. Legs bent at unnatural angles. No color rising from her still form. Only the cold, empty space of death.

"Jesus!" I stumbled back, trying to put more distance between us. Azirak didn't argue. It didn't want Sam dead anymore than I did. But it did want to feed. And showing me that gruesome scene with Sam as its star was enough to get me moving.

"Jax?" She reached for me, but I shoved her aside.

What the hell had I done? The goal was to stay away—not drown deeper. Reality came crashing down. I'd stayed, fueled by the energy I'd taken in from the demon kill. A single kiss. That's all I'd planned. Just to taste her one last time. But the energy in my system was like a drug. Some supernatural narcotic that stole away my inhibitions and good sense. Add that to the fact that Sam was already a problem for me and it was a cluster-fuck.

"Get away from me," I snapped, turning away. A bastard. That's what I was. The hurt in her expression was just another reason to hate myself. Distance. I needed distance. The demon inside didn't mean to feed from the pang of rejection radiating from Sam, but it did regardless. It couldn't help itself.

"Is it just physical? Is that it? I know—I know you want me. Do you feel guilty because you don't have any real feelings for me? I mean, I know you care, but it's been a long time. People's feelings change." She sucked in a deep breath and I had to force myself to stay where I was. I missed the feel of her in my arms. The warmth her body provided. "It's okay. Really. I'm a big girl, Jax."

The whole room darkened and I couldn't help laughing. I didn't mean to turn around, but the sound of her voice was like a beacon, forcing me back. "If it was just about sex, this wouldn't be an issue." One step. Then another. I stopped in front of where she stood, leaning close enough to feel her breath on my neck. Sweet and vital. "It's so much more than that with you. It always has been—and that's the problem, I think."

"Just so you know, from a girl's point of view, that's not

usually a big problem."

"It is." I took a step away. "Every minute I'm with you, I'm...happy. It makes the demon hungrier. I'm not meant to be happy, Sammy. I'm paying for what Cain did to Abel. It's been getting worse. It was bad in the beginning, painful, and now it's becoming unbearable."

I took a deep breath. "I'm not allowed to be at peace. And since I've been refusing to accept that, these stolen moments with you are taking their toll. They destroy my control. With the jacked-up energy I got from killing those demons, I should have lasted for at least two days—maybe more—just taking bits from people here and there. It should have kept Azirak sated. But I can feel the itch again. It's worse when—when we're close."

"You're saying you have to feed it again," she confirmed. "Something like what happened in the alley with that guy?"

How the hell could she ask the question like it was nothing more than an inquiry about the weather? "Yeah." The words were bitter. Knowing it and admitting it out loud were two different things. "I have to feed it again."

"And that would make it easier? To be close to me?"

Jesus. She was out of her fucking mind. "Maybe, but that's not my point. If you knew what I saw sometimes when I looked at you—the images—you would never put yourself in the same room with me again." I needed to drive the point home with cruel accuracy. "All I want right now is to kill you. I want to rip you open and spill you out, just to make the thing inside me quiet. Just to dull the pain."

She flinched as if I'd slapped her. "Well, then I guess we better get moving."

"Moving?"

"The sooner we find these things and what they want, the sooner you can leave. That's what the endgame is here, right? To get away from me? From this place?"

"That's the way it has to be," I said, doing my best to keep the chill in my voice. Then I remembered what one of the demons said about her in the field. Something about being *demon touched*. Fuck. I'd forgotten all about it. Too busy trying crawling all over her. "But there's something we need to talk about first."

She rolled her eyes. "Wonderful. Another secret? Are you related to Dracula? Maybe you have a cousin who's a troll?"

"Do you remember hearing something about being demon touched?"

She shrugged. "Vaguely. Why, what's it mean?"

"I don't know." I sank into the chair across the room. "But it can't be good."

She blinked. "You don't know?"

"I don't know," I repeated.

"Weren't you a card-carrying member of the evil-infested? You know how to deal with this stuff. That's what you said. How can you not know?"

"I may have overstated my expertise when it comes to demonkind." I pinched my thumb and pointer together and held it up for her to see. "Just a little."

"You— Are you serious?"

"Don't worry." I pulled my coat tight and took a step toward the door. "We need answers. I think I know just the place to get them."

Azirak kept flashing the fight in the field through my mind, remembering the feel of the demon essence and the virtual high it had given us. It wanted more—and that was fine with me. We needed to know what it meant to be demon touched, and there was only one way to find out.

Interrogation.

Normally the thought of beating the answers out of someone would have sent the demon into an excited frenzy, but unfortunately, I'd been inconveniently saddled with a sidekick. The thing seemed as unenthused as I was by the concept of Sam witnessing a repeat of what happened in the alley yesterday. But letting her out of my sight was out of the question.

I checked on Rick before heading out with Sam. He'd been asleep, so still that in a moment of panic, I slipped a small mirror under his nose. Only after it fogged could I breathe again.

Harlow was full of demons. Most places were. They were easy for me to find by simply inhaling, their acidic trademark scent stinging my nose. When I'd first come home, I'd caught the scent of a demon bar on the edge of town. A dive called the Inferno. I pushed open the door and took the lead, slipping into the decrepit building with Sam on my heels.

The first thing that came to mind was to make her wait outside. But she was determined to be in the thick of this. To prove that she could handle whatever my life might throw at her.

I'd made her wait around the corner on the way over when I saw a man try to rob an elderly lady. A quick round with him in the alley a block over and I felt a little more at ease. It didn't sate the demon completely, and wasn't nearly as potent as the demon kills, but it took the edge off the ache.

We took a seat as the bartender eyed Sam, then turned to me. "What'll it be, Tainted?"

"Excuse me?"

"Drink," the scruffy thing behind the bar spat. It wasn't a demon. I didn't think, anyway. It smelled wrong. Different from what I was used to, but most certainly not human. Then again, my nose was off lately. I hadn't caught a whiff of the bastard that attacked Sam on campus, and I'd been standing right there. "As in, what do ya want?"

"Coors," I said, scanning the room. Except for me, Sam, and the bartender, the place was empty.

Sam nodded. "Same for me, please."

The bartender disappeared for a moment. When he returned, he placed two open bottles on the counter without asking for ID. I eyed them for a moment, then looked up. "What?"

"Just don't get many of your kind in here." He inclined his head toward Sam and flashed her a flirty smile. "Hers either. Humans tend to keep their distance from places like this."

"My kind?"

"Tainted." He tipped back his own glass and set it down on the bar with a clatter. "With a human no less. An odd sight."

I took a swig of the beer and almost spit it back out. Crap was warm. "Mind elaborating?"

The bartender laughed and poured himself another drink. "Seriously?"

I set down the beer. I wasn't in the mood to play guessing

games. "Do I look like I'm joking?"

The bartender sighed. He rolled his eyes and grabbed the counter rag. Swiping it back and forth over the same spot, he said, "'Course not. Your kind doesn't have much of a sense of humor. Can't say as I blame ya, though. The normal demons simply got trapped in human forms and have limited *natural resources*. You Tainted have to share your space. Raw deal, man. Raw deal."

I gripped the beer in an effort to keep Azirak down. The demon was getting impatient and it seemed to have a singular dislike of the thing behind the counter. I felt the same way. Neither of us would be opposed to a little dessert.

The bartender tossed the rag over his shoulder and held out his hand. "Name's Heckle. Bel Heckle."

I didn't move.

Sam shook the man's hand instead. "Excuse him. His manners are only active between the hours of four and five p.m. every other week on Tuesdays."

Heckle guffawed and gave her hand a proper shake.

"Trapped?" I asked between clenched teeth. I knew the full-blooded demons were running around in human form, but had no idea they'd been trapped like that. "Who trapped them?"

With a shrug, Heckle leaned across the bar. He was wearing a grin that I itched to wipe away with the back of my fist. "Think of it as a punishment. Let's just say playtime got a little rowdy and they're in a timeout."

"I heard about this from the priest," Sam said. "Something about the devil casting them from hell, right?"

Heckle nodded. "Pretty much."

"And me? Why did you call me Tainted?"

"Because that's what you are. They're full-blooded demons walking around basically bound and gagged—you're a human with a stain on his soul allowing him to be cursed with a demon. Tainted."

I drained the rest of the beer and slammed the bottle to the counter. "Stain on my soul? And that means what, exactly?"

I could see it in the bartender's eyes. He loved having to explain it all. "When someone—a human—does something horrible, it leaves a stain. If the act is so horrible that the soul can't be redeemed in a single lifetime, it gets passed along to future generations." He leaned on the bar, winking once at Sam before continuing. "It's a blemish. A dirty spot on an otherwise pure thing."

Sam took a sip of her own beer, trying not to make a face. Guess she wasn't a fan of warm brew, either. "So you're saying Jax has a demon because of a stain on his soul?"

"That'd be correct, little lady. When a demon takes up residence in the body of a stained soul, that's what we call Tainted. Bad attitude. Short temper." He snorted. "Horrible fashion sense. Somewhere along the line, someone in your family committed a crime. You're the lucky bastard who gets to pay for it. It doesn't have access to its supernatural abilities, but unlike the other demons who need fresh feeds to access some of their latent talents—strength, speed, et cetera—a demon in a Tainted simply has to take control."

"Huh," Sam said, taking a pull from her bottle. "That gives new meaning to the sins of the father thing."

This was fascinating, and maybe under different circumstances I might have been interested in a history lesson, but I wasn't here about myself. "I need some information."

Heckle eyed me, suspicious, and sneaked a peek at Sam. "This ain't a library, man."

"And it's not a bloodbath, either. Might be nice to keep it that way."

"See what I mean? Bad attitude." With a pointed nod toward Sam, he sighed. "What ya lookin' for?"

Things were getting messier by the minute. I launched right into it. "What does it mean if someone is demon touched?"

Heckle wasn't putting off emotion the way a human would, so reading him was harder, but body language was body language. Heckle was scared.

"I'm not getting any younger," I prodded.

"Every demon is different. Most have no lasting side effects when feeding, flu-like symptoms or blurred vision for a few days—I'm betting you leave folks with quite a headache after you do your thing. Some, though, leave some nasty calling cards." The bartender's brows rose. "Might help if you told me more about the situation. What kind are we talking about here?"

"I don't know. Sam is being hunted by demons. We don't know why, but we heard one say she was demon touched. I need to know if we have anything to worry about."

Heckle watched me with an odd expression."You care about her, right?"

"Yeah. So?"

"And you have *no* idea why someone would target her specifically?"

My patience was officially drained. I slipped from the stool and leaned across the bar, stopping inches away from the annoying bartender's face. "If I knew, I wouldn't be asking, right?"

Heckle backed away and threw up both hands in an exaggerated show of surrender. "Okay, okay. To be demon touched means a high-ranking demon has fed from the human. Even the smallest demon leaves a tiny mark on their feed. Like I said, it's usually nothing that lasts, but the stronger ones can create a link."

"A link?" Sam asked.

"Think of it as a symbiotic relationship. What happens to the demon, happens to the linked human. If the demon is truly powerful, he can also control the human. Make it do his bidding."

Sam was pale. "What can we do to break it?"

"The first thing you need to do is find out who the demon was that fed from her. Some can be broken. Others can't."

"Any idea how we can do that? Find the demon?" Sam asked, voice a little shaky. She'd pushed the beer aside.

"There *is* someone that might be able to tell you. A demon named Havat Doyle."

Sam looked hopeful. "Where can we find him—or, is it a her?"

"Oh, Doyle is a he, all right. You can find him in the War Zone most afternoons and evenings."

"The war zone?" I asked, sure I didn't love the sound of it.

Heckle's bushy brows waggled as he poured himself another shot. "You never been in the War Zone? Well, you're in for one *hell* of a treat."

Chapter Twenty-Two

Sam

Heckle walked in front of us, whistling a vaguely familiar tune. I wasn't the violent type, but if he didn't stop, there was a chance I'd smack him in the back of the head. Obviously Jax had rubbed off on me.

He led us down a narrow, wooded path, looking back once to give the thumbs-up sign. Yeah. This was how horror movies started. The poor, stupid couple followed some weirdo into the woods only to be hacked to pieces and then eaten by sparsely toothed men wearing overalls and mismatched shoes.

"How much farther?" Jax asked coolly. We'd followed Heckle in Rick's car, all the way to a sprawling estate on the outskirts of town. From the state of the property, no one had been out this way in a long time. The grass was past my knees, and as we finally approached the house, I could see several of the windows broken out.

"Just around the back of the house. There's a cellar underneath."

Jax paused. Grabbing my arm, he pulled me to a stop. "Tell us what we're doing here."

Heckle turned and sighed. "I'm going to introduce you to Havat Doyle. Remember?"

"What exactly is this War Zone thing?"

"Demons are a nasty, volatile bunch." Heckle tapped Jax on the shoulder. "But like you, they have their limitations. They're bound by the frailties and boundaries of a human body. Maybe not to the same extreme as you—full-blooded demons weren't born into their humans, they were forced into them. They still retain some of what they were."

"So what does this all have to do with the War Zone?"

"Like I said, volatile bunch. They need to let off steam. That's what the War Zone is for." Heckle glanced back at the house. "Are we done playing twenty questions?" he called over his shoulder, walking away.

We had no choice but to follow.

Around the house and past a set of rusty cellar doors, Heckle led us through a wine cellar that would have made Kelly drool all over herself. We snaked down the aisles, stepping over forgotten bottles that had fallen from collapsed shelves, and when we came out on the other side, there was a door that opened to a narrow, unlit staircase.

Once we arrived at the bottom, Heckle turned and prevented us from going any farther "A few things before we go in." Gaze swiveling to Jax, he frowned. He cringed a little. "I can only take one of you in. It has to be Sam."

"What?" we exclaimed in unison.

"You're out of your fucking mind," Jax raged. He tried to push past Heckle, but the smaller man, surprisingly strong, shoved him back with ease.

"I'm sorry," Heckle said. "There's no choice. It has to be her."

I was terrified of slipping into the unknown darkness ahead with only this weird stranger as a guide, but if the answer to this whole mess was in there, I had to at least consider it. "Why? Why does it have to be me?"

"I know what he is," Heckle said, sniffing the air in Jax's direction once. He scrunched up his nose as though he'd just caught wind of something foul. "So will the others. You're going to have to trust me when I tell you that this is not the place you want to be."

Jax snorted. "I'm a demon," he said with a grin that made the butterflies rage in my stomach. "I think I can take care of myself."

"Technically you're a human with a demon. That makes you, at best, half a demon." If I didn't know better, I would have sworn Jax actually was insulted. "You're big and bad, sure, but there are too many to count down there. Unfed demons might be easy for you to take down, but with sheer numbers on their side, you'd be toast. There are demons beyond this hallway that would rip you to shreds at first whiff just for being what you are. "

"Why?" Jax asked.

Heckle shrugged. "Purists. You're a human—something they consider nothing more than a means of sustenance. Yet you've been gifted with the great power of a demon."

Jax's eyes widened and I forcibly bit back a giggle. He looked like a cartoon character who'd just received the surprise of his life. "Gifted?"

This was getting us nowhere. Gently, I pushed Jax aside and focused on Heckle. "If I go in there with you, what's to stop them from feeding on me like the other demon did?"

"You will be under my protection. They will have no claim to you," he said solemnly. I didn't know him from a hole in the wall. He could be an excellent liar. Still, something about the intensity in his voice made me believe him.

Jax, on the other hand, wasn't convinced. "Your word?" He grabbed my hand and tried tugging me up the stairs. "Let's go, Sammy. This is a waste of time. I don't trust this guy as far as my demon could—"

"Fine," I said, pulling away. "I'll do it. I'll go with you."

"The fucking hell you will."

"Sorry, but I've got a little news flash for you, Jax. You don't own me. Last time I checked, I was free and clear to do whatever the hell I wanted. And right now, I want to go with Heckle."

"Fine. Then I'm coming, too." Jax turned to Heckle. "You can't stop me."

"No," Heckle said. His voice got cold, and the look in his eyes, a spark of dominance mixed with anger, chilled the air. "But you can't enter without me, and I simply won't take you. Either of you. I take Sam. Alone. Or I take no one. I leave it up to you. It makes no difference to me either way."

Jax wasn't going to budge. That much was clear. I turned to him, and with one final plea, said, "It's this or nothing. You said you didn't think this thing would stop until I was dead. If that's true, then we need to find it, and whatever connection it *might* have to you, and we can't do that alone. We need to know what this Havat knows."

He didn't answer.

"Jax, think about it. You can't watch over me every second of every day for the rest of my life. You don't plan on sticking around, for one thing. We need to finish this."

He was quiet for the longest moment, turning from me to Heckle with an angry scowl. "If anything happens to her, I won't kill you." His voice was low, dangerous. "I'll leave you alive. I'll torture you in ways you can't possibly imagine." He tapped the side of his head and gave the other man a wicked grin. "This demon is very creative."

Heckle nodded and returned Jax's smile with one of someone humoring a spoiled child. "No harm will come to her. I give you my word." Turning to me, he held out a hand. "This is very important. Take my hand, and whatever you do, do not break contact. Not even for a second. Do you understand?"

I wound my fingers through his and nodded. His skin was cold. Not corpse-cold, but not normal body temperature, either. I fought back a shudder. "Yeah. I understand."

And with that, we stepped into the darkness. I didn't look back. Seeing Jax would only twist the knife. To be told he had to wait this round out was bad, because he felt responsible for the situation, and therefore, me. Having no control had to be killing him.

We reached the end of the hall and came to another door. Heckle wordlessly pushed it open and what waited on the other side stole my breath away. The War Zone was a perfectly accurate word for this place. A sea of bodies fanned around a sunken circle where two hulking men—demons, I guessed—fought in the middle. One brutal blow after another, the men slugged it out with vicious enthusiasm.

A chorus of cheers and boos filled the room as Heckle tugged me along, heading for the far end where a tall black man sat in an ornate chair. A scantily clad blonde girl on either side watched the room with a bored expression, rubbing the man's shoulders every so often. The girl on the right was breathing heavy, running her fingers down her right thigh repeatedly like she was trying to wipe something away.

"Havat," Heckle said, stopping in front of the chair. "Might I have a word or two?"

Havat narrowed his eyes, but nodded. Obviously he wasn't thrilled about the interruption.

"We're looking for a demon. One that fed from this human girl."

"And you're asking me this, why?" Havat grabbed the girl on the right, yanked her down hard, and kissed her. When she pulled away, there was a thin trail of blood, and an angry-looking wound on her bottom lip.

My stomach roiled and bile rose in my throat. He'd bitten her. The girl didn't seem to mind, which made it even worse. Her tongue darted out, licking at the blood, as a twisted smile spread across her lips. With a low giggle, her eyes rolled back like she was deep in the throes of passion, and she ran her hands down the length of her body before crumbling to the ground and rocking softly.

"Because you have the best nose this side of hell," Heckle said. "Are you going to tell me you can't smell it on her?"

Havat laughed, and for the first time, turned to me. His eyes skimmed my body with an appreciative gleam as he took a deep breath. Instead of an answer, the demon laughed.

I opened my mouth to ask what the hell that was

supposed to mean, but Heckle cut me off. "Who was it?"

"We do not give information for free here. You of all people should know, Keeper."

"What do you want?" I blurted before I could stop myself.

Havat smiled. "And she has the nerve to speak to me. This gets better and better." He leaned back and swung his right leg over the arm of the chair. "I would like a stone."

"A stone?" That seemed harmless—which probably meant it was anything but. "A particular one, or will just any rock do?"

Heckle squeezed my hand, and Havat looked angry for a second before bursting into laughter. "I don't meet many humans with your…charm. It's amusing."

"Glad I could entertain you. Now, about the stone?"

"It's called the midnight stone and it was taken from me by a witch named Sadie Gray. Retrieve it for me and I will tell you the name of the demon that fed from you." He turned to Heckle. "I assume my acquiring the stone will be fair. Am I correct?"

Heckle nodded. "It's acceptable."

Havat clapped his hands together and stood. He held out his hand, and said, "Then we have a deal."

It was an unconscious gesture. Something society had ingrained at an early age. Without thinking, I let go of Heckle's hand and reached for Havat's. The room went silent, and for a moment, no one moved.

Then all hell broke loose.

Chapter Twenty-Three

Jax

There was a crash at the other end of the hall. But even with the demon's improved vision, I couldn't see what it was right away. I took two steps forward, and that's when I heard it. A dull roar, followed by a chorus of footsteps pounding against the concrete. A few seconds later, Sam and Heckle came barreling out of the darkness.

"*Go!* Up the stairs. Fast," Heckle huffed as they dashed toward me. Behind them, the roar grew louder and the sound of two racing footsteps became many, many more.

I took Sam's hands and propelled her up the steps, Heckle on our heels. "What the fuck did you do?" I growled as we crashed into the cellar at the top of the stairs. "Rip you to shreds. Make you wish for death. Any of this ringing a goddamn bell?"

"It was her fault," Heckle yelled. "She let go of my hand.

The moment she did, they all smelled her."

"No blame," Sam huffed, breathing fast. "Spank me later." She must have realized what she said, because out of the corner of my eye, I saw her cheeks redden. "I—"

"No, it's fine. I'm more than happy to spank you later."

And that was it. All the air we could expend. Now was all about running. A single glance over my shoulder revealed that the large group that had chased Sam and Heckle from the basement had splintered into several smaller ones. Heckle glanced back, but he wasn't quite as graceful as me. He tripped, going down hard in the mud. It was horrible leaving him behind, and I'd regret it later—maybe—but I held tight to Sam's hand and kept going. The crowd wasn't after him. It was after her. He'd be fine.

Angry yelling grew closer and something crashed into me from behind. I went down hard, just enough air to yell to Sam, "Keep going! Don't st—" Something hit my jaw, and stars exploded in my eyes.

I managed to dodge the next blow, rolling over to see a blond demon's feral expression. It swung again, this time catching me in the gut. Azirak stirred and fury spread like fire. With renewed strength, I bucked the demon off and jumped up.

I was about to throw myself forward, but another demon came charging up, knocking my opponent down with a brutal blow. A quick twist, and the other demon's neck lolled at an unnatural angle as its body hit the ground. Climbing to my feet, my unlikely savior flashed a disturbing smile. "Hurry, my lord."

It reached for me but I jerked away. "Your lord? What the—"

"You need to—"

Another demon came up behind him and, in a move I'd never forget, twisted and pulled, removing my ally's head clean off its body. *Fuck!* I started running. Azirak didn't fight it, either. It seemed as eager to get away as I was, and that scared the shit out of me. It didn't run from fights. It ran toward them.

It flashed an image of the decapitated demon, and then another of Sam. Sam. It wanted to find Sam.

The crowd had thinned, fights breaking out among the ones that had been chasing us. It seemed the crowd had split into two distinct sides. Ones who wanted us, and ones who, oddly, wanted to help. Ahead, a small circle gathered around something. As I got closer, my heart sped up. It was Sam. Heckle was in the middle trying to hold them back.

"Sam!" I yelled, bolting forward. I expected the demons to turn on me, hoping it would give her the chance to make a run for it, but instead the crowd split, clearing a path. Carefully, I moved forward as the crowed—a group of ten—whispered and stared. Several even stepped back.

A second later, they all fell to their knees.

"Azirak," one of the male demons said. He was the only one to then rise and come forward. "It is not safe for you here. Zenak's army is close."

"What the fuck are you talking about?" To Sam, I said, "Are you okay?"

She nodded and made a move to come closer, but the crowd was on its feet and closing in a heartbeat. Heckle threw up his hands. "It's okay. The human means him no harm. She, um, belongs to him."

Sam started to protest, but I shushed her. "What the hell

is going on here, Heckle?"

The same demon that stepped forward first held his ground, eyes on Sam. "She is not his. She stinks of Zenak."

"Whoa." I whirled on Heckle. "Zenak? Is that the name of the demon that attacked her?"

"She has been tasted by one of his clan," a demon wearing a young woman's face said. She bowed her head and flashed a tentative smile. "My lord."

"Your what, now?" Sam squealed. At the sound of her voice, the crowd tensed.

"Be calm," Heckle warned her. "No sudden movements."

"Who is Zenak? And you're the second one to spit that lord shit at me. What the hell is going on?"

"Zenak is the leader of our opposing faction," the female demon supplied. "He has, apparently, turned your human against you."

"No, he hasn't." Sam shouted. "And just so we're *all* clear, I'm not *his* human."

The female demon looked confused. "Not his? Isn't that your attachment to each other? To mate? I mean, humans are amusing, but that's all. Sustenance and toys, really."

"A toy?" Sam let out a strangled cry, and I was sure she'd launch herself at the female demon, but Heckle grabbed her arm and slowly shook his head.

The female demon glared at Sam. "Please, my lord. If you would step away from the human, we would all feel more at ease."

My patience was wearing thin and I wanted answers, so to humor them, I stepped to the outside of the circle. Azirak rumbled, but I stuffed it down. "Someone better start talking."

The male demon bowed his head. "Do you not smell the link on her?"

The female smacked the male in the back of the head. "Fool. It's obvious that Azirak's mind is clouded. He doesn't remember who he is and what he must do. Do you really think he'll be able to smell a link?" The female bowed her head and sighed. "I'm sorry, my lord. There are rules we are bound to. I can say no more."

"Say no more?" I roared. Azirak raged, flashing pictures too fast for me to really understand. There was blood, and an uneven, rocky terrain. One I recognized from earlier flashes the demon had shown. Thousands of bodies strewn across a blood-soaked field. Fire burned on scattered patches on barren land, the smoke drifting toward a pale gray sky. When it ended, I felt like someone had punched me in the gut.

"Are you well, my lord?"

"If you call me that one more time without telling me what the fuck it means, I'm going to rip your goddamned heart out," I spat.

The demon cringed, nodding enthusiastically. "Yes, my— Azirak."

"We want nothing more than to tell you of the glorious past, and of the future we plan to forge, but it is physically impossible. The words will not spill from these pathetic human lips."

I took a deep breath in an attempt to stay calm. "Okay. So what *can* you tell me? Anything useful?" I turned to Sam. "Anything about the demon that fed from her? Or how about this link you're talking about?"

"We do not know the name of the demon that has fed from the human, only that he is one of Zenak's—your enemy. There is one among us who might be able—"

"Havat," Heckle interjected. "That's why we're here. He's offered an exchange."

The male demon nodded. "As expected. When some demons feed, they have the ability to create a link between themselves and their prey. Think of it as a symbiotic relationship that's beneficial to the demon."

This sounded bad. "Beneficial how?"

"The linked human is like a limited extension of the demon. It's the part that takes all the bad so the demon doesn't have to. If the demon is injured, the linked gets the wound."

"What about the human?" Sam asked. The crowd turned, surprised. It was almost like they'd forgotten she was there. "What if I got hurt?"

The male demon kept its eyes on me. "It might feel pain, but it's not going to do the demon any real damage. However, if the demon dies, the feed dies."

"And the reverse?" Sam asked. "If I die?"

"If the reverse were true, and your death would kill our enemy, you would be dead already," the female replied with a steely grin.

The idea of Sam taking physical damage because this demon, whoever the hell it was, had fed on her made me sick. We had to find a way to break this link.

"You said something about using Sam against me." I had to keep my head in the game. "How do you mean?"

"If the demon is strong enough, it can actually control the feed. Make it do what it wants. Hurt itself—or someone else." The male demon gave me a pointed glare. "If you have an attachment to this particular human, then it is no wonder

Zenak sent one of his stronger soldiers to feed from her. It could easily have her attempt to assassinate you while you are using her."

"Whoa," Sam sputtered. Her face turned bright red. "Using me? No one uses—"

I cleared my throat while Sam glared at me from inside the circle. I'd definitely hear about this later. "If that was this Zenak's plan, wouldn't it have gone down already?" It was horrible, but the look on Sam's face was priceless. I couldn't help pushing it. Besides, it'd be worth whatever *punishment* I got. "My human toy was attacked a month ago."

"There are many possibilities," the male demon said. "Perhaps the link is weaker than anticipated. Possibly the soldier didn't get enough to finish it. Or, maybe Zenak is biding its time."

The female nodded. "Either way, Azirak is in danger. With even the weakest links, if the human is compromised in any way—substance abusers make great feeds—the demon can control them. This means any rested or altered state."

"Great," Sam mumbled. "So as long as I don't do shots or fall asleep, I'm no danger to him?"

"Why, though?" I asked, ignoring her. "If it targeted Sam specifically to get to me, there must be a reason."

The demon hadn't followed Sam back to Harlow to kill *her*. I was the target all along. It linked to her to get to me.

"You are Zenak's sworn enemy. It wants you dead, of course," the male demon supplied. "And if that should happen, then we all lose." He took a step toward me, and for the first time, flashed a truly threatening smile. "Your fondness for this human is a liability now that she is tied to your enemy, but out of respect, we will give you a chance to find the demon and get it to break the link. If you fail, we will break it ourselves."

Sam brightened and a swirl of hope surged around her shoulders. "So we *can* break the link?"

"Of course," the female said. She flashed Sam a disturbing grin. "Should the demon who fed from you choose to break the link, you will be free."

Sam snorted, deflating. "Like that would happen."

"Your death will also sever the connection," the female added "It may not harm our enemy, but it will free Azirak from the danger you present."

"Not my favorite option," Sam mumbled, folding her arms.

The male shook his head and turned to me. Bowing, he repeated, "If you are unable to break the link, we will be forced to break it for you."

He was saying that I had to find this demon and get it to break the link; if not, and I understood them right, they were coming to kill Sam? No fucking way.

"If I'm your leader, then I command you to leave her alone," I seethed, drawing myself up. I'd take them all on if necessary. One by one and piece by piece.

The demon seemed unimpressed. With a resolute shake of its head, it said, "We cannot take chances with your safety, my lord."

Chapter Twenty-Four

Sam

I was beyond tired. I'd been sitting on the edge of the tub for almost twenty minutes. The steam from the shower had all but dissipated, leaving the room cold and damp, and any minute now, Jax would be banging on the door to see if I was still alive.

We'd made it back to Kelly's a little after five in the afternoon. Heckle bid us farewell, promising to look into ways to break the link that didn't require talking the enemy into giving up its best resource, or me taking the stairway to heaven. The look on his face said he wasn't optimistic.

Jax ran over to check on Rick, then offered to scrounge up something from the kitchen to eat while I took a shower—probably in hopes that it would make me forget all about the "human toy" crap. Maybe that's why I was stalling. If memory was correct, Jax couldn't even manage macaroni and cheese without lighting something on fire. Unless things had drastically changed, I was going to starve.

Food or no food, I couldn't stay in the bathroom all night. We needed to deal with this thing, but I had no idea how. There was a long, twisted history between us. Jax's years away had built up the wall I kept around my heart, but the longer we spent together, the more it crumbled. I was sure the same thing went for him. One moment of weakness would be all it would take. I could slit his throat while he slept. I didn't really believe there was anything that could make me hurt him, but it wasn't a risk I wanted to take.

"Sammy?" Jax's voice came from the other side of the door, followed by a soft knock. Right on cue. "Please tell me you didn't fall asleep in there. I don't want you going all demon assassin on my ass."

Time to suck it up. I yanked open the door. "Yeah. I'm good. Just taking my time. Trying to process and all."

He stepped aside to let me pass. I rounded the corner, aware that he was following right behind, and froze when I got to entrance to the living room. On Kelly's fifty-two-inch television was the starting menu for my favorite cartoon—*Lilo & Stitch*. On the coffee table in front of the TV was a huge bowl of popcorn and two cups of steaming liquid—coffee. I could smell it from here. Jax was the only person I'd ever met who didn't make fun of me for dunking popcorn into coffee. "What's all this?"

He came around to stand in front of me. "A chance to process."

"Shouldn't we be, I dunno, out looking for a way to break the link?"

"Where would we look, Sammy? I talked to Heckle

while you were in the shower. He's still looking. No luck so far, though. His resources are better than mine. Our best bet is to sit tight for now."

"Well, what about that witch? Sadie Gray? Shouldn't we get the midnight stone from her? At least then Havat will give us a name. If we have a name, maybe we can — "

"Can what? Find the demon that fed from you? Get it to set you free out of the kindness of its heart? Kill it? Are you feeling particularly suicidal?"

Shit. That was right. Kill the demon and the link — aka me — died, too.

A lump formed in my throat and I sank onto the couch. He was right. There was nothing to do but wait it out and hope to God Heckle turned up something useful.

We'd done this so many times as kids. When Kelly worked late nights at the hospital and I was scared and alone at home, Jax would sneak over and we'd spend the night in front of the television. How many mornings had we missed the school bus? We'd spend the entire day in the woods at the fort behind Rick's house. In reality, it wasn't that long ago…so why did it feel like another lifetime?

Jax settled on the couch — close, but not touching — and pressed play. The opening credits rolled and the movie started, but I found it impossible to pay attention. Every few minutes I felt Jax looking at me, but when I glanced over, he'd turn away.

We sat there, silent and staring at the screen, but I knew neither one of us was paying attention. After about twenty minutes, Jax grabbed the remote from the table. Hitting pause, he sighed. "This isn't helping."

I sat up. "Sure it is. I feel much better."

"You're lying."

"I am not."

"You are," he insisted. "I can tell."

"Really? How exactly can you *tell*?"

"I can see your sadness." His voice got lower. "Your confusion, too." He leaned a little closer and inhaled. Arm outstretched, he waved his hand in a circle around my head. "Demons feed on negative human emotions, remember? We can smell them, but we can also see them."

"So what color are mine?"

He looked at me. For a moment it almost looked as though he was holding his breath, and when he spoke, it was soft. Just barely above a whisper. "Dark blue, mostly. Sadness. There are traces of gray, too. Fear."

"Makes sense," I said, twisting so I was facing him, too. "Since I'm scared and all."

"We'll figure this out."

"Will that be before or after your demon buddies come to kill me?" My eyes stung, and my heart thumped. No. Not now. Not when I'd done such a good job keeping my shit together for the most part. But it was no use. The tears gathering spilled over, blazing trails of warmth down my cheeks. "Or I kill you."

"You won't kill me," he said. "Right now, I think you should get some sleep."

"Sleep?" Was he insane? "Didn't you hear what that guy—"

"Demon," Jax corrected.

"Whatever. Didn't you hear what it said? I'm more susceptible when I'm sleeping."

"I thought about that," he said, standing. I watched as he crossed the room and disappeared into Kelly's bedroom.

When he came back, there was a pair of old silver handcuffs dangling from his right hand. "And I have a solution."

I didn't know whether to laugh, or blush. "Where the hell did those come from?"

He strode across the room, swinging the cuffs, and winked. "Kelly doesn't clean anything. They've been there for years. I can't believe you never found them."

Without another word, he tugged me from the couch. My pulse quickened. A moment ago I'd been exhausted. Now though, every inch of my body hummed like a flash of lightning. The idea of being cuffed and at Jax's mercy did odd things to my stomach. A nervous flutter and a rush of heat washed over me. Stupid, since that's not where he was going with any of this. Preventive measures. That was all this was.

Jax's hand lingered at my shoulder for a moment, before skimming down my arm and gently guiding it behind my back. There was a metal snap, and the cold feel of the steel cuff against my skin tickled.

Or maybe not.

He stepped behind, between me and the couch, and took the other arm, restraining it as he had the first. "This is selfish," he whispered, leaning close. The warmth from his breath and the deep, dark sound of his voice in my ear brought goose bumps to the surface.

"H-how so?" I managed.

He came around to the front, expression severe. "You're restrained. Not a danger to me at all. But—" Jax ran a hand over my cheek, then trailed his fingers down my neck and over my left breast. "I'm still a danger to you."

Ho-lee crap.

Talk about a total body meltdown. I did my best to keep breathing evenly, but my body had other plans. Pulse spiking, I said, "Do your worst."

The war between what he truly wanted, and the fact that he'd been insisting we couldn't be together, raged behind his eyes. I saw the exact moment he broke. The tension in his body melted away. With a gentle push, I toppled back onto the couch. Jax was on me in an instant.

His lips crushed mine, violent and possessive, stealing my breath away. "I want you so fucking bad," he breathed against my lips.

Tingles exploded from the top of my head to the tip of my toes, making me warm in all the right places. I made a move to grab his shoulders and the sound of metal filled the air.

Jax laughed. A dark sound that nearly made my heart explode. "You're at my mercy," he growled. In a single yank, the shirt tore in half, and a chill raced across my exposed skin.

"Holy shit," I breathed, straining against the cuffs as his mouth came down to nibble on the tender flesh beneath my bra. When he got to the nipple, I twisted and bucked, squirming against the electric feel of his eager mouth.

My reaction only seemed to drive him harder. He chuckled against my skin, teeth tugging at the edge of the bra. "I love the sounds you make. Music. They're like pure fucking music."

I wanted this. Badly. Almost badly enough to keep my mouth shut and enjoy the ride. But the conversation we'd had in the field after what happened in the car came rushing back. The pain. I hated the thought of him in agony, and to let him continue would be selfish. "Jax, I think we need to stop."

"Stop?" He panted, trailing a line of kisses up my neck and lingering at the edge of my jaw. "No way. I'm not stopping this time. I've wanted you forever, Sammy. You want it, too."

"I do," I said through clenched teeth as he slid the right side of my bra aside, exposing bare skin to the chilly air. "But it's not worth the fallout. You'll be in horrible pain. Lose control."

"I've already lost control," he growled, taking me into his mouth and sucking hard. The pull, with the slightest pressure of his teeth, drew an involuntary moan from my lips. "You do that to me."

I gasped as he ground himself against me, the sensation nearly making me scream. The friction was mind-blowing, sending wave after wave of heat pulsing throughout my body. But I couldn't let this go on. If he wasn't going to put the brakes on this for his own good, then I'd have to be the one who stepped up. With as much force as I could muster, I said, "Jax, stop."

He went completely still. Pulling away, he slid from the couch and backed away several steps. The look on his face was pure guilt. "God, Sammy. Right now you smell amazing. I've wanted you for the longest time, you know that, but the lust you're putting off is driving the thing inside me insane. I don't want to stop—but I do. And Azirak…"

"Wants to devour me?" God, how I wanted to be devoured…

Jax grinned. "You're so inviting all trussed up and ready to go." He took another step back, then two forward. "God, Sammy…"

The way he was watching me, like a drowning man desperate for rescue, would be my undoing. I squeezed my eyes closed for a second and took a deep breath. When I opened them again, it was even worse.

He was standing over me again, face contorted and shoulders stuff. "It wants—" Jax brought both hands up to his head, tangling them into his hair as he dropped to the ground beside the couch. "Fuck!"

Suddenly the idea of being cuffed and helpless wasn't as appealing. "Jax?"

"I can't keep it—" His body convulsed twice, and when his head rose a moment later, both eyes were the color of coal.

"This body burns for you," he said. It was Jax's voice—only it wasn't. A deep breath. Azirak. "I can taste its desire to touch you, and yours to touch it."

It took every ounce of self-control to stay as still as possible. Here I was. Face-to-face with the thing that lived inside Jax again—only this time I knew who I was talking to. "And you?"

Jax—or Azirak—blinked, tilting his head to the right. Every movement was fluent. Controlled. So inhumanly graceful that it was eerie. "You speak to me?"

"Should I not?"

A grin. So familiar, yet so wrong. "Please do. I like it. The sound of your voice is—oddly pleasant to these ears." His eyes traveled down the length of my body, then up again. "You are pleasant to look at, as well, Samantha Merrick."

Creepy. "So, then it's safe to say you don't want to kill me?"

"Accidents happen, but no. I have no *wish* to harm you."

"Good. That's good." I was afraid to say anything else in fear that I'd piss it off somehow.

He laughed. "Though I have no doubt you would be a rare delicacy, to harm you would be detrimental."

I suppressed a shudder. "Detrimental?"

"My human cares deeply for you. To bathe in your blood would destroy him. We are one, even if he has yet to accept it. I try to make things as easy on him as nature will allow."

"That seems like a contradiction," I snapped before I could stop myself. "Making him hurt people is pretty much the opposite of easy."

"That is a dangerous tone to take. Your brazenness is amusing." He rolled his shoulders, eyes never leaving me. "I lead him to filth. Volatile life forces wrought with rage and greed. When I don't feed, it becomes painful for my human—like you are to him. I understand his hesitance to indulge in you, but there are ways. If he is willing."

Ways? For us to be together without Jax being in pain? "What ways?"

But he didn't answer. Instead, he stood and crossed to the other side of the room, sliding down the wall. Tilting his head back, he closed his eyes. Dismissed. I'd been dismissed by a demon.

Chapter Twenty-Five

Jax

When I came to, I was scrunched up on the floor, leaning against the wall across from the couch.

"Jax?" Sam twisted her head to the left an inch. She was still lying on the couch. "Is that you?"

It took a moment to find my voice. My throat was dry and burned like I'd been yelling for hours. "Are you all right?" The movie ended long ago and had circled back around to the start menu. I wanted to ask her how long I'd been asleep, but there was a knock at the front door. A beam of sunlight shone through the window. Morning. Fuck. It was morning already. I climbed to my feet and crossed the room, feeling guilty that Sam had gotten stuck on the couch, half-naked, bound. "Did Heckle call?"

She rolled to the side and struggled to sit up. "Phone didn't ring."

"Did you fall asleep?" I asked, helping her off the couch. There were angry red marks, indentations from the cuffs, on both her wrists, and she seemed to be moving slow. Like she was stiff. Her clothes were askew, and I averted my eyes until she turned, feeling a spark of lust festering beneath the surface.

Sam stood with her back to me. "I dozed off for a little while, but it was uneventful. Unlock these so I can see who's at the door?"

I slipped the key from my pocket and unlocked the cuffs. They fell to the floor with a clatter. "Really? Didn't you learn anything the other night?"

She rolled her eyes and pulled on the sweatshirt that was draped over the back of the couch as the door jingled, then opened. "I find it hard to believe the demons are now using keys to get inside."

A second later Chase stood in the doorway with a tray of coffee and a brown paper bag from Musso's bagel shop. "Hey. Careful," Sam said, stepping over to peer into the bag. "An everything bagel with grape jelly. The breakfast of non-champions. A girl could get used to this."

My brother winked and stepped inside. "Last time I saw you, you were having a rough night. I wanted to check in." Chase's gaze fell on me. He looked disappointed. "Apparently you're fine."

"Chase," I replied, eyes narrow.

"Jax," he responded coolly.

Sam tensed, like she was ready to jump between us if needed.

"Didn't know you were here." Chase squared his shoulders and stepped away from the door.

The demon shifted, anticipating violence. I pushed it down. "What are you doing here?"

"I came to check in on Rick. Plus, I got Sam's voice mail. I knew she was here, figured I'd bring breakfast. What are *you* doing here? Is it such a good idea?"

"She knows everything," I said. "Our family. The demon. All of it."

Judging by the expression on Chase's face, the confession threw him for a loop, but he recovered quickly and turned to Sam. "Even after finding out the truth, you're still hanging around him? What the hell is wrong with you, Samantha?"

"Careful, Chase. You sound a little jealous." I came around the couch.

Chase squared his shoulders. "Jealous of what? You?" He took a step forward. "You really don't see how stupid that sounds?"

I tensed. Azirak wanted to lunge at my brother, raging to feel bones snap beneath his fingers, but I resisted—barely—and flashed him a knowing smile. "You want her but she doesn't want you. Burns your ass, doesn't it?"

"Okay," Sam said, stepping between us. Leave it to her to play peacemaker. "Knock it off."

I ignored her and stepped forward. "Must really piss you the hell off that she's, what, the one girl in Harlow who hasn't blown you?"

"Whoa," Sam said as color fanned to life in her cheeks. "Could we please focus—"

Chase laughed. "Putting a lot on assumption, big brother." He leaned forward and winked. "Who says she hasn't? Maybe I've been in those pants already."

Sam turned an impressive shade of red. "Oh my God.

No one in this room has been in my damn pants but me."

We whirled around to stare at her.

"Perverts." She rolled her eyes and said to Chase, "Something happened at school."

"Sammy," I warned, taking a step toward her. Involving my brother in this was a bad idea.

She kept talking. "I was attacked."

Chase stared. Face pale, his eyes settled on me. "Attacked? By who?"

"By what," Sam corrected.

Wonderful. Just what I needed. "It was a demon."

Chase's face turned scarlet. He stalked the rest of the room, stopping inches from me. The accusation in his eyes was plain as day. "Why the hell would a demon attack her, *Jax*?"

Azirak roared. It flashed a barrage of images. A million different ways that it could kill Chase right then and there. Snapping his neck. Hitting him at just the right angle to send fragments of his nose shooting into his brain. Grabbing the pen that sat inches away, on the coffee table, and jamming it into the hollow of his throat.

I pushed the thoughts from my head. It would probably upset Sam if I ripped Chase to shreds right here on Kelly's living room floor. "Back away from me before I rip your throat out." Thankfully, he did as told. "As for why Sam was attacked, it was to get to me."

"Get to you? Why?"

"Not really clear on that part, and really, it doesn't matter."

Chase slammed a fist against the small table by the door." Like hell it doesn't—"

"There are bigger issues to deal with. When she was attacked, this thing linked to her. If it gets hurt, she gets hurt.

If it dies, *she* dies."

"Then we break this link." Chase turned to Sam, and the expression on his face, unadulterated fear and concern, pissed me off. Suddenly the time he'd gotten to spend with her over the last three years was the only thing I could think about.

"We're working on that, but we don't even know who the demon is," I said as evenly as possible.

"Assuming it matters?"

I clenched my jaw and silently counted to ten. He was still looking at Sam. "It matters," I said coolly.

Chase was oblivious to my near meltdown. "The attack happened at Huntington, right? Let me do some poking around. I know a lot of people. Let me see what I can find out. Maybe someone saw something."

"Suit yourself." It's not like he'd find anything. Sam said the police were no help, and if everyone at the party had been drinking, the likelihood of someone having witnessed anything helpful was slim.

Chase nodded and started toward the door. Stopping for a moment, he turned to me. "Keep her safe."

Sam had been trying to get me talking since we hit the interstate. While Chase was off chasing his tail, we decided to move on plan B. Sadie Gray. If we got Havat his stone, he'd tell us the name of the demon that'd fed off Sam.

She asked, "Will you still leave? After all this is over?"

"For everyone's sake, yeah."

I could see her face from the corner of my eye. Disappointed. Somewhere deep down I hated that she felt that way, but a larger part was glad. If she begged me to stay, there was a good chance I'd consider it. "Where will you go?"

"Nowhere particular. I try not to stay in one place too long."

"So you move around a lot? Where have you been?"

"All over, really. Most of the fifty states. Parts of Canada. Even Australia for a few months."

"Why? I mean, why bounce around?"

"Is there a point to all this?" I snapped, gripping the wheel tighter. The more she talked, the more the deeper feelings fought for attention.

"Just trying to make conversation."

"Well, don't, okay? No point in making this harder on yourself than it has to be."

"What's that supposed to mean?"

Why did she keep pushing? Why the hell would anyone in their right mind dig themselves in deeper with someone like me? "Pretty sure we went over this earlier and I'm not sure why you think it might have changed."

Her jaw dropped. In that moment, I was thankful to be behind the wheel instead of her.

"Know what I think?"

"No," I responded, even though she'd tell me anyway.

"I think you're using this thing as an excuse to run away."

I opened my mouth, then closed it, stunned. "Weren't you listening when I told you what I wanted to do to my brother? Did you see what I did to those men in the field?"

"They weren't men, though."

Now she chose logic? Great fucking timing. "Your point?"

"My point is, you've been in town for days now and you

haven't really hurt Chase. You haven't hurt me. And as for the *non-men*, they were trying to hurt us. You didn't just go out and randomly attack someone on the street."

"Actually," I said. Either she was blocking out Gutierrez, or she had serious memory loss issues. "I did. You were there, or don't you remember?"

"Technically, you saved lives. Didn't you tell me he was dangerous?" She kicked at the dash. "Jesus, Jax. You keep trying to make yourself out to be the devil, when really, you're just a guy dealing with a shitty hand. Get over it."

Get over it? Was she fucking kidding? I was forced to live each day caught up in a storm of violence that there was no way to escape, and she tells me to *get over it*?

I wanted to yell. At her. At life. At fate. Instead, I laughed. "There aren't many people who would ever have the nerve to say that to me."

"Yeah, well I've seen you puke all over yourself. That's bound to screw with your badass factor."

We were quiet for a few minutes. I knew I should keep it that way, but as usual, Sam's nearness wreaked havoc on my common sense. She was like an electric current that shorted out all my damn fuses. "I'm sorry."

"For?"

"What happened last night." Even though my eyes were glued to the road, I could still see her stiffen. "At the house. With Azirak…"

She didn't respond.

"I—we—" Fuck. Why the hell was this so damn hard? "The demon might have been in control, but I was there. I wouldn't have let it hurt you." I swallowed back the admission, but it came out anyway. "I liked it. I'm a fucking bastard, Sammy, but I liked it. It's hard to be with you when I'm me, but when the demon takes over, there's no pain. I'm still there, and I can see and feel everything. I almost wanted to let it…"

"To let it touch me," she finished for me.

"I told you," I said darkly. "I'm a fucking monster. I wanted you so bad that I almost didn't care how I got you."

"That's what it meant," she said, twisting in her seat. "When it said there was a way if you were willing."

I refused to answer. Refused to even think about it. There wasn't any way it would ever happen. Not like that. "What the hell do you want from me, exactly?"

"How about the truth?"

That pissed me off. "Truth? Except for the demon, I've never lied to you. In fact, you're the only person I've never lied to."

"You did," she insisted. "You told me you loved me and that you would always have my back."

Of course I loved her. Loved her so much that it was in danger of killing me. It was in danger of killing *us.* But I'd never told her how I felt. Sure, she knew I cared, but the L-word had *never* been spoken out loud.

"Trying to remember? Don't bother." She shifted back until she was facing forward. There was a cold edge to her voice. Hard and broken. It was almost enough to make me pull the car over. "It was the night before you left. The night before we kissed. We were in Rick's living room, watching a movie. You were half-asleep."

I should have been surprised, but I wasn't. I'd loved Sam from the moment we met. Holding a large umbrella over her head as the priest said kind words beside her parents' graves. We'd never spoken. Hadn't even been introduced. Rick had gone to support his friend and neighbor, Kelly Merrick, whose brother and sister-in-law died in a tragic home invasion.

Standing beside Rick and Chase, I'd watched the girl with the long brown hair stand eerily still. She didn't cry. Didn't speak. Only stood there staring at the ground as her parents were lowered into the cold, wet earth. Even then, so early in my life, I saw pieces of myself mirrored in her eyes. Lost. Alone. Separated.

Ruined.

It was another one of those defining moments. I'd known, even then, that this girl would play a monumental role in my life. We'd grown up close. Inseparable, really. Friends. Partners in crime. It was that last step—love—that pushed me to leave her behind.

There was no stopping it. The words came tumbling out. "The night I kissed you—I almost killed Chase. That's why I left, Sammy. I knew I was too dangerous." I kept my eyes front and center, afraid to see the expression on her face. "I think I knew even back then that you were a trigger. Being with you, it made me happy. The demon doesn't do happy. It needs despair and rage."

"Jax—"

I kept going. Had to get this out before I lost the nerve. "Kissing you…it was the most amazing thing, but it hurt. The pain was unlike anything you can imagine. Physical, mental, emotional… But I could have sucked it up. I would have. For you. But when I left you that night, the demon was going nuts. I ended up standing over my brother's bed with a blade. Everything became so clear. You've seen enough violence and death in your life. I won't be the one exposing you to more—especially when it's all my life is now."

"You have no right to decide what I should and shouldn't have in my life."

"Maybe not—but it doesn't change things. It won't ever change things. I *am* leaving when we clear things up. Everyone I care about is at risk when I'm here."

"Fine," she snapped. "Then I'll go with you. Not like you can stop me. I'll just keep following you until you cave."

I shook my head. "You'd never be able to follow me."

Chapter Twenty-Six

Sam

We drove the rest of the way in silence, pulling up in front of the address we'd found for Sadie Gray just before noon. There was a part of me that dreaded what we were about to do. This woman wasn't going to just give us what we wanted. Not without something in return. I didn't have anything left to give.

The house was a modest Victorian with a well-manicured lawn and a tire swing that hung from a sturdy-looking oak tree.

"What's the plan?" I unbuckled the seat belt as Jax killed the engine. "She's not just going to cheerfully hand the stone over. If it was that easy, Havat wouldn't need us."

"She's going to give us the stone," Jax said, getting out of the car. He slammed the door as I did the same. "Whether she wants to or not."

It was moment likes these, despite the deeper feelings between us, that I was truly afraid for Jax. There was no doubt he'd do whatever it took to get what we'd come for, and that worried me. I followed him up the walkway, cringing when he assaulted the door with enough force to rattle the windows.

A woman appeared. Tall with wild raven hair and exotic features, dressed in a low-cut top and long, curve hugging skirt. "My, my, my," she drawled with an accent I couldn't place. One part Southern drawl, one part European—equal parts annoying. Her eyes skimmed Jax's body from head to toe, lingering just below the waist of his jeans. *Bitch!* Obviously I had no official claim on the guy, but come on. A man shows up on your doorstep *with* a girl in tow and you proceed to drool rivers on him? "I didn't realize Chippendales delivered."

"Sadie Gray?" Jax asked. If he noticed her appreciation, he was polite enough to ignore it.

Sadie leaned against the doorframe, stretching like a cat on a couch and puffing out her chest. Admittedly, I was a little jealous. I couldn't pull off sultry like that. With women like this throwing themselves at his feet, why the hell was Jax interested in me? Of course, that train of thought brought up *how many others were there while he was gone*? Which led to a round of mental flogging.

"For you? I can be anyone you want," Sadie purred.

"Good," he said, pushing her aside and stepping into the house. "I need you to be a witch."

With a wink, she said, "Whatever floats your boat, baby."

I snorted in disgust as Sadie attempted to let the door conveniently close in my face. "Do you moonlight as a prostitute, or are you just really skanky?"

The witch's lips twisted into a scowl. "Pissing me off isn't the way to get what you want."

"Then what is?" Jax asked.

She eyed him. "Depends. Tell me what it is you want."

"We were sent here by a demon named Havat Doyle. He said you have something he needs."

She threw back her head and laughed. "Are you blind, baby? I've got what *every* man needs." Her eyes met mine and she winked. "Some women, too."

"Actually, this dude Havat is looking for something you stole from him. The stone of midnight. Ring any bells?"

Sadie circled Jax, and said, "I can ring whatever bells you'd like."

"Oh, Jesus Christ," I snapped. My patience with the porn-star princess routine was officially gone. The witch had done everything except strip and wiggle her ass in his face. "You have it or not?"

"Maybe," Sadie said, eyes growing as cold as her voice. "But I have no intention of giving it to that bastard, Havat— or you. I acquired it fair and square. Not my fault old Havat is a sore loser."

Jax was across the room in the blink of an eye. "I could *make* you give it to me," he seethed, pinning her against the wall. "And I would enjoy every last second, I promise you."

I would, too, because something told me it would involve a serious hurt.

For a woman facing down an extremely pissed-off demon, Sadie Gray wasn't the least bit flustered. She chuckled and leaned in close. "I bet I would, too." She did a little shimmy, laughing. If it weren't for the fact that both our lives were on the line, I might have shot forward and yanked out all the woman's hair. "Maybe we can work something out. It wouldn't come cheap, though."

"Name your price," he said, letting go.

She backed away with a not-so-subtle shake of her ass and crossed the room. There was an old chest in the corner. The wood was warped and the hinges were rusted. Pulling it open, she rummaged around for a moment before exclaiming, "Aha. This is what you're looking for, yes?"

When she turned back to him she held a small green stone in the palm of her hand. It didn't look like much. No more than the size of peanut and the width of a marker. Sam expected something bigger and more impressive. Or, at the very least, black. Stone of *midnight*? Come on…

Jax made a move to grab it, but Sadie closed her hand and jerked it away with a giggle. Chin thrust, she said, "Not so fast. There's the matter of payment."

"Tell me what you want and give me the damn stone," Jax growled.

Sadie's head tilted and a lock of raven hair fell across her shoulders. On first glance the woman was nothing more than a pretty, if not pushy, face. Petite and unassuming. On second glance, however, I saw a gleam of power in her eyes. She might be a witch, but she was also someone skilled at manipulation. In her own way, Sadie Gray was just as dangerous as any demon. "You will feed from me. Enough to link us."

Wow. I searched the woman's face for signs that this was a joke, but there were none. Only the cold stare of determination. "Are you insane?" I snapped. I wanted to get rid of a link and this moron wanted to create one? "Why would anyone willingly ask for that?"

Sadie's expression was icy. "Being linked to a Tainted has its advantages."

Alarm bells started going off in my head. Neither one of us had said Jax was Tainted. "Such as?"

"Long life, for one thing. I will live as long as he does."

"I live a violent life." Jax said." If something should happen and I die, you die as well. You'd still be fragile. Even injuries I sustained could kill you. Doesn't seem like the best logic on your part."

Sadie giggled and let her hand rest on Jax's chest. "Let's just say I'm a betting woman, and I'm betting hard on you."

That was enough. I came forward and slapped the woman's hand away. "Back off, bitch, and keep your paws to yourself."

Sadie threw her hands up and took a step back, but there was a challenge in her eyes. A dare. She was convinced this would end in her getting what she wanted from Jax. *Everything* she wanted.

Over my dead body—although that was becoming an increasingly possible proposition.

"That can't be all," Jax said, slipping his hand into mine. "An extended stay on the mortal coil doesn't seem to warrant that kind of risk."

"Oh, it's not. Over time some Tainted links develop, shall we say, heightened abilities."

"And that translates to…?"

She shrugged and stepped away. With a grin, she undid the first four buttons of her blouse, allowing a patch of lacy black to peek through. "I suppose we shall see, won't we?"

"No. We won't," I snapped.

Everything from that point on was fuzzy. Watery at best. A wave of fatigue hit hard, and I swayed on my feet. Jax screamed my name as strong hands gripped my shoulders and the world tilted sideways.

A rush of images swarmed me. A watery face. A cold voice.

"Come to me tonight," it hissed. *"Come to the club."*

Shit. The link.

Everything went dark.

Chapter Twenty-Seven

Jax

I hadn't moved since I set Sam down on Kelly's couch. For a minute I thought about snapping the cuffs into place, just as a precaution, but changed my mind. I'd just stay alert. Watch for signs that something was wrong.

It wasn't a long wait. Less than twenty minutes later, she shifted and slowly opened her eyes. "Jax?"

"I'm right here," I said, kneeling beside the couch. "How do you feel?"

She pulled herself into a sitting position and tilted her head to stretch out her neck. "Sort of like someone used my head as a golf ball. All of a sudden I was so tired. I couldn't keep my eyes open." Sam hesitated. Several puffs of gray rose from her shoulders. "I hate to be the bearer of bad news, but I think we can say without a shadow of a doubt that, yes, I'm linked to this thing…"

"What happened?"

"It was there…the demon. Inside my head. I could feel it." She shuddered. "It spoke to me."

Fuck. "You heard its voice?"

"Yeah. Right before I passed out. But it's not *all* bad… It told me to come to the club tonight. We know where it'll be."

Five hours later, we were at the back door to the Viking. I hated this plan, but we were running out of time. Chase had called. He was still up at Huntington, but so far, hadn't had any luck.

Sam's plan to trap the demon by using herself as bait made me itch in my skin. Azirak, too. But we were out of options. "Let's go over it one more time," I whispered.

"Yes, Mom," Sam replied with a roll of her eyes. She was still tired, but seemed to hum with a renewed sense of energy. "I'm going to stroll in there as though nothing's wrong and do my job. Sling a little brew. Flirt with some guys. At the first hint of trouble, I'm going to give you the signal."

"And the signal?"

She puckered her lips. "I'm going to blow a kiss to one of the customers."

I nodded. I'd have eyes on her every moment we were in there. Nothing to worry about. That's what I kept telling myself. But even Azirak wasn't convinced. The demon churned and shifted, uneasy about the whole thing.

Heckle had called earlier with an update. While he hadn't found a more optimal way to break the link, he did say he was on the trail of something that might dampen it to the point that it wouldn't be an issue. He reinforced that we should still keep trying to find the demon Sam was linked to.

"Can I go in now? I can't afford to be late. I refuse to move back in with Kelly, so if I lose my job, I'm heading downtown to turn tricks..." She did a little twirl. "And looking like this, there's a good chance I'd starve."

"Go," I said, pulling open the door and trying hard not to stare. She wore jeans this time around, with a tight black tank top with the Viking logo on the front. I wondered what it'd feel like to slide my fingers beneath the hem and work my way slowly up her back. Azirak ran with the spark of lust, and flashed a scene inside my head. I had Sam pinned beneath me, against the hood of Rick's car. My hands were sandwiched between the soft, thin material of her shirt and her warm silky skin, the subtle thumping of her heart under my fingers. She moaned, arching off the hood and into me as my body responded, the need to take her, to possess her, hitting me with feral veracity.

"But be careful," I finished, shaking my head to clear away the scene. Not the right time for that.

It wouldn't ever be the right time for that.

I'd been standing by the railing on the second floor for almost two hours now. I was beginning to give up hope when the cell rang. If not for the demon, I never would have heard it above the noise in the club. I reached into my pocket and flipped it open. "Yeah?"

"Jax, I think I got him."

I held my free hand up to drown out some of the noise. "Chase? What do you mean?"

"The bastard that hurt Samantha. I think it's a demon going by the name of Hank Sutton. He's the TA from her history class."

"What makes you think he's our guy?"

"He was seen with a girl who went missing a month earlier. Several people also saw him leave the party right behind Sam. He's a regular at the Viking. He's actually—"

"Going to be there tonight," I said. "We know. We're there now. Sam's working and I'm keeping watch. Anything else?"

"I can text you a picture of the guy. That help?"

"Do it." I hung up without another word as the music changed from techno dance to a hypnotic rhythm that had couples swarming the dance floor below. A moment later, the phone beeped. Chase's text. On the small screen was a picture of a tall, lanky guy with wild, curly hair and an eerie grin. Fucking great. We were looking for a dorkier, demonic version of Carrot Top.

I scanned the room. Sam was on the other side flashing a flirty smile to a couple of college boys. It was still early, but the club was full of life and the bar crowded. There was no sign of Sutton. What was I supposed to do with the demon if he showed up? Wrestle him out to the car and lock him in the trunk? Someone would call the cops, and with my reputation, I wouldn't be given a chance to explain—not that I could come up with a reasonable explanation for stuffing someone in a trunk. Not reasonable to the rest of the world, anyway.

Song after song, the dance floor hummed with electricity

as bodies thrashed to the music. I watched the crowd, searching for anyone resembling Sutton, but there was no one. I pinched the bridge of my nose. There was too much crap in the air and it was giving me a headache. Perfume, alcohol, and emotion—thanks to Azirak, everything spun in a sickly swirl. Giving up on the balcony, I made my way to the stairs and across the room to the bar.

"Hey stranger. What'll it be?" Sam said with a grin. She leaned forward, bending low enough to give me an unintentional view down her shirt. My pulse quickened and I had to force myself to stay in place instead of moving forward to meet her. "Chase called a little while ago. Says he thinks the demon's name is Hank Sutton. Sound familiar?"

"Oh my God. Seriously? He was the TA at Huntington. Is he positive? Hank seemed so…normal."

"He's pretty sure. Is there anything you can tell me about him? Anything that might help pick him out in a crowd? Chase sent a picture but…" But Sam wasn't listening anymore. She was staring over my shoulder, at the bar. "What's wrong?"

"It's him. Hank. He's here."

Chapter Twenty-Eight

Sam

Jax flew across the room before I could stop him. Hank, who was chatting up a leggy brunette in a red leather miniskirt by the door, must have caught wind of him. The demon froze mid-sentence, looked up, and bolted into the crowd just as Jax hit the dance floor.

"Shit," I spat. The bottle of gin slipped from my hand and rattled to the bar. I ducked out from behind the counter and sprinted after them. By the time I reached the other side of the room, both men had been swallowed by the crowd.

I started across the dance floor, knocking into people with each step. Angry shouts and colorful words came from every direction as I plowed through the center, but as I reached the edge of the crowd, it all started to blur. Like I'd just stepped off a merry-go-round set on superspeed, colors swirled together, people on the dance floor becoming a single, shapeless blob. I reached out and caught hold of something—someone—as a vicious wave of vertigo washed through the room.

"He'll never catch me," the same voice I'd heard at Sadie's cooed inside my head, followed by a dark laugh.

"No," I whispered, continuing forward. I hadn't had anything to drink. I hadn't been to sleep.

"Come to me," the demon demanded. *"Walk right out the front door."*

Turn around and walk back to the bar. That's what I needed to do. What I *wanted* to do. But my limbs had other ideas. The command was like an industrial-size rubber band snapping against my will. One foot in front of the other, I wove through the rest of the crowd and approached the door, every step a war between my mind and body.

The cold night air stung my skin and the sounds of the club faded as I stepped onto the sidewalk. After a few moments, the only thing that was left was the sound my shoes made as they pounded the walkway. *Clop. Clop. Clop.*

"Sam?"

Thank God. Jax. Jax was here. He could stop me. Footsteps sped up behind, my pace never slowing. No. Not Jax. Way too noisy.

"Sam! It's me."

"Chase! Hurry," I called over my shoulder. "I can't stop."

He caught up and jumped into my path. I simply stepped around and kept walking. "What's wrong? Where are you going? And where's Jax?"

"He took off after Hank, but I think something's wrong. He's in my head. Forcing me to—"

"He's *controlling* you?" he asked, surprised. He tried

stepping into my path again, but I pushed him away and continued, undeterred. Chase cursed. "Okay. Forget the logistics. We need to stop this."

"Not sure what you have in mind. Other than throwing me over your shoulder, I don't see how you can stop this."

He chuckled. "Excellent idea."

One minute I was walking, casual but determined, the next my feet were off the ground and the world tilted sideways.

"How's that?"

I held my breath. The desire to keep walking was still there, but I didn't feel the need to kick and scream to get down. Score! But it only solved one problem. "We need to find Jax."

"Agreed, but let's get you someplace safe first. I don't think my brother would be thrilled to know you walked off to meet a demon. Dude might get jealous. Any ideas?"

I thought about it for a minute. How long would this last? And would it get worse? Chase couldn't hold on to me all night. Then I had an idea. "Kelly's house. There's a pair of handcuffs we can use."

Chase whistled, and I felt his shoulders shake with a laugh. "You in handcuffs? Oh, I'm definitely game for that," he said, and swiveled toward the parking lot.

"Are you okay?" he asked. The expression on his face was apologetic, and I thought about making a bondage joke, but decided against it. Chase had a habit of taking things a little too literally and that was the last thing I needed right now.

Him grabby and me in chains. The only thing that would top that would be Jax walking in on another kiss. Kelly had been talking about repainting the walls, but somehow I didn't think bloodred was really her thing. "Are these too tight?"

I twisted my wrist in the cuff. He'd secured my right hand with one side, and clipped the other end to the radiator. "As long as it keeps me here where I'm safe, then I'm good."

"Should try Jax again. Maybe we should use your cell?" We'd tried three times to reach him on the way over. There'd been no answer. If Hank was in my head, that meant that either Jax had been hurt, or he hadn't caught up to the demon. Either way, it equaled trouble.

"Can't. Mine's gone."

"You don't have it on you?"

"I don't have it, period. It ended up at the bottom of the river. Don't ask…"

He shrugged and pulled out his own cell, turning toward the door to make the call. The sound the phone made as he pushed the buttons echoed through the room. After a minute, Chase shook his head and snapped it closed. No luck. He looked as worried as I felt. They bickered and clashed, but underneath it, the Flynn brothers loved each other. "Maybe I should go look for him."

"Yeah," I said with a roll of my eyes. That would complete my craptastic week. Jax and Chase ripping each other to shreds while I sat chained in my aunt's house. "Great plan. Go in search of the guy who wants to rip your heart out. Lemme know how that turns out for ya."

He frowned again and set down his cell. "Good point. After all this time, you're still crazy about him, aren't you? All this crap that's happened is technically his fault, and you really *do* still want him to stay."

I didn't want to talk about this. Not with him and definitely not now, but avoiding it wasn't going to change things. Nothing would. "Doesn't really matter. He doesn't want me enough to stay."

He shook his head. "I don't agree with the thing you two have going. I never agreed with it. Jax is volatile and dangerous and I was always worried about him snapping on you. But he does love you. Don't think he doesn't."

"Sometimes it's just not enough, I guess." I'd lived after he left last time and I'd live again. He was a guy, right? There were plenty of those walking around out there.

The front door rattled.

"Jax?" I called, breath held.

Chase jumped from the chair and waved like a lunatic. "Shh," he whispered, frantic. "If you're linked to this thing, maybe it can track you down, too."

Well, crap. I hadn't even thought about that.

He crept toward the door, staying away from the windows. He'd almost reached the other end of the room when it burst open and a tall figure stepped into the light.

Hank.

"Look out!" I pulled against the restraints, digging into my pocket in a frantic search to find the key. Only I couldn't. I'd insisted that Chase take it just to be on the safe side.

Hank's head snapped up and his eyes zeroed in on me. There was a spark of madness there. A feral, violent gleam, and in that moment, I wondered how I'd never seen it before. How could you hide that?

He started forward. Thankfully he didn't get far. Chase jumped behind him, half-full bottle of Kelly's favorite wine in hand, and swung hard. The sound it made as it shattered across the back of Hank's head, along with the muffled thud his body made as it crumpled to the ground, was a symphony of relief to my ears.

Chase shuffled toward me, eyes wide and brushing tiny bits of glass from his sleeve. "You okay?"

"Me?" I laughed. "You're the one who went Rambo on a demon's ass. Quick. Unlock these before he wakes up. We have to find Jax."

He nodded and slipped the key from his front pocket. There was the tiniest blush in his cheeks. "Aw, shucks, ma'am. It was nothing."

I stepped away from the wall, rubbing my wrist and glad to be free. "Tell you what, I've officially decided I'm not into the whole bondage scene."

He took my hand. "Well, that's a shame. I hear—"

That's when it hit me. Or rather, it *hadn't* hit me. "Something's wrong."

Chase, growing pale, spun back around to check on Hank. When he didn't move, he turned back to me, confused. "I don't get it. He's down for the count. What could be wrong?"

"Exactly. He's down for the count. If we're linked, he'd be standing and *I'd* be down."

Chase considered it for a moment. "Well, maybe you weren't linked? Maybe he attacked you, but didn't do this link thing?"

"Impossible. I heard the thing in my head," I said, peering around him to look at Hank. He was still and bleeding from a nasty-looking gash on the back of his head. I knotted my fingers through my hair, working them across my scalp. Not a scratch. From what Heckle said, there should definitely be something there. "I didn't walk out of that club on my own. I was *forced*."

"So you're saying he's *not* the one who fed from you?"

"Sammy!" Jax appeared in the doorway. He looked down at Hank and frowned.

At the sight of him, relief washed through me and a weight equal to a Volvo lifted from my chest. "Jax! Thank God." I dragged Chase across the room and stopped a few feet from where Hank lay. The faint rise and fall of his back indicated he wasn't dead. "He found us. Chase got him, but I don't think he's—"

"Sammy," Jax repeated, this time softer. There was fear in his eyes. A kind of terror I'd only seen once or twice in all the time I'd known him. His gaze alternated between me and Chase as the fingers of his left hand twitched. "I need you to do something for me. No questions. No arguments."

"What—"

"Come here. Walk to me."

Chase stepped in front of me, and with a squeeze of his hand, shook his head. "Wait a sec." Turning to Jax, he said, "What's going on?"

Jax ignored him. "Sutton wasn't the demon. Do you really think my brother would have been able to knock him out so easily if he were?" He came a step closer. "Please, Sammy. Come to me."

"That's what I was trying to tell you. Hank followed us here, but when Chase hit him, I didn't feel a thing. I don't think he's the one I'm linked to."

I tried to go to Jax, but Chase's grip tightened around my arm. He was pale and looked just as worried. "Samantha, wait. Something's wrong here."

"I know," I snapped. Jesus. Were they deaf? "Have either of you been listening to me?"

Jax inched closer. The look on his face was terrifying. Furious. Eyes trained on Chase, he said, "I'm listening, Sammy. But now you need to listen to me. Sutton isn't the demon. He isn't even *a* demon. It's *my brother*. He's the one you're linked to."

Chase's fingers twitched around my arm, then tightened. He was shaking his head. "You've finally lost it, Jax. You're not making any sense."

Jax's expression didn't falter—neither did his pace. Slow and determined. "You're like me. Tainted. You've got a demon as well."

"I'm human, Jax. You know that."

But Jax shook his head. "All this time, it was you." His eyes darkened and his posture changed. Combative, tense, and ready to fight. "*You* attacked Sammy that night of the party. That's why I didn't smell another demon. You've never had a scent. What about all those girls that went missing? Did you feed from them? Kill them?"

This was insane. Chase was a letch, but a killer? There wasn't a chance in hell. I listened to their exchange, slightly detached and wondering if maybe the whole thing was one long, surreal nightmare. Any minute now I'd wake up, safe and sound in my dorm room at Huntington. The attack would never have happened. The car would be parked outside—minus the seaweed. And Jax... Jax had never come back to town. That was it. This entire bad dream was my mind's twisted way of dealing with lingering feelings for someone who had left me behind three years ago.

I probably would have gone right on believing that—if

not for the fact that Chase yanked me backward, laughing like a maniac.

"Oh well. Looks like ya got me. Surprised, *brother*? And I have a scent. All demons do. It's just not traceable by you."

All the breath rushed from my lungs and I had to concentrate in order to remember how to breathe. Simple thing, breathing. Normally an involuntary process. Now, though? My body seemed incapable. "Chase?"

"Shh," he soothed, patting my shoulder like someone would a scared animal. Despite having several very colorful replies on the tip of my tongue, I complied and swallowed my retort. Turning his attention back to Jax, Chase snickered. "I gotta know, man. How did you figure it out?"

My head was spinning. "But, Hank. What about Hank? Why would he run—show up here and attack me—if he wasn't—"

Chase rolled his eyes. "I was controlling him. Obviously." He turned back to Jax. "Now, you were saying?"

"It was something one of Azirak's demons said. About the one who was after me biding their time. It got me thinking. You're a selfish fuck, Chase. You always have been. You pushed too hard to keep me here, feeding me shit about it being for Sam's sake. I don't know why I didn't see it. You think too much of yourself to ever admit you couldn't take care of her on your own. Then I started thinking about the attack at Huntington. How I never smelled the demon—"

"We can't track each other by scent. Part of the rules, man."

"I didn't know for sure. Not till I walked in and saw Sutton down and Sam still standing."

"I'm sure you have a ton of questions."

Jax was the very definition of darkness in that moment. I'd seen him bend and twist, failing countless times to control his anger, yet now, there was an eerie peace. The calm before the storm. Like those few minutes right before hell broke loose when the trees were still and the water was like glass. "How long?"

"All my life—same as you."

"That's impossible."

"It's not. Just ask my link." Chase laughed again and gave my arm a good shake.

Jax gritted his teeth and took a deep breath. "So why not kill me sooner? If you've had the demon all your life, same as me, why wait?"

"I had to be sure I'd win. The demons inside don't really reach their full potential until they've festered in a human for twenty years." He clapped his hands together. "We're aged up nice and good now, bro. Time to settle up."

Jax paled.

"Seriously, if you hadn't spent the last three years of your life brewing in your own pity party, you would have seen the truth."

"And what truth might that be?"

"That this isn't a curse. It's a *gift*." He let go of my arm and commanded, "Stay." To his brother, he said, "The demon is power, Jax. Unbelievable power."

Jax was quiet for a minute. Underneath the darkness in his expression I could see the pain. He'd always been at war with Chase in one way or another, but he loved his brother. Loved him so much that to keep him safe, he'd given up everything. When Jax spoke again, there was an air of determination in his tone. "I don't know how this happened, but we can figure it out. Take back control. We don't have to go at each other. Not like this."

Chase laughed. A horrible sound that made me want to cover my ears. Not human. Not demon. "Take control? I never lost it! Unlike you, I embraced my destiny. My demon and I are in perfect sync." He nodded over his shoulder and said, "While you were running away from your true nature, I embraced my calling with open arms. I guess it just comes down to the fact that I'm simply stronger. Always have been."

"Stronger?" Jax's eyes darted from his brother to me, then back again. "You mean weaker. Strength would have been to resist. To fight. You caved like a little bitch."

"Aren't you the happy little hypocrite. You've got blood on those digits, same as me, bro. Don't pretend otherwise."

"I'm no saint," Jax agreed. The pain in his voice almost destroyed me. "But I don't—never have and never will—kill."

"News flash for you, Jax. You will. You'll have to, because in our *particular* situation, it's kill or be killed."

"What situation might that be?"

Chase grinned. The expression that used to make me smile now made me sick. "We're at war. We're bound to these weak, pathetic human bodies until one of us makes the other bleed. You and me, man? We're the key to it all."

Chapter Twenty-Nine

Jax

I tensed as Azirak raged like never before. The demon kept showing that single phrase, *You and me, man? We're the key to it all.* Over and over like a skipping CD. I had no fucking clue what it was supposed to mean.

Next came the images of that blood-soaked, barren field in his visions. Two impossibly tall figures faced off under a burning gray sky. The demon was annoyed, but I didn't understand what it was trying to get across. A message. A clue. Something I needed to know. I felt its frustration humming through every inch of my body.

"You've known Sammy almost your whole life, Chase. You don't want to hurt her. You'd rather hurt me, right?" Another step. We were a foot apart now. Possibly two.

Chase jerked Sam close, then ran a finger down the side of her face. Azirak went wild. "Hurting her hurts you, and that's my lot in life. I don't like it, but it is what it is." He licked his finger and sighed, then ran his tongue along the line of her jaw. "Besides, she tastes amazing. Can't argue that, can ya?"

Azirak roared, and all my muscles convulsed as the demon fought for control. *I* had to maintain control. It was enraged and there was always a chance it wouldn't show restraint. With Sam linked to my brother, if he went down, so did she.

"I walked away from her, remember? She's a fun distraction while I'm in town, but that's about it."

"Your stink is all over her, Jax. Nice try." He grabbed a handful of Sam's hair and tilted her head. A small noise escaped her lips and a rush of gray bled into the air. "Then again, so is mine. Just between us brothers, you fed from her too, right? Just a little? Good stuff, no?"

My jaw tightened. The demon pushed harder.

Chase laughed. "Go ahead. I know you want to take me out. Give it your best shot. But keep in mind it won't end well for her."

Jax held his breath and stood his ground. Poker face. This had to go down smooth. "So?"

Chase was silent. He smiled and stepped to the table where the pen sat. Grabbing it, he positioned the point at the hollow of Sam's throat. "You can't bluff me, Jax. We both know you can't touch me without touching her—and there's no way you're willing to do that. You don't have the balls to make that kind of sacrifice."

Chase winked and, before I could blink, he pulled the pen away from Sam's throat and jammed it into his forearm. She gasped and shuddered as blood began to drip from her own arm—not his. "Oh my God," she breathed, clutching her bleeding limb close.

"I think I made my point," he said with a grin. He threw the pen at my feet and started to back away, dragging Sam with him. "And I think it's time to finally end this thing."

The intention was to lunge forward and somehow get Sam away from my brother, but like a baseball bat to the gut, the breath left my lungs and in an instant staying upright became impossible. Thankfully, I wasn't the only one. Beside Sam, Chase also dropped to the ground.

"Sam," Heckle's voice boomed from the doorway. His eyes were closed while his hands made odd gestures. Air traffic control or magic. I didn't know, and didn't care—as long as it gave Sam a chance to run. "Come over here. Bring Jax with you."

Small arms slid beneath mine and lifted. I tried to help her, but the energy had left my body. It took several tries, but Sam finally managed to drag me to the door.

Chase, still crumpled on the floor by the couch, lifted his head to glare at Heckle. "You can't kill me. It's against the rules."

"But I don't have to let you kill them, either."

Chase chuckled. "You think that's going to change the outcome of this? I'll just get the fucker tomorrow."

Heckle shrugged. "Maybe. But you won't get him tonight."

"We need answers." We were back at the Inferno, Heckle's bar. I felt better, but had yet to get a straight answer as to what the fuck happened at the house. "What the hell was that whammy you hit us with?"

"Just a little something I picked up along the way."

"Magic?" Sam asked. Her eyes were wide.

Heckle laughed. "I suppose by the human definition, you might consider it that."

Sam rested her injured arm against the bar. Heckle had cleaned and dressed the wound, but from the way she kept wincing, I knew she was in pain. "What about breaking the link? Did you find an alternative?"

"Other than what we already know? Nope," Heckle said. He put a glass down in front of himself, and then another in front of me. Leaning across the counter, he winked. "Sorry. None for you, girly."

Sam slammed her fist against the bar. "There *has* to be something we can do."

"The only way that link is coming off is if you bite the big one or the demon chooses to let you go. Something tells me that ain't happening. Put your head tween your legs and kiss your ass good-bye." He paused, frowning, poured two shots of vodka. "Or at least, until Azirak's clan comes for you. There's that, too."

"What about that thing you were looking into? A way to dampen the effects? Will distance help? Or wearing some kind of…talisman?"

Heckle blinked twice, then fell into a fit of hysterical laughter. He grabbed the bar, chortling and stomping his foot so hard that the glasses on the shelf behind the bar started to rattle. "Talisman? What do you think this is? The movies?"

Sam's eyes narrowed and her small hands curled into tight fists. She reached across the counter, taking the bartender by surprise, and grabbed a handful of his shirt. Holy fuck, it was hot. With a hard yank forward, she said, "You can do better than that. Give us something useful or else."

Heckle's eyes widened—and he started laughing again. The guy was going to piss himself if he wasn't careful. "Or else what? You gonna pull my hair or something, girly?"

Sam's expression bounced from frustrated to furious before settling on vindicated. She let go of his shirt and grabbed my arm, tugging me close. I nearly fell off the damn stool. "Or else he'll eat you."

"Sammy, demons don't really eat other demons. Don't eat people either."

"Oh. Well…"

I grinned. Rick once said I looked 100 percent hell-spawned when I did it. I'd worked hard to perfect it, too. "But we do *love* to inflict pain. My demon thinks you look like a screamer. Are you a screamer, Heckle?"

Heckle hesitated. He was holding back. It was evident in the slumping posture and fidgeting fingers. "There might be something… But, and I know this sounds callous and I apologize, I wouldn't do it."

"She'll *die*," I snapped.

"Azirak's clan won't like it."

"If Chase doesn't kill her, the other demons will—not that anyone has told me why. You're all acting like I'm their demon Dalai-fucking-Lama."

"You are," Heckle said with a frown. "These demons are at war. Right now, the playing field is neutral. Neither side has an advantage over the other—it must stay that way at all costs."

Jax felt suddenly cold. "Why?"

But Heckle didn't answer. He poured himself a shot, downed it, and disappeared into the back.

Since I wasn't willing to risk Chase coming back to Kelly's, we went to a motel. The room smelled like mothballs, and the carpet was mustard yellow, but it was small and out of the way. Sam would be safe here for a while.

I couldn't keep her awake forever. Eventually she'd fall asleep and Chase would be waiting, if for no other reason than to make a point—he was stronger. I couldn't keep handcuffing her, either. First off, the scenario was too fucking tempting. A repeat of the earlier infraction wouldn't help the situation. Chase had the keys.

Why did the thought of killing my brother turn my stomach? It's what Azirak had wanted since I was old enough to understand the thing living inside me. Maybe if I did what the demon had craved, I'd have peace. Unfortunately, in order for Sam to live, we *all* had to live.

"Talk to me," she whispered. Sam sat on the bed across from me, legs tucked underneath her and face grim. She'd been quiet since we'd arrived, sitting pensive and watching me stalk the room. She was scared—the demon writhed to taste her fear—but she was also worried.

About me.

"I'll fix this." I had no idea how, but I needed her to know I was on it. That I wouldn't just let her die. That's why I'd stayed, right? To make sure she was safe? Bang-up fucking job I was doing. Spectacular.

"No," she said, stretching her legs and sliding from the bed. She crossed the room slowly, eyes never leaving mine. Damn me to hell if it didn't get my heart cranking. I wished she wouldn't look at me like that. With those hooded eyes and kiss-me lips. Hadn't she figured out what that did to my concentration? "*We'll* fix this. Technically this is my problem, Jax. Not yours."

"Bullshit," I snapped. At the outburst, Azirak stirred, excited. "Chase is my brother. That makes this mine to deal with."

A sad smile slipped across her face. "Didn't you once tell me it was us against the world?"

So beautiful. So fierce. So extraordinary. Fate was a cruel bitch with serious PMS. Why else would it let someone like Sam drift into my orbit? I'd never seen it as a child, knowing only that we were two kindred souls. But when I got older and saw myself for the monster I truly was, I never understood how she missed it. The darkness that was so evident to me seemed to slip past her unnoticed.

"We were twelve when I said that, Sammy. Obviously things changed."

"Why did they change?"

I blinked. Sleep deprivation had set in. What the hell kind of question was that? "They changed because even though I don't go out and slaughter innocent women, I'm no different from my brother. I'm a monster. Same as him."

She scowled, slapping a hand against the bed. "You're nothing like him. I've had years with you, *seeing*. At my parents' funeral it was you who held that umbrella over my head, not Chase. When I was ten, it was you who spent your entire summer helping Mrs. Fellows paint her house when she broke both legs."

I tried to protest, but she held up her hand. On a roll. No stopping her now.

"Yeah. I know it was you. I also know you were the one who sat up with Cora Michaels senior year after her brother committed suicide. It was you who shelled out the money to help save Old Man Harper's dog after it got hit by that car. You sent flowers to Ginny Finley for six weeks straight after her boyfriend dumped her for being *too fat*." She stepped closer. Our faces were so close. Everything about her—from the sweet scent of her shampoo to the way the breath moved through her body—was like an electric current running through the room making every inch of me feel alive. "It was *you* who saved me the night I was attacked on campus."

Everything spun. How did she know about any of it? Shit. What should I do? Lie. I had to lie. "No. You're wrong."

But it was pointless. She knew everything. I could deny it until judgment day, and it wouldn't matter. It's why the darkness in me never bothered her. She'd known it was there all along. Only in addition to the darkness I saw, she must see something else. Something bright.

Something *good*.

She shrugged. I hated myself for noticing how the material of her shirt shifted, pulling tight across her chest. Or how her hair fluttered, framing her face and neck in soft caramel waves. Every minute detail was like a flashing neon warning sign to back the fuck away. I didn't, though. Couldn't. She was a magnet and I was a slave to her pull.

"Doesn't matter that you won't admit it," she continued. "The truth is, you're a good man, Jax Flynn. You're a good man—*not a demon*—and I love you. I've always loved you."

Warmth enveloped me as she placed her hand on the side of my face. "Always been *in* love with you."

Parts of me were horrified to hear the words, while others had longed for them for so long. Inside Azirak shuddered, both happy and starving at the same time. Its hunger spiked, but it fought the urge to feed, flashing watery images of Sam's face through my head.

She smiled. "I know you really believe we can't be together, and you don't want to admit how you feel about me, but that doesn't matter. I know how *I* feel. And right now, that's enough for me."

I was so much taller than Sam. Six foot five to her five foot four. She rose onto her toes, pulling my head down the rest of the way, and brushed her lips to mine. The touch was soft. Warm. Electric. Not at all like the kiss at the club, or the one in her apartment. This was different. Needy, yeah, but so much more than that. It was full of the one thing I didn't deserve. That I'd never deserve.

Love.

The emotion overwhelmed me, at first in a good way. Sam loved me despite who I was. *What* I was. It was amazing. And terrifying. And excruciatingly painful. In my head, Azirak writhed and squirmed, unable to hold back any longer. It flashed images of red and black. Of dead things and pain. I pulled back and pushed Sam toward the bed. She stumbled, thankfully landing on the edge of the hard hotel mattress instead of the floor.

"Stay the fuck away from me," I cursed. I couldn't have her so close. Not with all the dark, horrible things swimming around in my head. Backing toward the door, I closed my eyes and held my breath. Every part of me was on fire, limbs shaking and ready to snap. I had to get out of that room. Away from her. Into the fresh air. "I have to—"

A shudder. Then, a flash of light and sharp pain. I felt the shift but couldn't do a thing to stop it.

"Jax," I heard Sam say. She was standing in front of me, but when I tried to reach for her, my limbs wouldn't obey.

Neither would my lips.

"Samantha Merrick," my voice said, my own mouth betraying me. "I must feed."

Sam slid off the bed and took a step closer. A tuft of gray rose from her shoulders, but with the demon in control, it looked different. The color was sharper and the smell… The smell was nearly as enticing as the sway of her hips and the way her shirt pulled to the left as she bent forward. I wanted to yank her close, but at the same time push her away.

"Feed from me," she said, grabbing my hand.

I opened my mouth to yell, but of course no sound came. Still, I could feel it all. The warmth of her skin. The erratic drum of her heart. And fuck me, but it felt good. There was no ache. Just the blissful feel of skin against skin.

My body reacted to her nearness, every inch of me coming alive and humming in anticipation. Even though I wasn't in control, I felt every euphoric, frustrating moment. Felt it in 3-D, even. Every sensation was amped with the demon in the driver's seat.

"I propose a trade," she said, this time bolder. "Feed from me in exchange for information."

Azirak was intrigued. "What kind of information do you seek?"

"This war—I need to know more about it."

The demon tensed, and I was horrified, worried it might

lash out at Sam. But it didn't. Instead, it said, "And how will you feed me? Will you truly be able to work up enough fear of this form to satisfy my hunger?"

She thought about it for a moment before shaking her head. "I'm not sure. Probably not. But Jax said something. That when we were...*close*...it drove you crazy. You wanted to feed."

"You speak of lust?"

"I guess so."

No!

"And you can feel that way? Knowing it's me you cavort with and not him?" I was hard.

Sam smiled. It was an odd kind of grin that made me feel at ease somehow. "I want him. I guess I've always wanted him. And he's in there. Even though it's you I'm talking to, I can see the spark in his eyes. He's not gone. If this is the only way I can have him, and you tell us what we need to know, then so be it. But make no mistake, it's him. It's always *him*."

Azirak paused, considering her offer. I pushed to regain control, but it was pointless. I'd waited too long to feed the demon, and it wasn't going back in its box until it had its fill. Of her. "His feelings for you are intoxicating. I will admit you are sweet. A delicacy I could savor. I would be curious to taste you. To try to understand the allure you hold for him. And for me."

"Please," she begged, and I knew then if it was me in control, I would have caved at that very moment. The curve of her lip and delicate slope of her neck... The sound of her voice was like a beacon, and I wasn't the only one who felt that way. The spike of desire I felt was twofold. I'd give anything to be with her, but Azirak would, too.

The demon stepped close to Sam, running my hand across her cheek. She shuddered, looking into my eyes. Me. She was looking for me. "What do you wish to know?"

"His brother told us one side needed to spill the blood of the other to be free."

Please don't do this…

"And Heckle said we couldn't let it happen under any circumstances."

My agony echoed into dead space. If Azirak heard, it was choosing to ignore it. The thought of it alone was enough to kill me. The idea of her with the demon. My hands running over her body under the monster's control. Hands that had spilled so much blood taking what I could never have…

"I want to know," Sam said, squaring her shoulders. "What happens if blood is spilled?"

"We are trapped," Azirak replied. It laid my hands on either side of Sam's neck. The quickened throbbing of her pulse was like a jackhammer beneath my touch. Azirak shivered internally, and after a moment, ran my hands downward. Over her shoulders, over both arms, finally letting them rest on either side of her hips. "The army of one thousand—five hundred of mine. Five hundred of his. Zenak's. Demons. Forced to live in human bodies. We are little more than dogs on leashes. What you humans refer to as neutered."

The demon stepped back and sat in the chair across from the bed.

"Eons ago, there was a great war. A century of battle that soaked our land with the blood of soldiers. Lucifer, having had enough of our games, banished the demons from hell. Zenak and I were punished more harshly. The instigators of it all, we were trapped in limbo. Not here. Not there. And then the Tainted came along. Born with a blemish on their soul, it created an opening. A doorway that we might pass through. It was a way for us to walk in the mortal realm as our brothers did."

"The other demons, you mean?"

It nodded. In an instant, it had my shirt over my head and on the floor at our feet. "As with most things in nature, there was a loophole to our punishment. An opportunity to gain back the power and standing that we'd lost. To be truly free again." The demon sighed. It was watching Sam hungrily. "Come here," it commanded.

She hesitated, but stood and crossed the room, stopping in front of the chair.

Azirak studied the planes of her face and the way the lines of her shirt hugged her curves. It listened to the sound of her breath, moving through her lungs at a slightly elevated pace and matching the beat of her heart. I felt the demon's desire. It was like standing in the middle of an inferno, burning with no hope of rescue. The thing wanted Sam. Images flashed before my eyes. Sam, naked and writhing beneath it on the floor. Calling out *its* name and begging for more.

"You asked what would happen if blood was spilled. You must first know that it isn't just any blood. It must be royal blood. If that blood is spilled, then hell will happen upon this earth," it said.

"What—"

"Enough," it snapped. "Touch me." Grabbing her hand, it held it up to my bare chest.

Sam's stayed like that for a moment, before pressing down harder and scraping her nails downward.

Azirak threw back my head and let out a moan. So did

I. There had never been anything like it. The pleasure. The pain. She wasn't gentle. The scratches left deep red trails, one even breaking the skin. A thousand razor-sharp needles mixed with alluring scent. Sam. Lust. It was the most erotic fucking thing ever.

When she came to the waist of my jeans, she undid the button and yanked down the zipper. Hard. Blood thundered in my ears. I didn't know how the demon was doing it. Staying so still. I'd have attacked her by now. Thrown her down and torn off every scrap of clothing on her body. Not Azirak. It retained control, standing statue-still as Sam slipped her hand into my jeans.

She cupped me, working her hand and squeezing lightly. Azirak gasped, and when Sam's fingers moved to the waistband of my underwear, fingers slipping inside, the atmosphere in the room changed. It darkened. Something shattered, and a floodgate opened. In that moment, all I wanted was to take her. Any way I could. Every way I could.

The demon lifted her off the ground and charged the bed, pinning her beneath my body. Its mouth was on hers, ravaging, while my fingers tugged—no, pulled—at her hair. It ground itself against her, and the noises she made, soft moans and surprised whimpers, drove us both close to the edge.

"I understand now," it whispered, pulling back, hoarse and short of breath. "The allure you hold for him. He wants you. As do I."

Sam sat up, her breath ragged, the expression on her face sad. "I want him, too. But only him."

Just when I thought it would tear her jeans off and finally in the most fucked-up way possible give me what I'd waited so long for, Azirak was off the bed and across the room. A new feeling filled me, coming from the demon and bleeding into the room. Blue. Sadness. The rejection it felt was stifling, choking out the air, and I couldn't breathe. When the reality of it hit me, I was stunned. I loved Sam. I'd loved her my entire life. But now, I wasn't the only one. Azirak loved her, too. I didn't know when it happened, or how, but I knew it just as I knew my own name. Azirak was in love with Sam. It wouldn't feed from her.

It bent to retrieve my shirt from the floor. "I am sorry. There is no him. There is no me. There is only us. You will both need to accept this."

My feet, still under the demon's command, carried us from the room and onto the street.

Chapter Thirty

Sam

I paced the hotel room for the six hundredth time. This was becoming an annoying habit. Back and forth between the cheap faux wooden desk and someone's sick idea of art—a horrible painting of a countryside pasture. Jax had been gone awhile and I knew I shouldn't worry—he was a demon for crap's sake—but I did. The way Azirak left concerned me. I'd made a deal with it. Information in exchange for… For what? Would I really have gone through with it? Screwed a *demon*? It gave a twisted new definition to the phrase "anything for love."

I sank onto the bed, too tired to keep moving. Sleep hadn't been something I'd gotten much of in the last few days. Since the dreams started, I'd been avoiding it. Coffee, caffeine pills. Whatever I could do to stay awake. Unfortunately, it was all about to catch up and the timing couldn't possibly be worse.

Moving. I needed to keep moving. That way, I couldn't nod off. I jumped from the bed and resumed pacing. No nightmare land, then no sleepwalking into the arms of the enemy. But with each step, resolve crumbled a little more. Grabbing the TV remote, I flipped it on and began channel surfing. Unfortunately, there were only two. Old game shows and infomercials. Both would have the opposite effect I was after.

Mashing the off button, I tossed the remote across the room and ran both hands through my hair. Just a few minutes. I wouldn't sleep. Just lie down and keep both eyes open.

No. Bad idea. My eyes fell to the chair on the other side of the room. Less comfortable than the bed. I made a beeline for the tacky piece of furniture, settling in and tucking both feet up. "Count sheep," I said to myself. "One, two, three…" No. Something loud. "Crickets. Crickets are annoying…"

Twelve seconds and I was out of the chair and moving again. Sitting still was no good. "Four, five, six…" With each step came a new number, and each new number brought me one step closer to oblivion. By the time the door opened and Jax walked in, I was ready to drop.

He was him again. The demon was gone, Jax's beautiful stormy eyes peeking back from beneath a mop of dark, unruly hair. He stepped into the room and closed the door behind him, watching me with a puzzled expression.

"I'm exhausted. If I sit—or stand—still, my eyes just close."

Still, he said nothing.

"I'm sorry," I said, shaking my head. Apologizing was stupid since none of this was my fault; still, I couldn't help it. "I didn't want to worry you. It's been a while." Because that's what he looked like right now. Worried. "So, did you get what you needed?"

He looked better than when he'd left. His color was closer to normal and he didn't seem as tense. Before, each and every movement was jerky and stiff. Even his voice had been different. Edgy and clipped.

He shook his head. No.

He hadn't gotten what he needed. For some reason, a rush of heat hit me.

Jax watched me. I wished I could see emotions like he could. At least then maybe I'd have some idea about what was going on inside that head of his. His gaze was unflinching and raw. Like he was holding something monumental back.

I fell back onto the bed. "I can't just sit here. I'm going to pass out."

Still, nothing.

He took a step toward me, then stopped and closed his eyes. When he opened them, they were black. "If I were to tell you the only way you could have him is to take me, what would you say?"

I swallowed. "I'd say…" What? What would I say? I wanted him, but could I do it? Knowing…

I stood as he came another step closer. My heart kicked into overdrive.

"I am a part of him. One cannot exist without the other. If you are with him, then you are with me. This is the only way. Does this revolt you?"

I wasn't revolted. Not by Jax. And the demon was right. Azirak was as much a part of Jax as his love of swiss cheese and Belushi movies. As his strong arms and unbelievably sexy grin. As his compassion and fiercely protective nature. "There is no part of Jax that I don't want," I said defiantly. "I want him. *All of him*."

Azirak growled and closed the distance. His lips came to my mouth. The kiss was fierce. Animalistic. It stole my breath and fanned the flame that had been building from the moment I'd seen him at the diner. His fingers dug into my flesh as he ran them roughly up my neck and tangled them in my hair. With a sharp flick of his wrist, he yanked my head to the right, exposing my neck. A spike of pain came and went as his teeth grazed the skin and I let out a whimper, arching up off the mattress and closer to him.

He laughed. Dark. Dangerous. Deadly.

Demonic.

This was what I needed. Wrapping my legs around his waist, I kissed him back as though life, *survival*, depended on it. Every night I'd dreamed of him. Every morning I woke thinking of him. All the things I'd wanted to share with him over the years. I lifted my head to reclaim his lips, pouring it all into the kiss. A kiss meant for Jax.

He moaned, a feral noise low in his throat, and lifted me from the mattress. His hands gripped my backside, palming and kneading the flesh, and just when I was about to cry out, we were moving. There was a breeze, my hair fluttering all around, then something hard and solid was at my back. Azirak crushed me between Jax's hard body and the wall. His lips came to mine again, with bruising force, and he moaned words I didn't understand into my mouth. When he was finished, he captured my top lip between his teeth and pulled, teasing the tip of it with his tongue. I bucked against him, the sensation of it shattering.

His hands were everywhere all at once. On either side of my face. Sliding greedily down my neck and torso. Over my hips. I never imagined feeling anything as potent as his raw, passionate need. No matter what he grabbed, he couldn't seem to get enough. Jax's blunt fingernails scraped across skin, leaving electric prickles in their wake. One part pain and five parts ecstasy.

"Oh my God," I gasped.

He responded by yanking my body away from the wall and shoving me onto the bed. I sucked in a breath as he stood over me, pulling Jax's black T-shirt over his head and letting it fall to the floor. Four angry-looking scratches from the base of his neck to his navel stared back. "You enjoy looking at this body?

I nodded, mouth dry.

"It enjoys looking at you, as well." He leaned in, face stopping inches away. "Take off your shirt and hand it to me."

I obeyed, and with slightly shaking hands, shrugged out of the shirt and handed it over. He was a blur as he moved, grabbing both wrists and binding them tight. The only move-ment I was capable of was a slight wiggle of fingers.

"I liked the way you looked with the bindings on your wrists."

"The handcuffs," I said, voice barely a whisper. The memory of being at Jax's mercy made the flame burn even hotter.

"Do not fear. No harm will come — "

Too much talking. I spun around and silenced him with another kiss.

"Fuck," he said with a sigh, and pulled away. His eyes

had changed. Now, instead of black, they were gray. Jax ran a hand across my cheek, sliding it up and threading it through my hair. "Sammy, I—" With a shudder, his eyes changed again, black, and an animal-like roar spilled from his lips.

I was off the bed and crushed in his arms. Four steps and my backside hit the dresser. Something crashed to the ground and shattered. The lamp. He kicked it aside as his lips trailed a savage line down my neck and to my breasts.

"I know you're in there," I said, throwing my head back as his teeth grazed the skin through my bra.

At the sound of my voice, he shuddered, muscles twitching, and in a single, smooth maneuver, had me on the floor, the buttons of my jeans undone and the denim roughly shoved down around my hips. The cool air nipped at my skin as eager fingers dug into bare flesh.

I gasped and leaned sideways, trying to shake the jeans off, but he bore down, eyes black as night. "Leave them."

Fine by me.

The jeans were forgotten as his lips worked their way down my stomach, and...then nothing. He pulled away, face hovering above mine, one eye now black, the other gray. "Sammy... I don't know if I—I fed on another demon but..." He hesitated, but his resolve was obviously just as weak as mine. He brought a hand to my face, trailing a finger down the side to my neck, and frustratingly slow, between my breasts. "I want this, but it's here. It's here and I can't ask you to—"

Without a word, I lifted my hips to meet his. The contact was dizzying. Electric and powerful. He inhaled sharply, muscles tightening, as the spark of need behind his gray eye exploded into an all-out inferno. We'd crossed the point of no return.

I guided his hand lower. "You should probably stop talking."

His lips met mine again, and this time, the fire nearly broke me. A small sigh escaped my lips as his hand trailed across my belly and traced its way downward until he came to my center. I gasped as his fingers worked, stroking a feathery line back and forth until I couldn't stand it anymore. I moaned, pushing up to increase the friction, and Jax chuckled. The sound alone almost sent me over the top. Dark and filled with the promise of something explosive.

Not Jax. Azirak. There was a subtle difference. I couldn't quite put my finger on it.

For a moment the pressure of his fingers disappeared, and I was about to protest, but they returned, sliding beneath the elastic of my underwear. As he teased me apart, he whispered, "Is this what you want? Does this please you?"

I gasped again. The response was answer enough. The world exploded as he slipped his fingers inside, rocking them back and forth and sending the world shooting to the stars. No one had ever touched me there. I'd had sex, but this— no one had ever done this. I never imagined... *Holy shit!* I bit down on my bottom lip, sure I'd scream out as his pace increased. And I would have, too, if he hadn't brought his mouth to mine. The kiss was all-consuming. Raw and possessive. I belonged to the man. I belonged to the demon.

"You feel so fucking good under me," he whispered against my lips as the movement of his fingers slowed, then disappeared. "So right."

"...Jax?"

He was still staring, but his eyes had changed. Gray.

Beautiful, amazing, and *all gray*. "Yeah, Sammy?"

The sound of his voice against the silence was like nails scraping down my back. Sharp and welcome. Like liquid heat. I didn't know where it came from, but I suddenly had to know. "I need to know... Did you mean what you said? That you loved—"

A sound filled the air. A mix between a growl and a laugh. Jax dove forward and pinned me to the floor with his body, tongue darting in to open my mouth and lips moving furiously. He swung his leg over so he was above me, trailing scorching kisses along my jaw.

"Love you?" he whispered at my ear. Breath warm and voice a deep, velvety whisper. "I fucking *breathe* you. Your face, your laugh, the way you chew at your bottom lip... All of it. *All of you.* Any light you think you see in me is an echo of you."

My heart nearly exploded.

"This," he breathed as he worked his way down my neck, "doesn't change anything. I'm still leaving." He moved back to my mouth, teasing my lips apart with the tip of his tongue. Pulling away for a single, agonizing second, he said, "But yeah, *I love you.* Always have."

"Can we do this?" The heat between us had reached critical mass, but the thought of him in agonizing pain was enough to give me pause.

"It's both of us, Sammy," he said with a growl. "Azirak is here and in control, but its letting me—"

Good enough for me. I kissed him hard.

In a graceful swipe, my underwear was off, as was his, and the feel of him, hot as the sun and hard as stone, pressed up against my skin—and then suddenly with a growl, inside.

He moved slowly at first, the rhythm sending glorious tingles through my body. He kissed me, never breaking contact. Lips. Neck. The curve of my breast. He was everywhere and I was riding a wave of pure ecstasy.

His strokes quickened as he nibbled at the corner of my ear. "There's only ever been you, Sammy," he panted, warm breath caressing my neck. I moved with him, finding the pace that would send us over the edge. Fingers clutching. Muscles tightening. Breathing ragged. Waves of intensity like nothing I'd ever felt before.

One last push and we both slipped over. Wildfires. Earthquakes. Tsunamis. All the shocking forces behind nature had nothing on this. This was perfect. This was right.

This was mine.

They were mine.

Chapter Thirty-One

Jax

I bit down on the inside of my cheek hard enough to taste blood. It was the only thing stopping the roar of pain that threatened to rip me in half. It started building moments after I kissed her, driving me closer and closer to the edge of insanity. Sam's breathing was soft and even, her body like an inferno beside me. More than anything, I wanted to stay in that bed, her wrapped in my arms, and forget the outside world existed.

Forget the demon existed.

"How bad is it?" she whispered.

I flinched at the sound of her voice. God. She knew me so fucking well. I thought about lying, but decided it would never work. She'd see right through it. Always did. Forcing a chuckle, I said, "How do you think it'd feel to have your lungs yanked out through your nose?" I threw off the covers.

Azirak was bouncing images again. It wanted to stay here with Sam, yet after being with her, it *needed* to feed again. The dizzying back-and-forth—blood and agony alternating with flashes of Sam—made everything spin.

She rolled over. "I'm thinking pretty unpleasant."

God. She was so fucking beautiful. Even with the slight frown tugging the corners of her lips down. A miracle. She was a miracle. One that loved me despite the fact that I'd shared her with a monster.

This wouldn't work.

"I—I think I understand how it works now. With us." I stumbled away from the bed, grabbing clothes along the way. Pants. Shirt. One boot. Through gritted teeth, I continued. "Being around you is hard, but not impossible. I think I can take little bits of emotion here and there to keep Azirak under control. A nip of anger or a shot of fear, and it won't do any damage. But when I get what I want—you, all of you—I'm flash-starving the demon. The good emotion just sucks the energy right out of us. Having it there while we—it made things…" God. This was so fucking hard. "Easier. We couldn't have… If I didn't let…"

"Jax, it's okay." Sam sat up, the thin, scratchy hotel sheet wrapped tight around her chest. "So you're saying it's like burning too many calories. When you're…happy?"

I turned away and pulled on the other boot, fingers shaking as I knotted the laces to keep them in place. Actual ties were impossible. Anything requiring too much coordination or focus just wasn't going to happen right now. "You're the ultimate demon diet wrapped up in a sexy package. It's—" A spasm went through me, stealing all the air. I needed to get out of there. Sam didn't need to see this, and I certainly didn't want her with me if Azirak took control again. The memory of the thing's excitement, and then pleasure, while we were with Sam killed me. "I need to feed it."

Sam adjusted the sheet and nodded, flashing a heart-stopping smile. How had I stayed away for so long? More importantly, how the fuck was I going to leave? Being around her again only reminded me how perfectly we fit.

Another spasm. Cutting it too close. Leaving her alone was risky, but it would be fast and I wouldn't go far. With a nod, I was out the door.

It took longer than I'd wanted, but I was able to hunt down a demon. I stumbled upon it just as I was about to give up and head in the direction of the club. That part of town was where all the drug deals went down. It'd be easy to find a lowlife or two to pick off. But the demon was preferable.

Though not as strong as the one earlier, it calmed Azirak to the point where the near-blinding tension in my muscles eased, and the pain in my skull dulled to a barely there throb. And bonus? It came with zero guilt and a little extra kick. This was something I could get used to. Taking demons instead of kicking the shit out of humans. Double the energy and ten times less guilt. If I'd known offing them would afford him such a jolt, I would have been doing it all along.

By the time I made it back to the hotel with a new shirt for Sam, I wasn't any closer to knowing what to do about the link. Sam's life was tied to Chase's, not to mention the whole hell-on-earth thing Azirak mentioned. I wasn't clear on exactly what it meant, but it couldn't be good. For anyone.

I balanced the coffees I'd picked up from Musso's in one hand, the shirt draped over my shoulder, and managed to unlock the door with the other without dropping anything. The bed was empty, the comforter tangled at the foot and the sheet piled on the floor. I set the coffee down. "Sammy?"

No answer.

There was a stillness in the room that left me cold. I tore across the floor and kicked open the door to the bathroom. It bounced twice, the rattle echoing off the tile, before stopping to reveal an empty room.

Air. Maybe she went out to get some air. I rushed the door and stepped out into the sunlight. There was no one as far as the eye could see. Rick's car was parked where I'd left it, the keys still heavy in my pocket. There was a noise on the other side of the room. The nightstand. My cell.

I nearly tripped over my own two feet to get to it. "Sammy?"

The person on the other end laughed. "Not exactly."

Azirak rumbled. "Chase, I swear, if you touch her I'll rip your limbs off one by one and feed them to you."

Another laugh. The same cocky snicker I'd heard my entire life. "Graphic. You kiss my girl with that mouth?"

Azirak raged and words were impossible. All that came out was a low, feral growl. If my fingers squeezed any tighter, the cell would be toast.

"You'll need to come down to Harlow General."

"The hospital?" My heart skipped a beat. I fell back into the chair, Azirak feeding me a thousand horrible scenarios in graphic detail. "Why? What did you do?"

"Just come down, Jax. Now."

The line went dead.

I made it in record time. Chase hadn't been specific, so I had no idea where in the hospital they were, but the best guess was the ER. As it turned out, I was right.

"Don't," Chase said, standing. He and Sam were seated in the chairs right outside the emergency room waiting area. Whatever the reason was for dragging me here, Sam seemed fine. "Before you attack me or make a huge scene, consider this. All it will take is one word from me and she'll do something nasty. Maybe to herself. Maybe to someone else. You're going to need to play this chill, brother."

Sam's eyes were wide and her lips pressed in a thin line. She sat without a sound and avoided eye contact with anyone who passed. He'd ordered her to be silent. That was the only way she wouldn't be kicking up trouble.

"Why are we here?" I asked. The anger Azirak was throwing off had me seeing double. Every inch of me hummed with the need to tear Chase apart.

"The doctors were wrong about the cancer. They underestimated the spread of the disease."

At first his words didn't make sense. Doctors? Cancer? But when understanding came, it was followed closely by an icy wave of panic and fear. No. Not now. I couldn't do this now.

Chase turned and quirked a finger at Sam, who stood and followed him down the hall without objection. Over his shoulder, he said, "Better hurry, Jax. There's not much time left to say good-bye."

I followed them down the halls and around corners,

numb. My uncle, much like Sam, was my lifeline to reality. I couldn't count the times I'd sat on the floor in some dump, curled tight and hating myself, while the eldest Flynn talked me through the guilt from hundreds of miles away. It was during those calls that I found the strength not to follow our ancestors' footsteps. Rick, along with Sam's memory, had been the rope that kept me from the hole.

When we rounded the last corner and Chase pulled back the curtain that hung around the last bed at the end of the long row, I felt sick. Rick lay with his eyes closed, surrounded by tubes and wires. There was a machine to track his heartbeat to the right, and something else that let out a soft beep every few seconds to the left.

"Rick?" Chase said, stepping up to the bed. Sam followed. "We're here, man."

I moved closer, torn between watching my uncle slip from this world, and watching Chase and Sam.

His eyes fluttered open, and despite the situation, the elder Flynn smiled. "My boys. I'm so glad you made it."

I took my uncle's hand. His skin was so cold. Like he was already gone. "We're here, Rick."

Rick sighed and closed his eyes for a moment. When he opened them, he was smiling again. "I was hoping to stick around for a while longer, but doesn't look like that's going to happen."

"Don't say that," Chase said, taking his other hand. I was glad our uncle would never find out the truth. It would have destroyed him.

Rick squeezed both our hands and pulled us together. He placed one over the other with mine in between, as a series of body-racking coughs shook him. When he managed to catch his breath, he said, "I'm so sorry."

"You have nothing to be sorry about," I said.

But Rick didn't seem to hear. "I put it off for so long," he continued. "And now I'll never have time to make it up to you—but you have to know the truth."

"Shh," Chase said. "Whatever it is can wait."

Rick shook his head. The movement cost him. It took several moments, wheezing and coughing, for him to catch him breath. "I thought if I kept you apart, I could change things. That I could keep one of you from destroying the other. History, though… History has a way of repeating itself, doesn't it?" He turned his head and stared at Sam.

She paled. "Rick, what are you—"

"They're born. Over and over again. Once every few generations, they find their way into a Tainted—but Tainted are rare. It takes a special kind of monster to leave a stain on his entire line. One or the other has come and gone through-out the generations of our family, but never both. Never at the same time. And now, with them both here…"

My heart thundered until I could barely hear what he was saying. "Rick, you're not making any sense."

"The intense anger you felt toward Chase growing up, the itch to hurt him—it was never your fault, Jax. It was the demon. One of two clan leaders trapped in mortal bodies. Demon royals." Rick's head rolled to the left, so that he was looking at Chase. "You were always better at controlling it, weren't you? I knew, though. I always knew."

Chase was pale. He was shaking his head and swiping the back of his hand across his eyes.

"You're good boys. Strong. You can beat this. You have to beat—have to beat this."

"We will," my brother said, voice cracking. He was squeezing our uncle's hand so hard that his knuckles had gone white. "We will. Together. All three of us."

I wanted to agree. We could do it. Together. But the words wouldn't come. This was it. The end of something and the beginning of another. Rick had always been the glue that held us together. Death wasn't just stealing the only father I'd ever known, it was stealing my entire family.

"No. For the sake of the world, you have to walk out that door and never, ever see each other again."

"Rick—"

Rick grew agitated, pulling at the sheets and shaking his head. "If you spill each other's blood, it will open the gates... Hell..."

His chest rose and fell for a moment, before falling still.

It was over. Rick Flynn was gone.

Chapter Thirty-Two

Sam

I wanted to scream. Of course, that was impossible. As we'd entered the hospital, Chase commanded me not to speak. I didn't get the chance to tell Rick how much I loved him. Now, standing over his bed with the Flynn boys on either side, the darkest parts of me were glad he was gone. He'd be spared whatever horrible things came next.

"Well, that's that then," Chase whispered, dragging his hand from beneath Jax's. He flinched when Rick's fingers slipped from his and fell still on the stark white sheets. There were tears in his eyes, but his expression had reverted to cold indifference. "You take care of things here. I'm going to take our girl here for a little ride. Obviously I have some thinking to do." He grabbed my arm and started toward the door, but Jax was in front of us in an instant. The expression on his face terrified me, while at the same time, sent a shiver of excitement shooting across my skin.

"Definitely not going to happen."

Chase growled and adjusted his hold. If he squeezed any tighter, he'd break the skin. I could almost feel the anger coming off him. Furious, he spat, "Are you that disrespectful that you'd fight with me over Rick's still-warm corpse?"

Jax cringed at his brother's words, then stiffened. There was a spark of something dangerous in his eyes and before I could blink, his hand shot out, fingers wrapping around Chase's neck. "Sam isn't leaving here with you. Let her go."

Chase stiffened. "Don't. Fucking. Push. Me. Not now..."

Jax stayed where he was.

"Kill me, then... Wait. You can't, can you? Hell on earth. Wouldn't want that, now, would we?"

Jax, without hesitation, pushed forward and slammed into his brother, hands tightening around his neck. The three of us flew backward, crashing into the tiled wall as Chase's airway closed off. How did I know?

Because *I* couldn't breathe.

I groped at the invisible hands around my neck for a moment before the room began to water around the edges. Jax had one hell of a grip. Swaying, I grabbed the edge of a metal cart, an echoing clatter filling the room as I fell, struggling for air.

Jax, momentarily pulled from his homicidal haze, whirled around as his brother's laugh filled the room. "Guess you forgot about that, too, huh? Seems to me like you're well and truly fucked, brother."

He stumbled away from Chase, horrified, and blessed air came rushing back. Jax took a step toward me, but Chase cleared his throat and waggled a finger. "Don't even think about it."

But Jax ignored him, grabbing my hand, helping me stand. "Let's go," he said, threading his fingers through mine.

I felt his warm skin, as well as a desperate desire to go with him, but my limbs wouldn't respond. No matter how hard I tried to kick my feet into motion, it wouldn't happen.

Chase laughed again, and a sliver of silver glinted against the light. A moment later a sharp sting bloomed at the hollow of my throat. The blade was pressed against his neck, the edge cutting into the skin ever so slightly. Just enough of a nip to cause a small trickle of blood to run down my neck.

"Stop!" Jax snapped. He threw both hands into the air and stumbled away.

Chase sighed. He rocked the blade back and forth, gently, each movement deepening the wound. It itched and stung. "Feel free to chime in with your thoughts."

"It's okay," I said, thrilled at the sound of my own voice. "It's just a scratch."

The look in Jax's eyes said he wasn't buying it, but instead of arguing, he asked, "Are you okay? He hurt you?"

"I'm okay." Overall it was true. Chase hadn't hurt me except for the cut, and really, it was just a scratch. A warning. He'd forced me to kiss him in the car before we came in. It was short-lived, though. He could command me to do whatever he wanted with my body, but he couldn't force the feelings he wanted to feed on. Lust. Now that I knew what he was—what he'd done—there was no chance of feeling anything but disgust for him.

Chase nodded and gestured toward the door. "Now that we've got that all cleared up, let's move forward, 'kay?"

"What is it you want?" Jax asked, a subtle quake in his

voice. I'd heard it once before, right before Azirak took over at my apartment.

"The same thing you want. My brother dead."

There was obviously a whole different side of Chase that I didn't know about, but what about the one I did? That had to still be there, right? He'd done horrible things, but he was still in there. That was obvious by the way he cried for Rick. "You don't want to kill Jax any more than he wants to kill you. There's a way around this. There has to be. Think about it. Hell on earth? Doesn't sound like a party."

His face twisted, a mask of anger and resentment, as he glared at me. "You don't think I tried? I embraced my demon, trying for years to keep it happy. To keep it away from you." He flicked a finger in Jax's direction. "Both of you."

Jax batted his hand away. "Don't fucking use me as an excuse for what you've done."

"Why? You're no better than me! How much blood have you spilled to quiet the thing inside *your* head?"

Jax didn't answer. He was staring at the door. Several nurses passed in the hall, one stopping to peer through the window. She nodded, giving a sad smile, and kept going.

"The college was my favorite place to feed," Chase continued, backing toward the door. He positioned himself in front of the glass so they couldn't see inside the room. "We were waiting for her that night. Saw her leave the party, and she looked so good. *Smelled* so good... We attacked her. The plan was to draw you out. To make you come running home—but you didn't. You were there that night and swooped in to save the day, but like always, you ran away with your dick in your hand."

"I stayed away to keep her safe," Jax growled.

Chase laughed. "I waited, sure you'd come home for her, but when you never showed, we had to change direction. I had one of my demons follow you, killing girls that looked like her wherever you went. That would bring you running for sure." He winked. "Guess I gave you too much credit. It took you forever to figure it out. Then Rick took a turn for the worse and you ended up back here anyway. I knew you'd leave the moment you saw me. The one way to keep you here long enough to end your life would be to put her in danger again right out in the open where no one could miss it. While you were waltzing into McCarthy's to kick my ass, one of my demons was cutting her brakes. I knew you'd save her, and there would be no way for you to ignore it."

"So, the plan was to draw me back home and what, kill me? Why go through all the trouble? Why not just find me yourself and do the deed?"

"A compromise I made with Zenak. I wanted you to have the chance to see them again. Once more. I hated the thought of you dying out there, and Rick and Sam never knowing what happened. I did you a favor. I did *her* a favor."

"A favor? You made her a fucking slave." Jax countered, taking a menacing step forward.

"I wasn't thrilled when I found out Zenak had linked to her, but there was nothing I could do about it. Damage was done."

"You could have done something to stop it."

"I told you, I embraced my demon a long time ago. *I* didn't want to hurt her, but we're a team. We coexist and that means sometimes sacrifices have to be made. I understand now that only one of us can survive. Zenak wants its power back, and for that to happen, you need to die. The others need to be free."

"So this is the part where you tell me you're going to kill me?"

"Almost," Chase said. The expression on his face almost looked regretful. "But regardless of what you think and how my demon feels, I love you, and I loved Rick. It's waited a long time. You'll have a day to get your affairs in order. Then we'll finish this."

"And Sam?"

"Since I have no plans on dying, she'll remain linked to me. Providing you follow through, I won't feed from her again. She'll remain alive."

"Alive and *free*?" Jax pressed, and Chase frowned.

"As free as possible. You worry about keeping up your end of things and I'll do my best to make sure she's safe and comfortable."

Jax squared his shoulders. "And what exactly is *my end of things*?"

I couldn't believe we were standing here having this discussion. Not that I saw an alternative at the moment, but still, it was surreal. We were discussing my life like it was something to be bargained for.

"We bury Rick, then you surrender yourself to me at a place of my choosing. You die with honor and Sam is free to live out her natural life."

"And let's say I don't?"

The thing inside Chase had swallowed his humanity. It'd turned him into a monster in the truest form and the worst part was, he'd let it happen. Unlike Jax who fought his nature every day, he'd rolled over and given in. "I'll leave you with this—there are so many things worse than death my demon could do to her. Things our simple human brains can't even imagine. I hate to have to say this out loud, but I need you to understand there's no room for compromise here. Not anymore."

Jax's face paled as his brother pulled me from the room. His lips moved in silence.

"I'll fix this."

Chapter Thirty-Three

Jax

Time passed in a haze as we fast-tracked the arrangements for Rick's funeral. Kelly was a huge help despite her dislike of me. No doubt she'd revert to her bitchy self the moment this was over, but for now, the reprieve was welcomed.

She let slip that Sam was out of town for a few days and would return for the funeral, but I knew the truth. Sam was with Chase. A hostage. Subject to God knew what. Each time it crossed my mind—which was almost every moment of the day—Azirak flashed images of destruction. Lapses in self-control had been the death of several pieces of Rick's furniture, fostered multiple holes in the walls, and caused the loss of nearly every dish in the house.

No matter how violent the emotion was I fed it, Azirak stayed restless, sending random images that ranged from childhood flashbacks, to Sam's face surrounded by swirls of color. Being with Sam essentially starved the demon and caused us both pain, yet we wanted her. Needed her. For the first time, the demon took on the role of ally, not enemy.

I'd dressed for the funeral, the silence in the house nearly as crushing as the weight settling over my heart. I wasn't ready for good-bye. Not to Sam. And not to Rick.

The wind kicked up, the chilly November breeze biting at bare flesh. I stood with the small group of people beside Rick's open grave, wearing one of his black suits. On my feet were my everyday shitkickers, knowing Rick would forgive it. He'd hated dress shoes. This was my way of paying tribute.

Sam stood on my right side, between Chase and me. Azirak smelled the pain and fear radiating from her in steady waves, taking small, negligible amounts as I slipped my hand into hers. As expected, her fingers didn't move, but her colors evened out. The ribbons around her head got just a little less gray.

There were only a few other faces in the crowd I knew. Kelly sat in the front row, on the end. The dark glasses she wore might hide her swollen eyes, but the subtle shaking of her shoulders as the deep blue lingered, and the way she fisted the tissue until her knuckles paled, made me regret the years of animosity.

There were others, too. Several of the guys from Rick's bowling league. Chip Mansen, an old friend from his construction days. Even Tim Henson from the post office.

The priest droned on and on about the how he was a pillar of the community and how charitable Rick Flynn was and how sorely he would be missed. A few minutes into the speech, I tuned him out. I'd made peace with his passing. This was fluff to soothe the masses. Dead was dead. It didn't matter what Rick had done—or hadn't done—in life. He wouldn't care that his body had been laid to rest under the shade of a large dogwood tree. The mahogany casket with deep-blue silk lining. The sharp suit. They were all tools to take the sting away from the living.

The priest finished and one by one, people paid their last respects. Kelly kissed Sam's cheek, then leaned in close to hug Chase. Before she walked away, she wrapped her arms around me, as well.

"He was a good man," Chase said once we were alone. My brother's eyes met mine and I was struck by the regret he saw there. "I know you hate me for this, Jax, and that's fine. In fact, it's better than fine. It's easy. You and me, we never got a choice in all this. We were born into this world as pawns. Just all there is to it."

"Not interested in bullshitting with you. What's next?"

Chase sighed. "Meet me at that place we used to go to as kids. Two hours. I can't—I don't want to put this off any more."

He was referring to the fort we'd built in the acreage behind Rick's house when we were younger. Nothing more than a clearing in the thick of a bunch of trees surrounded by several car-sized boulders, the three of us had played there as children. I hadn't been back to it since the night I'd left. It's where Sam and I had first kissed. The same place everything had started to unravel.

I nodded, not trusting myself to speak, and watched as Chase led Sam away. She looked back once, and powerful emotions hit me hard. Fear, yes, but also love. She didn't blame me for any of this.

And that hurt almost as much as losing Rick.

I had no intention of being a sacrificial lamb. For starters, the demon would never allow it. If push came to shove, Azirak would take over and fight back. If that happened, it might kill Chase—and that would kill Sam. Not an option. I needed a plan to ensure we both survived and that the link between Chase and Sam was dampened. My only hope was Sadie Gray. With just over an hour left, I stood on her doorstep, ready to offer the world on a silver fucking platter if there was any way to save the girl I loved.

"Well, well, well. Can't say I'm surprised," Sadie said with a wink. This time she was wearing skintight leather pants and a bustier that left little to the imagination. Her hair, like before, hung wild, and smelled of jasmine. She stepped aside and motioned for me to come inside. "Most men can't stay away."

"I could have," I said, meeting her gaze.

Sadie wasn't a woman who intimidated easily. "That so?" She shrugged and said, "Yet here you are. I'm still not parting with my midnight stone for less than the agreed-up-on price, if that's what you're after."

"Do you remember the girl I was here with last time? Sam?"

She rolled her eyes and faked a yawn. "How could I forget? Little Miss Stick-Up-the-Ass?"

Heckle told me there was no way to fix this, but I had to try anyway. "She's tied to a demon. A Tainted, like me. I need to break the link."

The sound of her laughter was a cross between delicate

chimes and a razor scraping metal. "Sorry, baby. Unless the demon has an attack of conscience and lets her go, or you off the big bad, which I'm sure you know offs the linked, Suzy Q is as good as a corpse."

"Fine. Then help me dampen it. Is that possible?"

She was quiet for a moment. "Hmm. There might be… First, tell me why you're so willing to save this girl."

It seemed like a perfectly normal question but I could tell by the look in her eyes that it was anything but. "Why does that matter to you?"

"Call it curiosity." She laughed. "Well, that and a bit of good old-fashioned jealousy. I made my interest in you quite clear, yet you prefer a simple, boring human. I'm dying to know what the appeal is."

"I love her," I said simply. Out loud the words sounded right. They were the natural conclusion to a lifetime of moments that defined who I was beneath the monster.

"But love is so fleeting," Sadie said. "And for someone like you, it's a bit dangerous, no?"

"Just because I love her doesn't mean I can be with her. But just because I can't be with her doesn't mean I'm willing to let her die."

"So you would sacrifice a part of yourself—because that's what my price is—for someone you can never have?"

Someone you can never have…

That's what Sam was. A distant star so far from my reach that it hurt to even try. I didn't hesitate. "Yes."

Sadie frowned, then snorted. "Blah. I'll never understand you Tainted. Your emotions are all over the place. But at least I can say I've finally seen it all." She held out her hand, fingers unwrapping to reveal a small red stone. "This is a hybrid stone. It's part moonstone and part quartz. It will not break the link—but it will dampen its effects. The demon would require physical contact to control her."

"A stupid rock? That's going to dampen the link?" I growled. "Don't fucking play me, witch."

Sadie rolled her eyes extended her hand a few inches. "Go ahead. Touch it."

I ran a finger across the outer edge of the stone still in Sadie's hand. A jolt like electricity crackled, sending a rush of warmth into my hand.

Sadie looked smug. "Got some kick to it, right?"

I nodded. "What about injury? Will she still be susceptible to damage done to him?"

"As long as the link is active, yes. There's no way around that. It's the very basis of the bond. The slave is there to endure the pain of the master."

It wasn't ideal, but it would have to do. For now. With luck, it would allow me to get Sam away from Chase. I'd figure out how to deal with the rest later. One step at time. "How does it work?"

"Your human simply has to have this on her person. The stone will do the rest."

I held out my hand.

Sadie laughed and waggled a finger. "You haven't agreed to my terms. They're the same as the first time you came a-knockin'. It's that or nothing."

I didn't like it. There was something she wasn't saying. Nobody would ask for this under the conditions I knew about. Unfortunately, there was no time to debate. I had twenty minutes to meet Chase at the fort, and still had one last stop to make. "Done."

She clapped her hands together, excited. "Wonderful."

"Now give me the stone."

"You feed and link us, then you get the stone."

I advanced and Azirak went wild. "Should I hurt you? Is that how you like it?"

She stepped forward and braced both hands against my chest. They lingered there for a moment before dropping to my belt. "I think I have a more pleasant way for us to do this."

I knocked her hands aside and pushed her away. "The demon prefers pain, plus I'm pretty sure I remember telling you I wasn't interested in what you were giving away."

A spark of annoyance flashed in her eyes. Under different circumstances, she and Chase would get along great. Both deviant, cocky shits who had a problem with the word no. "Your demon can feed off any human emotion except for happiness. That one's reserved solely for the good guys. Obviously each little hell-spawn has its favorites, but the link can be created using any of them. I'm not into pain." She came closer. "Now if you're interested in a little bondage…"

I seized her wrists as she went to reach for the belt again. "I'm not going to fuck you, Sadie."

"Luckily for you, I'm not turned off by your brush-off." She dove forward, crushing her lips to mine. The taste of her left a sick feeling in my gut. Metallic and foul. It was nothing like kissing Sam. Sadie's lips moved furiously, her tongue opening my mouth wider. I wanted nothing more than to pull away, but Azirak wasn't having it. Not when there was a snack being offered so freely.

Her wrists still in my hands, I squeezed hard and let the demon rise to the surface. The demon wasn't as put off as me. It squirmed and writhed, eager to ingest the orange mist rising from her body.

Me? I wanted her pain.

My fingers twitched, crushing her small wrists with bruising force, and she gasped. That, I liked. It was familiar and comfortable, and was all the encouragement the demon needed. The rush washed through me as the demon took in the emotion. The humming sensation of pure bliss as the essence passed from the air and into me. It was sick, but at times like this I understood the thing's need. The feeling never lasted long, but fuck it all if it wasn't amazing while it did.

When I finally pulled away, Sadie was breathing heavy and flushed. She was dazed and her wrists were deep red. There would be bruises there in a few hours. A small part of me felt bad. A bigger part was darkly pleased. She'd forced me to do something I didn't want. Even though there'd been no enjoyment in what had happened and technically we could never be together, I felt like I'd betrayed Sam in some way.

"How do we know it worked?" I asked, putting some distance between us. The sight and smell of her made me sick. Leaning to the left, I spat the taste of her from my mouth.

Sadie didn't seem insulted. She grinned and held out the stone while flexing her free hand. "Oh, baby, trust me. It worked."

Chapter Thirty-Four

Sam

"This isn't what I wanted, Samantha. Not really. I need you to believe me."

I refused to answer. He'd been talking for the last forty minutes, professing his regret and insisting that things had "gotten out of hand."

He knelt in front of me in the dirt. The fact that he didn't seem affected by the cold was annoying. The sun was going down, and flurries dotted the sky. The thin flannel shirt he'd given me from his closet did little to stave off the chill, and my feet were numb. The bridge had washed away in the last big storm, so we'd had to trek through the stream to get across. My socks and shoes were soaked. "I do care about you. I always have. That's never been a lie."

I couldn't hold it in any longer. I'd been giving him the silent treatment for the last few days except for the two times he demanded I speak to him. "Then *why* are you doing this?"

He deflated just a bit and sighed. "This is so much bigger than Jax and me. We got a raw deal. These two demons? Zenak and Azirak? You can't fathom the level of hate they have for each other. We have no choice. If I weren't doing this now, it would be Jax doing it later." His voice got darker, and he stood. "Anyway, you should *thank* me. Once I kill Jax, Zenak and its clan will get their power back and you'll be safe. Another outcome wouldn't end well for you. We're linked, remember? The other faction is hunting you down as we speak."

Anger and betrayal roared in my head. It was raw and ugly and in that instant I'd never hated anyone or anything more than him. "You and Jax have no choice? Do you hear what you're saying? Of course you do. You could *choose* to let me go. Break the link. You could *choose* to leave your brother alone. *Jax* did. He walked away. He felt so much anger toward you that he left everything he knew and loved to keep you safe."

"God," he yelled. "You act like he's a fucking *saint*. His leaving was weakness. He should have killed me that night he was standing over my bed. I knew he was there. Waiting. But he didn't make a move." He kicked a rock at his feet and came at me, gripping both shoulders tight and putting his face in mine. "You're always defending him. Always talking about him like he's a damn god. *I'm* the strong one. *I'm* the one who stayed for you. *Me*."

"Don't you get it?" I screamed. "I don't want you!" Deep breath. "Part of you must know that on some level. That explains the kiss in the diner. We were linked, right?

You had to command me to kiss you. There's no other way I would have ever gone there."

I saw it brewing in his eyes. The violent storm. "Bitch," he spat as his hand snaked out. It caught me across the jaw, rocking my head back. I saw stars for a minute. Beads of color and ribbons of light.

How could this be the same person I'd known my whole life? The guy who taught me how to pay beer pong and aces? The guy who loved animals and volunteered at the children's home on Wednesday nights? His anger scared me. I'd never seen him so riled, and with the demon inside, I didn't know what he might do if he didn't calm down. Impulse control had never been his strong suit.

"Jax could have taken you out at any point. Don't you think taunting him home was risky?"

Chase laughed. He shook his head and kicked at another small stone by my feet. The pebble rolled away, bouncing until it hit a nearby pine tree. "You've known Jax almost as long as I have, Samantha. He's always struggled with what he is. He fought Azirak's hate for me from the first moment it crept into his mind."

"You and this thing belong together. You're both disgusting."

There was a blur of movement and his hand was at my chin, fingers digging hard into skin as his eyes flashed black, then gray again. "Careful, Samantha. My demon just barely tolerates you for my sake. Don't give it an excuse to hurt you."

He held on for a moment before letting go. He paced from one end of the fort to the other. The movement was stiff and jerky. I recognized it from watching Jax. His demon was hungry. "Power, Samantha. Unbelievable power."

He stopped and leaned close, warm breath puffing out across my skin. He skimmed down the side of my face with the tip of his nose, sighing. "Stay with me and we can have it together. I look just like him. I wouldn't even be offended if you pretend."

I leaned in close and gave him a shy smile. He returned it, bringing his lips closer. Nearly touching, I whispered, "You might be his twin, but you look nothing like him. *You're* a monster—inside and out."

He pulled away, anger slowly changing to amusement. A flash of black, and the demon emerged. He continued backing up until he came to medium-sized branch that jutted out from the large pine tree beside him. "Fine. Have it your way. I prefer lust, but I can sustain myself on your agony just as easily." He drew his body back, then slammed forward, ramming his shoulder into the trunk of the tree.

Despite my best efforts, I screamed. I wobbled sideways, sliding from atop the large rock, and crumbled to the ground in a rush of pain. The world went dark for a minute, and when I could breathe again, I looked up. Chase, the demon still in control, was looming above me with a sadistic grin.

"You were never good enough for him," it said with a laugh.

"Fuck you," I spat through the pain. Silence. I wouldn't cry out again. Wouldn't give it the satisfaction.

"I'm the demon. I'm the human. You're not understanding. We're one."

"Aww," I said, forcing a smile. Involuntary tears welled as I swallowed back a painful whimper. "A cute demonic couple."

He hauled me from the ground by a handful of hair. That time I couldn't help it. I screamed. The sound bounced off the mountain and echoed into the valley. "That's more like it," it said, pushing me against one of the trees with enough force to shake some leaves loose.

Bending close, it closed its eyes and inhaled deeply, smiling. "We each have our favorite emotions. Azirak's are rage and pain. Wholly unpleasant. They leave a sweet taste behind. Lust, however, is tart. Like lemons. Refreshing. The pleasures of the flesh are where my interests lie. It's how I *will* feed." Right hand falling to Chase's belt, it slipped the buckle and undid the first button of his jeans.

My heart stuttered, skipping a beat before hammering into hyperdrive. I had to get away. Because the alternative...? *No.* I bent forward, pretending to accept my fate. When the demon laughed, I struck. Kicking off the ground, I brought my right knee up as hard as possible. The connection it made was both satisfying—the bastard screamed in agony—and sickening because I felt it too. He teetered back and I doubled over and stumbled away, gasping for air.

Something latched onto my ankle, and in a rush of dirt and air, I was on the ground and Chase was on my back. "Little bitch," it spat. Now its voice was different. Less human. It grabbed my arms and twisted, pinning them.

"Enough." Jax boomed. I twisted, and in the fading sunlight, he was there. Standing at the mouth of the fort, trench coat flapping in the wind like a superhero's cape. Larger than life, he was a mix of myth and magic made flesh and blood.

I wouldn't let him sacrifice himself.

"I wasn't sure you'd show."

"I'd never leave Sammy to die." Jax stepped over a fallen

tree, into the mouth of the fort, eyes never leaving mine. "Get off of her." The command left no room for argument. "*Now.*"

"Despite her less-than-friendly attitude, I'll keep my word. She'll be safe. I promise." The pressure on my back disappeared, and Chase dragged me up. His voice was normal now. The demon was gone.

"Your word means shit to me," Jax snapped, stopping a few feet from his brother. "I want a minute to say good-bye."

A plan. He had to have a plan. The Jax I knew would never just give up. He'd be smart enough to know that if he died, I would never be free.

Chase shrugged and stepped back. "Don't see what it could hurt. She can't leave, and if you make a move I don't like, I'll plunge a knife right into my heart."

"I'd never risk it," Jax replied.

"And that's exactly why we're here, big brother. Because you were never willing to take the risk."

"No," Jax said. There was a sad ring to his voice. How had we all ended up here? A few months ago my world was normal. Sure, Jax was gone, and Rick would have been sick either way, but there were no demons. No witches. No gate to hell swinging on rusted hinges. Life was simple. Now? I couldn't imagine anything more complicated. "We're here because you *were.*"

Chase looked like he wanted to say something more, but simply nodded. "You have your good-bye. I won't leave the area, but I will walk away. That's all Zenak will let me do."

"It will have to be enough."

Jax waited until his brother turned away to start forward.

"This is crazy. You can't do this," I whispered. Not that I

cared if Chase heard. What was he going to do, stab himself again? Head rush another tree? That wouldn't be as bad as watching him kill Jax.

"Sammy," he said, taking my face into his hands. There was something in it. It was smooth and cool with a slight point at the top. "I'm doing what I need to do." As he spoke, he slid the hand, and the thing beneath it, down my cheek and over my shoulder. From there, he skimmed my arm and ended by wrapping his fingers through mine. With a single squeeze, he took his hand back, leaving me with the small object. With a pointed stare, he gave a slight nod to my pocket. Whatever it was, he wanted me to hide it.

Ha! I knew it. A plan. Sniffling, I stuffed both hands into my pockets. "There has to be another way," I said, keeping the charade going. No telling what Chase would do if he thought something was up.

"I wish there was." He pulled way and slowly mouthed, "This might hurt. But when I make my move, I need you to run."

I shook my head. "I can't. He—"

His eyes darkened. The middle of each iris turned black, leaving only a thin line around the edge gray. "Trust me, Samantha Merrick."

He pulled away, eyes reverting to gray, and I let my head fall forward so that our foreheads rested together. "There's stuff I want to say…" I wasn't acting anymore. What if something happened and he was killed? What if we both were? I'd told him how I felt, but there was so much more to it than short, simple words.

"Tell me later, then. Over popcorn and coffee and cartoons." He brought his hands up to either side of my face,

skimming my cheeks with the tips of his fingers and threading them through my hair. When his lips met mine, it was
shocking. Like being dipped into an icy lake in the middle
of a snowstorm. Suddenly every inch of me was alive and
desperate for his warmth like my life depended on it. His
arms crushed my body closer, the kiss stealing the air, as I
fought to keep my balance. It was unlike anything I'd ever
experienced before. Love. So much love. Everything Jax felt
for me was there in that kiss.

A dizzying rush of images flooded my mind. Jax seeing
me for the first time, at my parent's funeral. The first time
he'd crawled out onto his roof to sit with me after a nightmare. Our first day of high school. Our kiss in the fort. Him
standing over Chase's bed with a knife, fighting back the demon inside. Seeing me leaning across the table at McCarthy's, kissing Chase.

I saw everything. I *felt* everything. His thoughts and
emotions in all those moments were buzzing around inside
my head, inside my heart, threatening to make my head
explode.

When he pulled away, it was like he took a chunk of me
with him. I could almost see it in the air as we separated, a
thick, silver strand wrapped around me, connected to him.
As he backed away, the silver faded, but the glow of it, faint
but unmistakable, remained.

Chapter Thirty-Five

Jax

The kiss left my heart thundering and the blood rushing in my ears. An unbelievable warmth filled me, slowly fading as I backed away from her. I didn't know what it was, but everything about her was amped. Her colors were brighter, expression more telling. It was almost as though I could see inside her head. It was always intense with her, but that kiss had been the kicker. Something close to desperation came over me, and all I wanted was to touch her again. To feel that warmth. But I had something to do.

I turned away.

What happened in the next few moments would either save us and damn me forever, or get us both killed.

I don't know how, or why, but you love her…

A picture of Sam flashed inside my head.

I'm going to need to give you control if we have any hope

of getting out of here in one piece...

An image of Chase, lying still and bloodied at my feet.

No. You can't kill him. Sam will die, too...

I felt the demon's irritation, but oddly, also its understanding. The rage it had for Chase's demon was there, but miraculously, the feelings it had for Sam overshadowed it. I hoped those feelings would ground my humanity and keep me from losing myself to the demon like Chase had, because I was about to gamble big.

"Time's up, Jax."

It was ironic that Chase had chosen this spot. "Of all the possible scenarios that have gone through my head over the years, this was never one of them."

My twin came forward and stopped a few feet away. He pulled out a gun. "You ready?"

I couldn't resist. "If I say no, can we take a rain check?"

"I know you think I want to do this, but I don't."

"Then don't," I said simply. I had to do this with as little damage as possible. The stone Sadie supplied would disturb Chase's control over Sam, but it wouldn't protect her from damage done to him.

Chase raised the gun. "Good-bye, Jax."

"Good-bye, Chase."

"Stop!" A voice boomed through the trees.

The inhuman echo bounced off the rocks and vibrated inside my chest. From the darkness beyond the fort, Heckle stepped forward, and I breathed a sigh of relief. I'd visited the bartender earlier to ask him to watch over Sam if something went wrong tonight. He agreed, but also said he had a plan. It was a risky one considering all the complicated factors of our situation, but it was all I had. I just hadn't been sure

Heckle could pull it off.

"Zenak, I'm sure you are aware that I cannot allow you such an unfair advantage."

Chase bristled and lowered the gun. "The gun?" He let it fall to the ground. "Fine. I'll kick his ass with my bare hands."

Heckle frowned and snapped his fingers. From above, a great flash of lightning lit up the night sky. It also illuminated the fort for several seconds. Long enough for me to see the large group of demons—at least twenty—standing in the shadows behind my brother.

"Oh. You mean them?" Chase laughed and gave a casual shrug. "Would you believe they're here for support?"

"Of course," was Heckle's reply. "So long as you grant Jax the same liberty." Another flash of lightning, and from the shadows behind Heckle, another group of demons came forward. I recognized several. The male and female demon from the War Zone. Azirak's clan.

Annoyed by the even playing field, Chase retrieved the gun and pointed it again. As he aimed, his clan came forward to circle me. The action engaged Azirak's demons, and they, too stepped forward. One let out a horrible wail and plunged into the crowd, fingers extended toward Chase. It was cut down by his demons before it reached the halfway mark.

And then hell broke loose.

I closed my eyes.

I'm ready. I'm ready to embrace *you.*

"Do it!" The words exploded, and the demon inside me twitched.

Unlike the other times Azirak took over, there was an electric hum. It unfurled deep in my chest, then spread quickly everywhere else.

Alive. I'd never felt so alive.

My eyes shot open and to my surprise, I was still in control—except I wasn't the only one. Azirak was there, right beside me in the driver's seat. I'd embraced the demon. It wasn't Jax and Azirak anymore. We were one. A single being. The demon's strength and speed were my own.

Chase was right. This was beyond anything I could have possibly imagined. Different. Everything was different now. Colors were brighter. Noises were sharper. Smells a thousand times more potent.

A noise rang out. The gun. I heard the click of the trigger above the chaos of the crowd, and the echoing boom as the bullet shot from the barrel. Even the whooshing noise as it split the air on its path to my head was like a song to my ears. I stepped aside. Nothing more than a slight shift in position. The bullet whizzed by, passing so close that it kicked up several strands of hair. I heard the projectile slam harmlessly into one of the trees.

"How—" Chase let out a feral growl. "You embraced the demon."

"You were right, *brother*. It is amazing."

We stood there for the longest time. Brother to brother—demon to demon—as once more, war erupted around us. Azirak squirmed, but it was different now. Not a separate thing on the inside, but a part of me. It wasn't just the demon anticipating the battle—it was me as well.

Chase lunged forward, fingers hooked and greedy for blood. I pivoted, dodging the blow by inches, and sprinted for the large rock in the middle of the fort. Jumping, I planted my right foot down, using it to push off again. The leverage shot me into the air. As I went, I twisted my body and landed behind Chase in a crouch. A few feet away, one of Zenak's demons tore the head from one of Azirak's.

Feeling Azirak's anger over the loss of one of his own, I leaped into action without giving it a second of thought. I grabbed the demon by the throat, fingers digging into muscle, straight down to bone, and yanked. A rain of blood and gore and the demon collapsed.

Chase roared, and when I turned, I saw he was cutting a bloody path to where Sam stood, on the edge of the crowd. She was surrounded by several of Azirak's demons. Their backs were to him as they closed in.

She was still linked to Chase. They were going to kill her.

I dashed around the thick patch of pine trees and went straight for them. There were footsteps behind me in the dirt, not far and moving fast. Ahead, the crowd around Sam was closing in. I picked up the pace. It was astonishing. In order to access this kind of speed and agility in the past, I would have had to surrender complete control to the demon. Now, it was mine. Balanced right at the tips of my fingers and ready to use whenever I wanted. Chase's obsession with the power was almost understandable.

Almost.

Fifteen feet. I was almost there. Something crashed into me from the right, sending the world sideways. Two somethings. One on either side, they held me down in the dirt and bracken. "My lord!" the male screamed. "Here! Azirak is here."

But Chase was nowhere to be found. I searched the bloody crowd and finally found him, halfway to the other side. Halfway to Sam.

A primal growl tore from my throat. Drawing on the

demon's rage, I freed my right arm, and with it, grabbed one of the demons. With a massive heave, I hurled her into the male demon on my right, sending them sideways. Then I was up and running.

Chase reached the crowd first. It was surreal to watch as he ripped through the other demons, tearing them down with a brutality that I'd never before witnessed. I'd seen violence. I'd seen death. I'd been the cause of them. But never anything so savage. Even after they fell, Chase continued to ravage their corpses. Like he needed to destroy them at the most basic level. By the time I reached them, my brother was covered in blood and smiling sickly.

"Don't do this, Chase. You're about to cross a line that there's no coming back from."

My brother kept his expression neutral, but I could see a hint of sadness in his eyes. The old Chase. Or maybe the fake one. Maybe I never knew him at all. "The line's already been crossed. That night at Huntington that I fed from Sam—that was when I knew how this would all end. Deep down, I knew."

I heard the rush of air as Chase's fist shot forward, and felt the vibration of impact with agonizing detail. My head rocked back, the scenery changing from the overgrown edge of the fort to the dark sky above, before I crashed to the grass. I could smell my own rage, spicy and potent. In embracing the demon, its feelings were now my own. There was no turning back.

It was about to rain hell.

Chapter Thirty-Six

Sam

Something had happened. The silver strand I'd seen connecting me to Jax after our kiss was out of sight, but I could still feel it. I had nothing to compare it to, but if not for the fact that I hadn't felt any of the blows Chase delivered, I would have sworn Jax had unintentionally linked us. Every once in a while I felt a flash of anger, and a rush of something like adrenaline — only a thousand times stronger. It was from Jax. I didn't know how, but I was sure.

Heckle pulled me aside as the great battle began. By the time he finished explaining what he was doing there, I had an idea of my own. Heckle, as it turned out, wasn't an ordinary run-of-the-mill demon. In fact, he wasn't a demon at all. He was something special. Something useful. Together, we'd hashed out an additional plan. Backup. Just in case…

But he'd disappeared, and Azirak's demons came for

me, intent on keeping their promise. Help came from the most unlikely source. Chase. But even though he'd taken down the group circling, there were more. Many more. And if they couldn't get to me directly, they knew they could get to me through Chase.

Through the link.

They rushed him, fists flying.

I turned to escape the chaos, but a sharp pain exploded on the right side of my head. Then, another to the gut, followed by air leaving my lungs. I crumbled to my knees as involuntary tears fell, and the world took on a blurry haze. Every blow dealt to Chase landed on me.

Something wet trailed down the upper right side of my face, tickling slightly as it went. When I lifted my hand and pulled it away, it was smeared with blood. Panicking was a bad idea, but I couldn't help it. I tried to take a deep breath, but it was like someone had wrapped a rubber band around my chest, making it worse. Ribbons of color danced before my eyes as spikes of pain rolled over me. I'd broken several ribs in high school. I knew how it felt.

I tried crawling to the patch of trees at the corner of the fort. There were demons fighting everywhere. I couldn't prevent the damage that came from Chase, but I could at least get clear of the rest.

But each movement was harder than the last. Whatever was happening to him was bad and it was taking its toll. At one point I had to stop and spit out a mouthful of blood, horrified when something small and white landed on the ground. A tooth. A few paces after that, I bit back a scream as my right elbow gave out with a soft but distinct cracking.

Just when I wasn't sure I could make it another inch,

Heckle was there. "Here," he whispered as he lifted me from the ground. It hurt. Everything hurt. But I let him drag me to the sideline. "This ends now."

Another flash, even brighter than the ones before, lit up the sky, but unlike the previous two, this wasn't lightning. It was something else. When it cleared, I gasped. The battle was gone. The pain, the other demons, the blood and bodies. All of it. Evaporated as though it had never been. The only things left were me and Heckle, and Jax and Chase.

For a moment, I was sure Chase had taken one too many knocks to the head. This was a hallucination. That, or death. "What—"

"This war is between your two demon clans. Using a mortal to gain advantage is unbalanced."

Chase stalked forward, stopping just shy of grabbing Heckle around the throat. "You have no right to interfere."

"On the contrary, it is my *job* to interfere." He stepped back and gestured to Jax. "This is your game board. You will play your hands out. Alone. Royal blood against royal blood."

Chase looked as though he might argue, but Jax simply nodded and stepped away. "Take your opportunity, Zenak. Let's finish this once and for all."

And with a grin, Chase lunged forward and threw the first punch. In fact, he was throwing the only punches. I backed away as they fought. Chase assaulted Jax with fury, but he refused to strike back. He did his best to dodge the blows, but dealt none of his own. He didn't want to hurt me.

"How can you let them do this," I whispered furiously. "You know he won't fight back. You said they couldn't use me, yet that's what Chase is doing."

"Do you remember what we discussed?" Heckle asked, voice low. "They are brutal and vicious, but I believe Azirak to be the lesser of the two evils."

I nodded as a chilly breeze whipped the leaves into a frenzy above their heads. The nearly bare branches stretched into the sky like skeletal fingers, reaching for heaven.

In the middle of the fort, Chase stood over Jax with a mix of hate and pity. "What are you going to do? You hurt me and you hurt her. We both know you don't want that. I don't either. Just roll over and die. Make this easy on everyone. End your pathetic existence. No more feeding the demon. Isn't that what you've always wanted?"

It was there in Jax's eyes. He was buying his brother's bullshit. I had to do something to tip the scales in Jax's favor. There was one way to get him to fight back.

Heckle was right. It was time for the backup plan.

"You're sure. You can do what you said?" My insides trembled at the thought of going through with it, but something had to give.

A faint shimmer surrounded Heckle's left hand. A moment later, he held out a pristine-looking blade. "I can. But as I warned, it will come with a price. You may lose him regardless of this sacrifice. There is no way to predict the outcome. It will all come down to choice."

If I agreed to follow through, then it would give Jax the freedom to kill Chase. The good part about that was, it would ensure that Zenak would never have his powers restored, and that Jax would live. The bad part was, Azirak's powers would be restored. It would break the curse that bound the demons and give them the freedom again. Forever. Heckle didn't know what would happen to human Jax.

It was a gamble. And in the end, that's all life really was. A series of gambles. "Chase!" I took the knife and positioned it above my forearm.

He froze for a second, glancing up from a weary-looking Jax, and laughed. "Come on, Samantha. You're the biggest chicken when it comes to pain. You freaked out two weeks ago when you got a splinter."

He was right. I stubbed my toe and screamed about it for an hour. But this was different. This was for Jax. Nothing I could do would kill Chase, but I could take the wind out of his sails.

I could take myself out of the equation.

"What's the point? You can't kill me. The link doesn't work that way." He eyed the knife. "I can still kill you, though. One swipe across my throat and you'll be choking back your own blood. Don't make me do it, Samantha. Please. Just step aside and let this play out."

"I can't kill you, but I can make you miserable."

"I'm commanding you to put the knife down."

I smiled and reveled in the shocked expression on his face. "And I'm *commanding* you to go to hell."

He took a step toward me, mouth wide open. "How the hell—we're still linked. I can feel it."

Behind Chase, Jax climbed to his feet with a frightening smile. A sickening crack sounded as he tilted his head to the left, and then the right. "You've got no control over her."

Chase spun on his brother. Lightning-fast, he whipped his fist forward and caught Jax in the jaw. Without a moment of hesitation, Jax retaliated by dropping to the ground and sweeping the back of Chase's knees. He went down hard and all the air whooshed from *my* body as the sting of impact sent a dull twinge through my muscles. But he wasn't down long. Jax was unwilling to do any real damage—but Chase wasn't. In a graceful arc, Chase launched into a kip up and delivered a jab that caught Jax directly in the throat. He struggled for air and stumbled back, crashing into the large rock at the center of the fort.

Chase turned to me. "What's the plan, Samantha?"

"Jax can't hurt you because of me," I said. "If I'm not in the way, he'll take you down." When I'd gone over this with Heckle, I expected to get to this point and freeze up. There was nothing. No second thought. No hesitation. Just conviction. Chase had to pay for what he did. Jax had to stay safe.

Chapter Thirty-Seven

Jax

Sam was a mess. Multiple gashes across her face, right eye swollen along with her bottom lip. She held her left arm at an odd angle, and it was easy to see she was having a hard time holding on to the knife.

And where the fuck had it even come from?

"I'm giving you one more chance," she said. I had a bad feeling. It was more than the strangely energized colored smoke swirling around her head. I shouldn't have been able to see them in the darkness of the clearing, but for some reason, it was brighter than normal. Almost neon. It was a whisper in my head. Something jumbled and indistinct, but somehow I knew in my gut that it was bad. "Let me go. Release me from the link."

I wondered if this was where I would have ended up if it hadn't been for Sam. If the situation had been reversed and she'd bonded with Chase all those years ago instead, would I have been the killer? Would I be standing in my brother's place?

Chase shook his head. "I'm sorry you were dragged into this, Samantha, but you're the only insurance I have. I can't break the link."

"Sam..." The broken, low whispers in my head cleared, and I didn't know how, or where they'd come from, but I knew what she was going to do. "*NOO!*"

She ignored me and smiled. It was beautiful—but wrong. Loaded with the promise of something cold. Something final. "Your insurance has just been canceled."

We shot forward at the same moment.

We were too late.

Chase and I reached the center as Sam buried the knife in her gut. Her eyes went wide as her heart sped up, then shuddered, falling still. I heard every single fucking beat as though it echoed inside my own head. Then, I heard nothing. Her body collapsed and everything inside me went cold.

After that, everything turned red.

Azirak roared. A sound that vibrated and shook loose every ounce of anger I'd ever kept bottled inside. I threw myself at my brother with all the rage I'd held back over the years. The burning need to feel my fingers covered in Chase's blood. The ache that came with wanting a peace I knew would never come. Wanting Sam. Finding her again.

Losing her...

It all spilled out.

With a boom like thunder, we collided and crashed to the ground, rolling sideways and trading blows. Chase gained the upper hand, throwing me off-balance and into the large rock. "You're responsible for...for her death...not me."

I dragged myself out of the dirt as he did the same. Her body was two feet away. Maybe less. It was all I saw. All I felt. What was that shit they tried to sell? Death is peaceful? Sam looked anything but.

"That's right," Chase said. "Look at her. Look at what you did."

The words barely got through, and I didn't care. There was a storm brewing. Not above our heads, but inside. The sound Azirak made—an echoing, mournful keen—caused the hairs on my arms and at the back of my neck stand on end. It wanted blood, but not for power. The demon wanted revenge.

For Sam.

Chapter Thirty-Eight

Sam

I watched the whole thing, seen only by Heckle. Death wasn't what I expected. There were no flying angels and large golden harps. The light at the end of the tunnel—or in my case, the woods—was a brewing storm with occasional lightning overhead. The gates of heaven hadn't appeared, along with Saint Peter, to welcome me in.

Probably because of the deal I'd made.

I couldn't see it from here, but when we'd sealed the deal, a small black mark appeared on the inside of my wrist. It sort of resembled a star, only with an extra point. There was no way for Jax to win this thing. Not on his own. This was the only way I could help.

With my life attached to Chase, Jax would be crippled by his feelings. The only way to give him an advantage was to remove myself from the situation. So I had.

Jax was savage. With me gone, he attacked Chase with a ferocity that was both beautiful and frightening. But he and Chase were evenly matched. They traded blows, Jax bearing down and kicking hard as Chase crumbled to the ground, then in an instant, Chase recovering and delivering a blow that brought Jax down.

"I'm glad you decided to fight," Chase said as they got to their feet. "With all the past between them, Zenak didn't want an empty victory."

Jax's expression stayed stony. He dodged to the left, avoiding Chase's next blow, and followed with one of his own. It landed in the center of his brother's chest, sending him sprawling back into the trees behind them. "There's no victory here. No matter what the outcome is, we all fucking lose."

As the men fought, Heckle came up beside me. "The deal we made is keeping your soul here, but it can't stay in the void for long. Are you sure you want to continue?"

"I sure as hell don't want to stay dead…"

After Heckle confessed to being something more than a normal demon—a keeper of balance—I'd laid out my plan. Stop my heart long enough for Jax to take Chase down. He said it would be easy—with the proper payment—to bring me back, but warned that the aftereffects would be unpredictable. And that was besides the whole *hell on earth* thing. If Jax did kill Chase—which I assured him wouldn't happen—we were in a whole world of fucked.

Heckle didn't share my faith in Jax. He felt that, after seeing me fall, he'd be enraged enough to take his brother's life, spilling royal blood and restoring Azirak's clan to its full glory. If I was wrong and Jax did in fact kill Chase, balance would need to be restored—starting with the nullification of our deal. I'd stay dead.

I'd made my choice knowing all that. I accepted it. If there was ever anyone I'd bet my life on, it would be Jax Flynn.

Chase launched himself forward and hurled his brother in the direction of the rock, but Jax threw his weight to the side, reversing their direction and strengthening the momentum. It was Chase who crashed against the boulder, not Jax.

"Do you regret it? Any of it?" Jax growled.

Chase struggled, but not as hard as he could have. "I regret *all* of it. And at the same time, none of it." His head fell back against the stone as his body went limp in Jax's grasp. "You were right. She was right. You were the strong one. I gave in far too easily and you were able—*willing*—to fight. My demon is strong, but you…the human is strong. When you found out Rick knew all along, didn't you wonder?"

It was dark now, and in the distance, a coyote howled, followed by the hoot of an owl.

Chase stopped struggling, but Jax was no fool. He didn't let up. "Wonder what?"

"Why he sent you away instead of me?"

"Yeah." I couldn't see his face, but his voice sounded sad. "It crossed my mind."

"I think it's because he knew I'd never be able to handle it. He sent you away because you were stronger. He had more faith in you, man."

"There's still time." Jax finally loosened his hold and pulled away a few inches. I felt a bubble of justification, and turned and stuck my tongue out at Heckle. I knew it! "Neither one of us has to die."

"You're wrong, Jax. I've got the wheel, but it won't last much longer. You need to take me out, because I swear to you, if you don't, I will kill you. It might not be today, or even tomorrow, but it'll happen. Zenak won't rest until its clan is restored, and I won't lie. I hate you. I love you, brother, but I hate you, too."

Jax hovered over his brother and I held my breath.

After what seemed like a lifetime, he stepped away and let Chase get up. "Go as far from here as you can get. Don't come back. Don't even think about this place."

Chase hesitated, sliding off the rock's surface and taking several steps away from his brother. He had to be thinking the whole thing was a trick. A ploy to catch him off guard and close in for the kill. "That's it? You're going to let me walk away?"

"You're my brother," Jax said. "Despite everything, I love you—but, like you said, I hate you, too. A kind of hate I'm sure you can sympathize with. I could *easily* kill you. I want to. More than you can possibly understand, I want to. After what you did to all those girls. And Sam... Don't mistake this for mercy, because that's *not* what it's about."

"What is it about, then?"

"Azirak, unlike Zenak, learned from its mistakes. It understands that if the clans are restored, there would be nothing left of this place. Everything, everywhere, would be laid to waste. Spilling royal blood would mean the end of earth as we know it, and Azirak likes it here. *I* like it here. This is my only choice."

"This is a mistake," Chase warned, and began backing away. His eyes fell to my still form lying in the dirt, and he shook his head. I couldn't see clearly through the trees, but

I thought there were tears in his eyes. "A huge mistake. Zenak's not going to give up."

Jax stared at his brother, saying nothing. Mistake or not, it was the only choice. The world would never be ready for either clan to regain dominance. With a final nod, Chase turned and bolted into the darkness. He was gone. It was over.

For now.

With the immediate threat gone, Heckle bent to retrieve my ruined body. Laying me on the ground in front of the rock, he stepped aside and Jax was there in an instant. I couldn't feel his fingers as he brushed the hair from my eyes, and there was no sensation as he ran his palm over my forehead and across my eyes to close the lids. I could still hear, though. And that was worse than the pain I'd suffered as the knife pierced my skin.

"Good-bye. I'm sorry. It was my fault. It's all shit. Empty fucking words that don't mean a thing," he whispered. "My life was always dark. From the moment I opened my eyes, all that surrounded me was black. And then there was you. The single brightest thing in this world. *In my world.* Now you're gone. You're gone and all I can see is black. If this is what Chase saw, I can understand—"

"What's happened here changes nothing," Heckle said, pulling Jax to his feet. "We made a deal."

Jax was on his feet and in Heckle's face. "It changes everything." He jabbed a finger at my body. "*She's dead.* Your terms mean nothing now."

"Stand down, Tainted, and be calm." Heckle knelt beside me. He whispered words too low to hear and placed a hand on either side of my head. There was a ringing noise and a rush of icy wind. Suddenly, I couldn't breathe—which was insane since I was technically dead. A single word echoed. *Rise.* And everything went dark for a minute.

When my eyes opened, I was staring up into a sea of stormy gray. I didn't need his ability to see emotions. It was all there on his face. Love. Shock. Hope. Awe. That, and more. The silver strand was back, wrapped and pulsing like a heartbeat around Jax, and connected to me. "Sammy? How—"

"She made a deal with me, too," Heckle said as Jax helped me up.

The macabre stain running down the front of my shirt was a chilling reminder of what had happened. I gently pulled away from Jax and took a deep breath. There was a sense of freedom now that hadn't been there before. My temporary death had done it. It'd broken the link between Chase and me. But even though that link was gone, there was still something there. Something different. This was bright and hopeful. Beautiful.

Jax threw his arms around me. The warmth from his body sent a shiver of contentment through me—until he was almost squeezing tightly enough to cut off all the air. "I thought I'd lost you."

"I'm not that easy to get rid of," I said, returning the embrace. As I sat there, cradled in his arms, the feeling grew stronger. More intense. I pulled away, searching his face, and the silver strand pulsated. "Do you see it?"

"See what?"

It was beautiful. Shining and warm and radiating. It was more pronounced than it had been right after the kiss. An almost-electric buzz that sent tingles up and down my spine. "I think—I don't understand how, but I think *we're* linked."

He watched me for a moment, face paling. The look of horror made my breath catch. "No. It's not possible. I didn't—"

I shook my head. It wasn't possible. Couldn't be. Yet there was something there. It was unmistakable. "I know, but I'm telling you. There's *something* there."

"You two are linked," Heckle confirmed, standing over us.

"It happened when Jax kissed me, didn't it? I—I *felt* it. That didn't happen when Chase linked us though."

"There are different kinds of links. Ones created out of violence and necessity and ones created out of love. They each have their boons and faults. They each feel different."

"Love?" I said. "Is that even possible from a demon?"

"Yes," Jax said. He looked up at Heckle. "Demons can love, but I'm pretty sure they can't bring the dead back. I don't know a lot, but I know that. You—what are you?"

"As I told you both, I am a keeper of balance. For lack of a better term, I *am* balance. I'm not good or evil. I simply am. It is my job—mine and several others, that is—to ensure that the world keeps an even balance of good and evil." He smiled. "I made a deal with both of you. I gave you the opportunity to make a choice. One would have kept the balance, and the other would have upset it. You both chose to sacrifice something in order to maintain it. You passed the test."

I'd sacrificed my life to take away Chase's unfair advantage and Jax sacrificed Azirak's powers—and a peaceful existence—to keep the world free from the demon's clan.

Heckle sank onto the large rock. "As I told Sam earlier, it was me to whom God came after your ancestor Cain slaughtered his brother, Abel. It was me who cursed his family."

"*You* started all this? You—" Jax started forward, but Heckle held out his hand and Jax froze in place.

"This is not a fight you want, Tainted. *Trust me.*"

He lowered his hand and Jax could move again. But instead of lunging forward, he stayed by my side.

"Cain brought violence to the world. What was peaceful and perfect, he stole when he murdered me."

"Murdered you?" Surreal had taken on an entirely new definition. If what he was saying was true, then we were talking to—

"I am Abel." He afforded me a small smile. "Until my death, there was no need for someone like me. No need for balance. The world was pure. And then, with a single violent act, it was tainted. Blackness that you cannot imagine fell across the lands. It was like a plague, infecting every living creature on earth. In an effort to restore what was lost, God gave me Cain's soul. It was poisoned by the crime he'd committed and had soiled the world beyond repair. The best I could do was bring some sort of balance."

I shuddered, though I wasn't sure it was from the cold. Abel. We were standing here with Cain's brother, Abel.

"The damage was greater than you could possibly imagine," he continued. The leaves rattled as the wind blew. "I couldn't wipe the slate completely clean, but I was able to take the bulk of Cain's darkness and redistribute it. It's why your demon feeds off the darkest human emotions. They festered inside Cain, driving him to commit the crime that corrupted the world. Now, each one of his descendants is born with a small piece of that soul. Cursed to make a choice—carry out his crime again or fight until the stain is finally wiped away. Over the years, more Tainted came.

Individuals whose horrific crime blackened souls were shattered and redistributed, but Cain's… His was the first. His was the worst."

Jax stared, mouth open and eyes wide. I knew exactly how he felt. "If you're Abel, then why help Jax? Technically he's *part* of the man who killed you."

Heckle laughed. The sound was more eerie than amused, though. "I've been a long time on this earth, Sam. What my brother did to me doesn't matter now. All that matters is maintaining a balance. I will never allow the blackness to overtake this place again."

"But why stop at balance?" Jax asked. "Why not tip the scales in favor of good?"

"If only it were that easy. No," he sighed. "Those days are gone. The best we can hope for is balance."

"But how was letting Chase walk away balance? Why strike a deal with Jax and me?"

"Because in the long run, it will bring balance. As I said, you've passed my test." He smoothed his shirt and stepped forward with a smile. "You both work for me. Think of it as subcontracting. From now on, you will help me maintain and restore balance."

That was our agreement. Heckle allowed me to come back to the land of the living, and I offered up my services—whatever the hell that meant—to his cause. It seemed innocent, but now I wasn't so sure. "Which I still don't get. I get recruiting Jax—he's a freaking demon—but me? What can I do?"

"There is much more to you, Samantha Merrick, than you are aware." Heckle winked at me. "It wasn't Jax who created the link. It was you."

Chapter Thirty-Nine

Jax

For three days after Chase disappeared into the night, I kept a watchful eye on Sam. That had been interesting. I'd officially moved back to town, taking up residence in Rick's house, and had convinced Sam, for the time being at least, to move in. The place was huge and there was plenty of room. Plus, telling Kelly was fun. It was like a scene right from our high school years, complete with gasping and screaming.

Everything was quiet. Wherever Chase had gone, it wasn't here. I was betting he'd lie low—at least for a while—but knew we hadn't heard the last of him. Like he'd said, Zenak would never give up.

And that was fine.

But we weren't out of the woods yet. We had a lot to deal with, including a new link, the one between us, that we knew nothing about. Heckle dropped the bombshell that the link had been Sam's doing, then disappeared into the sunset. He'd resurface eventually, but until then, we were in uncharted territory. Again.

I pulled the car up in front of Sam's apartment building. We were here to get the rest of her things. "This is a bad idea, Jax."

"Things are different now," I said. I agreed, but leaving her on her own for the time being was an even worse choice. The living situation would be hard for both of us—harder than she knew—but it was necessary. "You said it yourself. *You're* different. I think until we know what that means exactly, we need to keep each other close. For now, we're roomies."

"I'm sorry," she said, fiddling with the seat belt button. It felt like decades ago we were reversed—me in the passenger's seat and Sam in the driver's—sinking to the bottom of the river.

"About?"

"That you're being forced to stay." Heckle wouldn't let me leave. The bastard said I needed to be on call and therefore had to stay within shouting distance, so to speak. I wanted to put up a fight, especially since the deal I'd made was a two-parter, and staying in town was going to make the rest of the arrangement harder, especially with this new link, but my hands were tied.

I was sweating. Clammy palms and a nervous tremble in my gut. I would have blamed the demon, but Azirak—Azi, I'd started calling it—had been different since the day in the fort, too. Not gone and definitely not peaceful—I'd needed to feed it just last night—but more a part of me now. We had the same goals. And one of those goals was keeping Sam safe and controlling the fallout from its clan.

Understandably, they were angry. They felt we had betrayed them by letting Chase and Zenak walk. They wanted to be free and I knew we hadn't heard the last from them, either.

And then there was the witch, Sadie Gray. Heckle said in most cases a link could be dropped if the demon chose to, but when I'd tried, nothing worked. I planned to ask Heckle about it—just as soon as he popped up again. In the meantime, I'd have to keep my eyes open. See what Sadie's real motives were. Because there was no doubt she had something up her sleeve.

"I love you, Sammy."

She started to speak but I placed my hand across her mouth. This was hard enough to say without her constantly interrupting. "Just lemme finish. 'Kay?"

She nodded, and I slowly removed my hand.

"I love you, but you know that already. You've always known that. And yeah, Heckle is forcing me to stay and I hate it. I want to leave. For so many reasons… You and me, Sammy, it can't happen. I stand by what I said before. I'm dangerous. When we're close—when I'm really happy—it causes Azi pain. It causes *me* pain. Too much pain."

They were lies and every word burned as it left my tongue. Things were different with the demon now. Since embracing it, being close to Sam still hurt, but wasn't excruciating like it had been.

"I know," she whispered. There was a glisten in her eyes and I had to look away. The deep blue mist filling the car was already too much to deal with without seeing her cry.

"Eventually my brother will come back. If we're

together, like, *together*, together, he'll use you against me."

"But the link is gone. He can't—"

"Control you," I finished for her. "But he can hurt you. *Kill you*. It would destroy me." I reached across and ran a hand across her cheek. The skin beneath my fingers was heaven. So soft and warm. So perfect. So out of reach.

She leaned into my touch. The simple feel of her skin against mine sparked a fire. How the fuck was I going to get through this?

By just doing it, as Chase would have said. Suck it up and get the rest out.

"There's also another reason… The deal I made with Heckle required sacrifice. You offered your life, and I offered mine." Now that Azirak and I were one, a relationship with Sam might have been possible. It would have been complicated and tough, but possible.

"I don't understand…I thought you sacrificed Azirak's power?"

I forced myself to look at her. Balance. One thing in return for another. Heckle demanded the one thing I wanted more than anything. He'd ripped it away just as it finally fell within my reach. "That wasn't my sacrifice to make. It was the demon's. It had to be something I loved. The only thing I loved. It had to be you. You're my life, Sammy. I gave up you."

She was pale, and I realized she really hadn't bought the speech up to this point. She was probably right. All this righteous crap would have meant nothing in the face of my feelings for her. I would have caved.

Except now, I couldn't.

"So that's it?" Her voice was shaky. "We don't get to be

happy?"

It took a second to find my voice. The lump in my throat was thick, threatening to choke off my air, and hearing her voice crack only made it worse. "Guess that's why they call it sacrifice."

She pulled away and got out of the car without another word. I let her go, watching as she walked down the path to the apartment doors. She didn't look back once. When she was out of sight I followed, slipping from the driver's seat and making my way up the path.

Things were going to be hard with us living under the same roof. Life had brought us together, then ripped us apart. Again. Only this time it was rubbing our noses in it. Sam Merrick was my world. The universe and heaven and hell all wrapped into one. Somewhere out there was something that would tip Heckle's precious fucking balance and allow me to be happy. At peace. To be with her. I'd find it.

I'd find it because there was no alternative.

I'd find it because I couldn't live without her.

Acknowlegments

As always, a huge thank you to my family—especially my parents and husband. I wouldn't be sitting here writing this now if it weren't for them.

To my first readers, Gia, Mary, and Lori. Thank you so much for your time and feedback. Priceless doesn't even come close. And I promise, if I ever find myself in the forest chained to a llama, you three will be the first I call! ;)

To everyone at Entangled, from editing to publicity, thank you for your dedication and support.

Lastly, and most important, to the readers. You guys are the ones who make my world go around. Thank you to the moon and back for all your support and time. You continue to blow my mind in the best possible ways. Hugs and chocolate flavored coffee to all of you!

About the Author

Jus Accardo is the author of YA paranormal romance and urban fantasy fiction. A native New Yorker, she lives in the middle of nowhere with her husband, three dogs, and sometimes guard bear, Oswald. When not writing, Jus can be found volunteering at the local animal shelter or indulging her passion for food. After being accepted to the Culinary Institute of America, she passed on the spot to pursue a career in writing and has never looked back. As far as she's concerned, she has the coolest job on earth—making stuff up for a living.

www.jusaccardo.com

Other books by Jus Accardo